TO BIND A DARK HEART

A DARK FANTASY ROMANCE

ATLEY WYKES

ALDER CIRCLE PRESS

Copyright © 2023 Atley Wykes

All rights reserved. No part of this book may be reproduced

or used in any manner without the prior written permission of the copyright owner,

except for the use of brief quotations in a book review.

To request permissions, contact the publisher at atley.wykes@gmail.com.

Ebook ASIN: B0BTXQ5XJ7

Paperback ISBN: 9798387589935

First paperback edition March 2023

Cover art by Atley Wykes

Layout by Atley Wykes

Edited by Ginger Kane

Printed by Amazon Printing Services in the USA.

Alder Circle Press

P.O. Box 115

Somers, WI 53171

atleywykes.com

Contents

Dedication	V
Maps of Maeoris	VI
1. Chapter 1	1
2. Chapter 2	15
3. Chapter 3	29
4. Chapter 4	39
5. Chapter 5	49
6. Chapter 6	58
7. Chapter 7	67
8. Chapter 8	80
9. Chapter 9	90
10. Chapter 10	100
11. Chapter 11	109
12. Chapter 12	118
13. Chapter 13	127
14. Chapter 14	137
15. Chapter 15	146
16. Chapter 16	153

17.	Chapter 17	161
18.	Chapter 18	169
19.	Chapter 19	181
20.	Chapter 20	190
21.	Chapter 21	200
22.	Chapter 22	208
23.	Chapter 23	216
24.	Chapter 24	224
25.	Chapter 25	233
26.	Chapter 26	240
27.	Chapter 27	247
28.	Chapter 28	257
29.	Chapter 29	266
30.	Chapter 30	274
31.	Chapter 31	282
32.	Chapter 32	289
33.	Chapter 33	298
Acknowledgments		302
About the Author		305
Blurb for To Etch a Promise in Bone		307
Maeoris Wiki		308

This book is dedicated to Henry Zebrowski. The only person I know of that loves DUNE and fucking as much as I do.

Maps of Maeoris

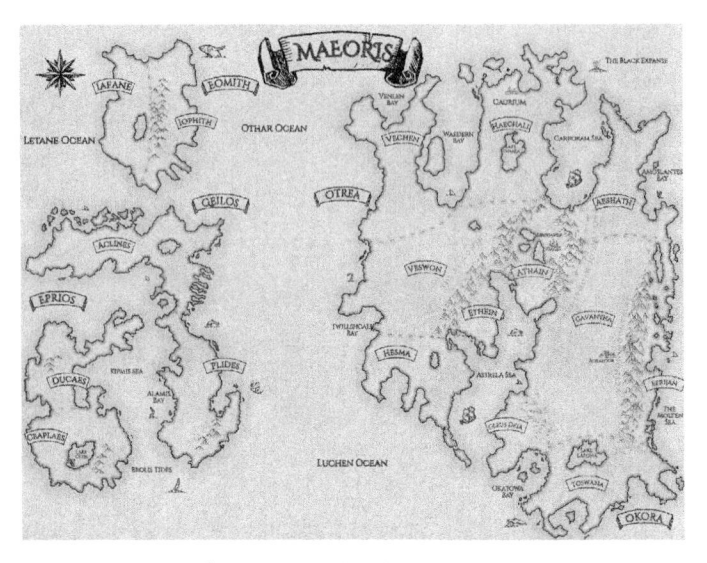

For more maps of Maeoris and Adraedor, visit atleywykes.com

Chapter I

Kael

I needed to stop glaring at the Elves inspecting me and the line of other slaves, their mouths pursed as they tutted about our appearances, or I was going to get caught. Sharp-eared assholes. Taking a slow breath, I imagined stabbing my bone sword deep into the heart of the Elven female eyeing me with distaste. Her blood would match the crimson dress she held next to my face and everyone would scream as she collapsed, scattering as I pulled my blade free and advanced on them... It was a pleasant thought and gave me enough wherewithal to plaster on a vacant smile as they inspected the woman beside me. Not that I had my beloved sword or even clothes. I was alone in enemy territory. Defenseless. And it was my fault.

My adopted brother, Gavril, had begged me not to take the mission, to let someone else go instead. All of them had. They thought I'd blow it within an hour if I saw the Marshal... But I'd insisted, and when that didn't work, I'd slipped out of the hideout without permission, only leaving a note explaining where I'd gone. Now here I was, standing naked in front of a group of Elvish cunts as they decided which slaves to pick as prizes for the winners of the gladiator games, attempting to prove all of them wrong.

But it would all be worth it if I could complete the mission.

"They're all so dirty," a female Inferi Remnant complained. "How're we supposed to tell what they look like under this muck?" She wore golden silks, her horns polished to a shine. A royal concubine, for sure.

"The same way I did with you, Zija." The lead Elven woman replied in a tiresome tone as she stopped at the slave next to me, lifting one of her breasts with a single finger and frowning. "A few piercings can cover a lot of issues, can they not?"

The courtesan started to lift a hand to the hoop in her nose before she caught herself and narrowed her eyes. "These slaves are an embarrassment, Carita. We need the best for today. Rhazien wants everything to be perfect."

My ears pricked at the name of the governor of the desert city, though he was better known as the 'Beast' to me and my cohort.

"Mind your tongue." Carita snapped. "I don't care who you're fucking, you're not in charge here. I am. Understand?"

I held in a laugh at the Inferi Remnant's expression. Did she really think that an *elf* would treat her as an equal just because she was in the Governor's harem? The arrogant bastards thought they were better than anyone else and had fought a war with the gods to prove it.

"Then it'll be on your head," Zija responded with a sneer as she swept out of the room, a few other similarly dressed Remnants falling in behind her.

Carita laughed under her breath, waving away her assistant's questioning look as she continued down the line.

"Name and age?" The assistant asked, not even looking up at me from the ledger she carried.

"Kael. Twenty-four," I answered, my tone just a touch too hostile, and she glanced up at me sharply. I gave her a bland smile, hoping I'd covered my mistake. Before Orya died, I'd been able to fake it. To keep my head down and survive. But that part of me had died with her and now all I wanted to do was fight, regardless of the consequences.

"This one is interesting," Carita said, stopping in front of me.

I studied her as she inspected me; her hair was dark and straight, flowing down to her waist, her dress black and red with golden touches. A member of the royal household, then. She was tall and beautiful, as all the Elves were. Perfect in her immortality. Something they'd stolen from all us Remnants.

She stepped closer, scrutinizing my features. Her metallic eyes seemed to take in every detail of my body—absorbing it all as she categorized each flaw. She ran her fingers through my long silvery hair, causing a gentle shiver to run down my spine.

"This one has a unique look," Carita said finally. "What are you, a Wraith Remnant? Or maybe a Sirin?"

"I don't know," I answered truthfully. My father had been human and my mother had died when I was a toddler. The rest was a mystery.

"No matter. This one should work with a few changes. She will be our 'Desert Lily.' With her skin and hair, it fits." She listed a few criticisms about my appearance that her assistant jotted down.

I clenched my jaw, which according to her was too sharp, determined not to punch the Elves talking about me like I was chattel. To them, I was.

"Step over here," another elven woman barked as Carita made her way down the line, selecting more women and men to join me on the other side of the room. A Sirin Remnant with olive skin and lavender hair pulled back into a tight bun shuffled over to stand beside me. Shimmery scales dotted her face, glistening with the tears silently streaming down her cheeks. She stood so still—only her hands trembled as her breath stuttered—that it seemed like she barely even registered what was happening around her.

I wanted to reach out, to comfort her. But I hesitated. How did one comfort someone who'd been reduced to a possession? To be used by others however they wished? Anything I said would be a lie.

I leaned closer and caught her eye, though my voice came out more awkward than comforting. "It's going to be alright," I said, wishing it was true, even as the lie tasted like ash in my mouth.

"It's not."

Her voice was so soft I barely heard her. "Just stay close to me. I'll keep an eye on you."

She stared at me dubiously before nodding. "What's your name?"

"Kael."

She wiped her eyes as she stared at me. "I'm Aella," she whispered, her voice wavering slightly.

My heart ached, memories of Orya crowding my mind. She'd been a Sirin Remnant, and too soft for Adraedor, just like the woman beside me. I wanted to protect Aella, as I hadn't been able to protect my best friend.

"Why are they choosing so many?" She whispered, her eyes darting around at our growing group.

I shrugged, a shiver of worry snaking through me. There were at least thirty slaves selected, almost quadruple the amount of the last games. Atar's balls. What was going on? I didn't even have time to wonder how monumentally I'd fucked up before the lead woman spoke again, directing us to follow her. A few of the unselected women looked disappointed, but most sagged with relief to have not been chosen.

Aella whimpered as we followed Carita into the hallway, her movements shaky. We were somewhere deep in the colosseum; the sounds of the gathering crowd were muffled but still recognizable. I couldn't smell any blood or animal waste, so we weren't near the gladiator barracks. The walls were made of the same red stone as the exterior, without the fancy adornments in the arena itself. It was still grander than anything I'd ever known.

Carita opened a door, and a blast of humid air hit me, so foreign that I didn't understand the sensation of moisture coating my skin initially. Aella cried out, seeing what I couldn't.

"Stop." The elf's voice rang out, cracking like the whips we were all familiar with. "Over here first."

Aella's shoulders fell as she moved with the rest of the group, and I could see what had captivated her. Massive pools of water spread throughout the room, the floor tiled in the colors of the royal house, with stairs leading into the baths. I hadn't seen this much water since before the Niothe sent me to the desert. Not even the Water Forums in the wealthy parts of Adraedor boasted this much clean water.

I tore my eyes away from clear pools and looked around, noting the exits and potential weapons as they directed us to a table laden with cups and bowls, filled to the brim with drinks and food. Honeyed locusts were piled next to skewers of spiced fruits and tureens of tortoise soup. There wasn't a sign of seffa anywhere and I swallowed against a dry throat, my stomach growling.

"Drink and eat. Slowly." Carita warned, eyeing us with undisguised scorn. "I don't want any of you drinking the bathwater and getting too sick to service whichever lord selects you."

Shit. Something big had changed. I'd assumed the games would be the same as usual, no one daring to beat the Beast in the arena, with him claiming all the trophies for himself. This was bad.

The others stayed back, no doubt expecting a trick. Water wasn't given freely in Adraedor. Every drop had to be earned. To see so much just waiting to be soiled by our bodies while so many in the city died of dehydration made me sick, but I strode forward anyway and selected a goblet. I drank deeply, letting the cool, clear water wash away the grit that always seemed to coat my tongue. The liquid hit my empty stomach with a pang, but I didn't stop until I'd drained the entire cup, reaching for the jug to fill it once more. Aella joined me, no longer hesitant, as she clutched her cup close to her chest.

"What if it's poisoned?" Aella whispered, eyes wide with worry.

"It smells fine," I said. The water was cold and refreshing, and the food looked incredible—better than anything I'd ever seen before. "Besides, if they wanted to get rid of us, they could have done that already."

I picked up a skewer of spiced fruits and took a bite, savoring the sweet and tangy flavors that burst on my tongue. It was so good that I forgot my fear for a moment, until Aella prodded me in the ribs, reminding me of our situation as she glanced pointedly at the Elves.

Carita and the others mocked us in Elvish, either unknowing or uncaring that I understood them.

"It's fine," I whispered. "They're just laughing at how we're eating." She looked at me dubiously before eating as well.

I picked up a bowl of soup, humming in pleasure with the first sip of the silky broth. Living in hideouts had its drawbacks, and one of those was living on seffa and dried meat.

"How do you know what they're saying?" Aella asked.

"I learned Elvish when I lived in Haechall—"

"Now into the baths." Carita interrupted me to direct us into the pool, her voice laced with a hint of cruel amusement as she watched those born in the desert approach with trepidation. I went in, eager to be clean for the first time in years. Aella hesitated at the edge, face pale and eyes wide as she looked around her. I reached out a hand, beckoning her closer.

"It's alright, it's not too deep." I called, and she stumbled forward until she was standing next to me waist-deep in the water. She blinked rapidly, tears spilling down her cheeks as she gazed around us in wonder.

"I've never—" She stopped a sob in her throat that tore through me. Sirins had ruled the sea; water was their home. For one to have never felt the sensation of cool water lapping around her... Unsure how to comfort her, I patted her shoulder and slipped under the water to avoid saying the wrong thing.

The others followed suit, some still fearful but none daring to refuse Carita's orders. I floated languidly, memories of my early childhood drifting back to me. Of the days I'd spent swimming in streams with my father, the sun on my skin warm and comforting, not the fearsome orb it was here. I couldn't remember much of him anymore, half of my memories of my father blending with Haemir, but I remembered his smile as he taught me to swim, splashing in the city fountain together as water cascaded from the fey statues. Caurium had been beautiful before it burned.

"Clean yourselves." Carita's voice snapped me out of my reverie, directing us to scrub ourselves with the bars of soap provided. The sand washed from my body coated the bottom of the pool and I wiggled my toes to dislodge it from my feet. It had been almost fourteen years since I didn't have grit on some part of me and I hated that I was grateful to the Elves for giving me this moment.

This was their way of controlling us. They would take and take, breaking us down until simply being clean felt like a blessing, blinding us to the other offenses they committed against us.

I stepped out of the pool, water streaming down my too thin body, and Aella followed me reluctantly.

"I didn't know." She touched her hair, marveling at the drops of water on her fingers. Anger licked through me like flames. The Elves had stolen so much from her. From all of us. I snatched my towel out of the attendant's hands and stomped over to the adjoining room, where more slaves waited with supplies to prep our bodies.

"You. Come here." One motioned for me and I stalked over to her, flopping onto the leather bench before she asked me to.

"What?"

She raised a delicate brow but didn't respond to my attitude.

"Give me your arm." I did and watched as she spread a thick, waxy substance onto it before yanking it away, and taking all the fine hairs on my skin with it.

"Vetia's horns!"

She rolled her eyes as I glared at her. "Calm down. It's just wax."

Fuck, that hurt. I took a deep breath, blocking out the pain. I could do this. Just one more step until I killed the Beast and set our plans in motion.

"Fine."

I clenched my teeth as she guided me into new positions to remove my body hair from the neck down. I kept quiet even as she ripped almost all the pale hair from between my legs, only leaving a small triangle of curls at the apex of my folds. No part of my body was untouched; every inch was plucked, polished, and trimmed before they covered me in scented oils until my pale skin glimmered like pearls. I felt even more vulnerable than when I'd worked in the mines—as if my skin was too thin and would break apart at the slightest touch.

Carita approached, nodding at my curling hair that cascaded down my shoulders. "Excellent work. Now, let's begin her enhancements. Sit."

She grabbed a pair of strange tongs and held them next to my chest as I watched in trepidation. With a swift motion, she clamped my nipple and I shouted. Ignoring my exclamation, she pierced it horizontally and threaded an electrum ring through behind the needle, keeping enough pressure that it would stay in place as she spun the opal bead to close it.

"Ydonja's stars, that hurt." I hissed, my eyes welling up with tears as Carita inspected her work, tugging on the ring.

I couldn't hold in a growl as she did the other breast, her movements as practiced as before. Her eyes narrowed in concentration before flooding black until no whites or irises remained as she touched the opals simultaneously, power flowing from her as magic activated the stone and metal. My breasts heated and swelled painfully, growing from their modest handfuls to enough to fill even the palms of a Zerkir Remnant.

She smiled, her mouth twisting into a satisfied expression as she motioned for me to stand up. My newly augmented breasts were heavy on my chest and flushed as the intention of her magic took root inside me. I'd known I would be on the receiving end of some enchantments. I just wasn't expecting this. My body felt *wrong*.

"If you all want us to have bigger tits, then you should feed us more." The words slipped out of my mouth before I could call them back and I winced, hearing my brother's voice in my head. *Too foolhardy, Kael.*

"If I wanted to give you a tail, I could." Carita smirked, her lips curving into a cruel smile. "Don't tempt me."

I dropped my gaze to avoid making eye contact with her, my urge to retaliate growing stronger. If I saw that smirk, I'd slap her and ruin everything. I could sense her delight in my obedience, and my self-control began to slip away. I nodded, and the laugh she couldn't contain only increased my need to attack her. To dominate her and show her I wasn't weak. Not anymore.

"Good," Carita said. "Turn your head to the side. Oh, your ears are already pierced. They're permanent. Hmmm." She inspected them, a line forming between her brows as she concentrated before glancing at me when I spoke.

"Why are you piercing my ears?"

"To prevent you from conceiving. And to keep your body hair from growing back." She answered, her gaze going far away as if deep in thought before she shook herself. She pierced my ears again, heat running through them to the rest of my body as she threaded more electrum rings and opals through my lobes. I knew different metals and stones were used in their magic, like all the slave collars had onyx, for example, but I didn't know what anything did. I assumed it had some healing effects since my breasts had already stopped aching, but that was only my best guess.

One of her assistants approached with a tray of more metal rings and gems, an array of needles beside them. I cringed, wondering what horrors she'd wreak on me next.

She gripped my chin, turning my head from side to side before motioning the girl onward. "Her face is suitable now that it's clean. Only one piercing left."

Joy.

"Spread your legs."

"What?" I asked in alarm, instinctively closing them.

She gestured to where Aella clutched the bench tight as an Elf threaded a ring through the hood of her clitoris.

"Oh, fuck no." I tried to stand, and she grasped me by the arm, holding me in place.

"It's a kindness," Carita explained, a hint of pity entering her expression, at odds with her brusque demeanor. "It'll make you enjoy any... attentions you receive."

I glared at her, disgust and shame swirling in my stomach. Over the years, I'd said a lot of cruel things about the concubines kept by the nobles, their bodies water-fat and soft. *Cetena's scales.* It was bad enough to be assaulted, but to be made to like it…

I didn't realize just what a mind-fuck they had to deal with. Could I do this? Even to complete my mission? I didn't plan on fucking the Beast. Only getting close enough to kill him...

"Fine."

I spread my legs and waited for the pain. Gritting my teeth didn't prevent a groan from escaping me as she pierced my delicate flesh, spinning the stone in place. I waited for the pain to subside, as it had in my breasts, but it didn't.

"Why isn't it healing?" I hissed as she gestured for an assistant to bring my dress, a column of white fabric so sheer that I could see through both layers easily.

"Your lord will activate it to the level he desires." She answered, looking over the floral hair pieces the attendant had brought, selecting two white desert lilies. "Put these in her hair. And hurry, we have to present them in less than an hour."

Finally.

The attendant helped me tug the dress on, looping the fabric over my neck and crossing my breasts, leaving my stomach bare as she wrapped my hips in more sheer fabric and arranged my hair. All the other slaves were dressed similarly in an array of colors, each with a unique flower in their hair, their dresses, and sarongs displaying all their freshly waxed flesh. There weren't any mirrors for me to inspect myself, but judging from the changes in the others, I wouldn't recognize what I saw anyway. Gone were the waifish, dirty slaves of before. Now their bodies appeared toned and curvaceous, with plump lips and glossy hair.

"Line up. Quickly." Carita demanded as she looked us over, her expression nowhere near as sanguine as before when she'd told Zija off for dismissing this crop of concubines. Aella walked to stand beside me, choosing her steps carefully to avoid jostling her new piercing. I clicked my tongue, my nerves getting the best of me, as Carita led us out the doors back into the hallway.

I followed our procession through the colosseum halls, noting all the turns, past the vendor stands filled with human 'guests' from all corners of the empire. The press of people grew thicker as Carita led us to the viewing platform opposite the royal booth, where we'd be displayed for the entire arena. Aella shivered beside me despite the blast of heat as we went outside and I gripped her hand.

Movement in the royal box caught my attention as a man clad in leather and bone armor stood, towering over the others. His black hair flowed loose on his wide shoulders, framing a face that didn't hold any kindness. It was hard, outlined with barely restrained anger that promised pain and destruction to his enemies. His bronze eyes glimmered in the sunlight like molten gold as he made his way across the platform to where an Elf I didn't recognize sat on the throne. Theron Axidor, the Marshal of this hell and my personal nightmare.

My lip curled as he smirked and I had to fight to keep from vaulting over the banister to attack him, regardless of the consequences. But I held back, forcing myself to think of the mission instead. This was why the others didn't want me here. They didn't believe I'd be able to handle seeing him again after what had happened.

I took a shuddering breath as Carita moved us into place on the viewing platform and Theron's gaze settled on me. His lips twisted into a wry grin that made my heart pound in my chest, the urge to end him almost overwhelming. I glared back, unable to school my features to anything other than rage. My brother was right. I shouldn't have come. And now I was going to get myself killed.

Chapter 2

Theron

I pressed my lips together, ignoring Theodas as he attempted to impress the Emperor with tales from the front line. He flashed me a haughty grin as he sipped frostberry wine, a delicacy from Vechen that Rhazien had shipped in for this visit. As much as I'd been dreading the court descending upon Adraedor, my brother's distraction for the last few months had been a welcome change. He hadn't tried to kill me once.

"The Zerkir Remnant strongholds are tough, but the Niothe are making headway with me at their head." The corner of his thin mouth lifted as he shot me a cruel look, his cobalt eyes locked on me, as if to drink in every drop of my impotent anger. I ignored him, stepping to the rail to watch the battle below.

Asshole.

I'd lost my position as Lord Marshal to Theodas Vennorin five years ago after I'd disobeyed the emperor and had been stuck here ever since, spending my days chasing slaves and picking sand out of my ass crack as I avoided Rhazien's attempts on my life.

"Theodas hasn't done shit for the Niothe," Zerek said in a low voice behind me, his red hair glinting under the bright sunlight of the colosseum as he tossed a grape in his mouth. "He just watches from the rear while the Senthenna does all the hard work. Then he acts like some kind of warrior prince."

Raenisa laughed dryly. "More like a court jester," she muttered as her sharp eyes scanned the crowd. She hated these things almost as much as I did; always seeming more comfortable at battle than in court functions. She'd refused to wear a gown, instead wearing her golden armor.

"He doesn't care about clearing out strongholds, only appearing to do so with few losses." Our naval force, the Senthenna, had seen more battles in the last five years than centuries before under his command.

"Think he'll be the heir?" Zerek asked, leaning against the rail as his hawkish gaze swept the packed stands. As much as he tried to separate himself from his family, the Amyntas' blood ran true in him.

I shrugged, not wanting to dwell on it. "Who knows?"

"You and Rhazien have the strongest claim. The Vennorins are only married to the throne. The snakes shouldn't even be here."

"We all know why the She-snake is here," Raenisa said with a smirk. I winced as the warrior fighting a taudrin lost an arm to the great lizard-like beast, ignoring Raenisa's pointed comment. Another fighter sprinted forward with a pike, pushing the creature back into its pen. Atar's hammer. What was Thanja thinking when she created these desert beasts?

The smell of sweat and blood filled the air as I looked around the Colosseum. Rhazien had spared no expense; showcasing Adraedor's wealth at every turn—gilded armor on the guards, waving scarlet flags with the Carxidor sigil, and ladies fanning themselves with spider-silk against the desert heat. The arena was an impressive sight; a massive circle of sand lined with carved red sandstone pillars and topped by stands that seemed almost too high to reach. Vibrant mosaics depicting the Godsfall adorned the walls, and the stands below filled with excited faces eager to watch the bloodshed. The entire spectacle was absurd; a show of affluence and authority more akin to a game of chance than an actual way of choosing the next ruler.

And at the center of it all was Emperor Varzorn.

He sat atop a throne constructed from bloodstone and quartz, his elfin features stark against its glow. His jet-black hair was cropped at his shoulders and his golden eyes shone with an unnerving intensity. I shivered as his gaze swept over me, my skin prickling under the weight of his scrutiny. He was more tyrant than emperor; cold and calculating, but with an air of power that made even Rhazien take pause. Rumors abounded about his ruthlessness in court, with the murder of his brother an open secret. And I had the bad luck of being his sister's son.

Varzorn surveyed the crowd before pinning Theodas with his stony stare. "Why don't you join them? Show the court what you can do on the sands."

His eyes shone with cruel mirth as he smiled at Theodas, whose mouth snapped shut before he plastered on a smile.

"Of course, your majesty. Trying my hand against these desert creatures would be an easy warm-up." Theodas' gaze darted to mine, and I sighed, ignoring his comment.

Varzorn caught the look that passed between us and his teeth shone in a smile that sent a fissure of fear down my spine. "No doubt these beasts wouldn't pose a threat to the Lord Marshal of the Niothe." Theodas inclined his head, not seeing the obvious trap he'd led himself into. Vennorins may strike true, but that wasn't a match for a Carxidor. "Only our formidable warriors would present a challenge to you."

"An excellent idea, uncle," Rhazien called, striding into the space, his favorite concubines trailing behind him in a flutter of golden silk and horns. He always favored Inferi Remnants for his harem; said their cunts were warmer. "I prepared prizes should you desire an exhibition. If you'll allow me?"

Varzorn gestured for him to continue, an amused smile twisting his cruel lips.

The crowd hushed as Rhazien paused at the edge of the platform. His bald head shone in the sunlight, tattoos snaking across his scalp and down his neck. Living in the same palace with him for the last half a decade hadn't lessened my fear of him, only increased my cunning. Every day was a gauntlet as he sought to eliminate the only other male heir with Carxidor blood, not that I claimed it.

"For the victors of today's games, I have prepared a special prize," Rhazien announced, arms spread wide. "A bounty of courtesans to reward the strongest fighters; each one named for a different type of flower. As you can see," he gestured towards the platform opposite them, revealing dozens of beautiful Remnants with exotic eyes and luscious bodies, "they are a truly exquisite bouquet." Rhazien continued, and I ignored him, grabbing a glass of expensive wine and tossing it back.

Fuck.

Rhazien loved to host gladiator games every month with courtesans as prizes, and they always ended the same way. Him winning since none of the nobles would truly stand against him. On the few times I'd been forced to take part, I'd conceded without ever touching the sand, having no interest in giving

Rhazien a chance to kill me with an audience. But those days didn't have nearly as many concubines for him to claim or the emperor in attendance. I was going to have to fight today. No doubt all the potential heirs would, at least if they wanted to be noticed by Varzorn.

A few of the lords had already begun eyeing the courtesans hungrily, ready to take whatever they could get. Across the sands, a woman stood on the platform in stark contrast to the rest of them. She wore all white, the thin material revealing her lush body, her hair cascading down her back like spun silver, interwoven with lilies. Her eyes were a deep green, piercing in their intensity, and something about them seemed familiar. But mostly I noticed how she was looking around her with utter disdain for those gathered there, as if she hated them as much as I.

"The winner will get a first choice of which flower he'd like to… pluck." He grinned as the audience laughed.

"Or she." The eldest Sarro daughter called out, the one they nicknamed the 'Young Bear,' since she was just as hard headed as her grandfather.

The crowd parted as Caelia Sarro strode through them, her dark hair cropped short above her ears and armor clanking with every step. Her muscular frame was impressive and Raenisa tensed beside me in admiration of the woman before us. The Young Bear had been feared for years, not because she was cruel but because she refused to follow the traditions that bound us all and damned anyone in her way. I'd admire her more if she and her siblings hadn't been grasping for the throne since before I was born.

"We'll go first. Come on, Theodas." She announced, her gaze never wavering from Rhazien's smug face. He smirked back with a nod and gestured for her to join the crowd of fighters below.

The audience held their breath, eagerness filling the arena like a current of electricity as the oldest Sarro stepped onto the sand, Theodas quickly putting on armor on the edges of the coliseum. Gold, copper, and silver adorned him and I snickered.

"Someone needs a lot of help, it seems."

Zerek chuckled, his sharp eyes following Theodas as the snake shouted at the servants below. "With that much silver and copper, he has to wear the gold just to walk."

Caelia wore mostly gold, going for brute strength in her fighting style, unsurprising. Her face betrayed no emotion as she stepped forward and bowed.

I held my breath as they began to circle each other, both looking for an opening to strike. Caelia advanced first, sending a volley of blows towards Theodas' chest plate.

She was graceful and powerful as she moved, every action economical and precise. Theodas followed suit, but with a much different grace; his movements were wild and untamed, combined with strength that only comes from battles fought time and time again—something I knew all too well.

I raised a brow and nodded to Zerek. "Black Theo has been training."

The Young Bear seemed unconcerned by the ferocity of Theodas' attacks, blocking them with her shield or dodging them completely. No matter how powerful his blows were, she always stayed one step ahead of him.

Until he managed a scratch.

Her movements slowed, and she shook her head as if trying to clear it, and he pressed his advantage. She tried to dodge his strikes but soon found herself backed against the wall of the arena, arms shaking with exhaustion. Theodas lifted his sword high and brought it down hard, slamming it onto her helmet and knocking her out. He stood, lifting his blade in the air in victory.

"Poison?" Raenisa murmured, and I nodded in agreement.

"Fucking snakes," Zerek swore. "You expect that shit from a Lazan."

"You forget who their mother is." I pointed out, glancing to where Theodas' mother lounged with the empress, a knowing smile curving her lips. "This clutch of vipers has fangs."

Raenisa made a face as Caelia's brother rushed out, pulling his sister to safety and shooting Black Theo a sinister look.

Rhazien clucked his tongue in mock surprise. "What a shame. Why don't you teach him a lesson, Theron?"

I looked at Rhazien and Varzorn. Their faces were nearly mirror images of one another, both eager to see me fall to my rival. I sighed, feeling the weight of their combined gaze. There would be no bowing out this time. To do so would mark me as an easy target for the others vying for Varzorn's attention.

I stood up and squared my shoulders. "As you wish, brother."

The crowd erupted in cheers at the announcement as I followed Raenisa down to the arena, tightening the straps on my armor until it was snug.

"He feints left before he attacks. 'Strike true,' my ass."

I grunted in response. I'd noticed the same.

"Make him pay," Raenisa growled, her eyes locked on Theodas with a bloodthirsty look. The Taelyrs were fiercely loyal; I didn't think Theodas understood just what kind of enemy he'd made in Raenisa when he'd stolen our assignment. He performed a show of stretching his sword arm, confident now as he strutted around the arena. His expression fell when he turned and saw it was me he faced.

"Theron? Why are you—?"

"Varzorn." I shrugged. "And you know why."

There were no bows or niceties this time; both of us waited for the announcement, staring each other down before circling one another warily. My bone armor was nearly impenetrable but didn't offer me any enhancements of speed or strength, not like the mass of metal he'd strapped onto his body.

"What kind of poison did you use on the Young Bear?" I asked conversationally, keeping in step with him as we moved in a circle.

"Wyrmbane." He smirked, and I laughed under my breath. The wyrm was my family's sigil, no doubt something he'd planned.

"You have the antidote?" I asked, sand shifting under my feet. He wouldn't have as much experience fighting on the sand as I, especially compensating for his magic.

"Worried you'll need it?"

Theodas moved first, swinging his sword in a wide arc. I blocked it easily, and we went back and forth, both of us testing the other's skill. I could feel his confidence increasing as I parried his blows one by one; his strength and speed growing as he funneled more magic into the metal.

But putting power behind a blow wasn't enough.

He left himself open for a split second and that was all I needed. With a quick twist, I turned his own poisoned blade against him; he winced in pain as the blade sunk deep into his arm.

He stumbled back in shock, dropping his sword with a loud clang before sinking to his knees. Theodas shook his head in confusion, just as Caelia had done only moments before.

I stepped forward, pointing my sword at him menacingly before lowering it to press against the side of his neck until it forced him to bare his throat or be cut.

"Yield."

His lips thinned further until they were no longer visible, his cobalt blue eyes glaring up at me.

"I concede," he murmured before collapsing back into the sand. His brothers ran forward, the lumbering one scooping his older brother into his arms as the one with the silver eye shot me a venomous look.

The crowd cheered in approval as he carried away Theodas and I made my way to the sidelines where Raenisa waited, the next pair of nobles already hitting the sand to duel for the emperor's favor.

"Well done." She said with a nod before turning away to survey the arena. My gaze searched the throng only to settle at the top of the stands on the same beautiful white-haired concubine who had been watching me since she'd walked out. Her eyes were filled with loathing and hatred as she stared at me, and it felt like I was looking into a mirror.

I shook my head, attempting to rid myself of the strange feeling and focus on the battle in front of me.

The courtiers murmured as they watched the next skirmish. It didn't take me long to realize what they were discussing; after Varzorn had pulled me from the Niothe, they had dismissed me as an option. My quick defeat of Theodas had shown them I was a genuine threat, and now everyone else who wanted to be the emperor's heir would try to kill me, too.

But I had a bigger problem. I couldn't take my eyes off the courtesan.

No matter how hard I tried, my gaze kept wandering back toward her. I'd contemplated forfeiting after beating Theo, but the mental image of someone else laying claim to her made my blood boil.

I forced myself to look away from her and toward the arena, where two more nobles were beginning their duel. Steel clanged against steel as both opponents fought for dominance, each trying their best to outwit and overpower their opponent.

The crowd cheered them on, though my focus quickly shifted away from the fight as a movement in the corner of my eye caught my attention; it was that same white-haired courtesan again, now standing at the edge of the balcony looking down on us all with a strange expression on her face. As if she wanted to kill every last one of us.

I watched her throughout the rest of the bouts as the afternoon wore on, even during my other fights with distant cousins who were determined to make a name for themselves. Her gaze never wavered, tracking me as if she wished it was she on the sand, able to skewer me herself.

"We've come to the last bout of the day. This battle will determine who will be crowned champion and have the first choice of the prizes. Prince Rhazien Carxidor versus Prince Theron Axidor!" The announcer declared. My stomach sank, and I looked up, my gaze locking with Rhazien's. He smirked, his eyes glinting with cunning. *Fuck.* Had he planned this?

Varzorn made a face when they announced my father's surname, as if annoyed I still claimed the Axidor name instead of his, as Rhazien did. The emperor had never had children—they tended to kill their fathers in the royal family—but he enjoyed Rhazien's claim of his Carxidor heritage.

I took a deep breath and steeled myself. Rhazien was bigger and stronger with all that gold on, but I had trained harder than anyone else in the Niothe. Memories from my childhood crowded my mind, flashes of blood and pain with Rhazien's face hovering over me, and I shoved them away as he sauntered down the steps to the sand.

"It looks like it's you and me, brother," he mocked, his voice carrying through the arena. My stomach roiled, a strange mix of fear and determination flooding my veins with adrenaline, but I pushed myself to stay focused. "Unless you're ready to concede?"

"Not today," I replied, drawing my bone sword once more, wishing I still had its twin. Godsdamn Striker. Rhazien's expression hardened, and I realized his plan. He'd expected me to yield, as I always did. Then it would appear as if the man who'd defeated everyone else was too afraid to face him. Any other day, he would be right. I didn't give a damn what Varzorn or anyone else thought of me. But I wasn't about to forsake my claim on *her*. I glanced up at the concubines, unsurprised to see the silver-haired beauty's gaze still locked upon me.

We advanced slowly, testing our swords against one another as we circled, neither of us willing to give up an inch of ground. My weapon was sharper, made of bone from the god Rhaedos, but Rhazien had more power behind his attacks. His movements were lightning quick, his metal armor and magical metallurgy giving him unnatural speed and strength as he staved off my strikes with almost no effort.

My muscles strained with every parry, sweat dripping down my face as I desperately tried to gain some kind of advantage against his massive power. But Rhazien was too swift, his sword always faster than mine.

"What's wrong brother? Don't tell me you're scared?" He taunted me from across the sand. More memories threatened to overwhelm me, my body remembering the pain he'd inflicted on it, and I had to fight the urge to flee.

I didn't respond; instead, I gritted my teeth and redoubled my efforts, determined to show him I wasn't that frightened little boy any longer. Our swords clashed together in a flurry of sparks until it seemed like we were both about to collapse from exhaustion and I cursed myself for forgetting my bronze. I was tired, and he knew it.

"Poor Theron, never has what it takes. Just like father." He attacked, driving me back as he swung for my throat.

My gaze shifted away from Rhazien and towards the balcony, where the white-haired courtesan was watching us intently. Somehow, in that moment of distraction, I found a spark of renewed energy and determination that pushed me forward. If I wanted her, then I had to win this fight. I didn't know why I was so desperate to claim her. All I knew was that she was *mine.*

I held my sword aloft, sunlight glinting off the pommel as I advanced toward Rhazien. He shouted something at me I couldn't understand, his words lost in the tumult of the cheering crowd, but I had no care for what he said—my only thought was to win this battle and claim her. I ducked and twisted out of the way as Rhazien lunged for me, my movements so swift it felt like I was flying. A cutting blow from my blade slammed against Rhazien's back, forcing him to one knee. The crowd roared thunderously as our blades clashed, their cheers and jeers pushing me onward as I fought. I sprang at him, my motions so fast it seemed like I had been given wings like a son of Kearis as I moved around him.

I landed a solid blow against Rhazien's shoulder that sent him sprawling back onto the ground. The crowd roared as our swords collided, reverberating in my ears as I advanced, determined to not let Rhazien best me this time. Never again.

Rhazien scrambled to his feet, his face a mask of rage as he lunged at me with one last desperate attack. I parried his blade with mine, holding it away from my body as I pushed him back. He stumbled backward and fell to the ground, his weapon getting lost in the sand as I leaped forward and pressed the blade against his neck. His eyes widened in surprise before hardening as I pushed the tip of my sword into his pulse.

"Go on, brother. Finish this." He hissed, waiting for me to prove my strength. That I was as much a Carxidor as him.

I glared at him, clenching my teeth in silence as a swirl of raging emotions swelled within me. I wanted to do it. To rid myself of the man that had tormented me all my life. I glanced up to where Varzorn watched, his expression impassive as he motioned for me to show mercy.

I stepped back, and the crowd roared. Whether or not in support of my decision, I didn't know. The populace hated Rhazien, but they disliked me as well. My brother scowled, his face an ugly puce color as the announcer declared me the winner, but I barely heard it. My attention locked on the white-haired concubine once more and I stalked forward, intent on claiming what was mine.

Chapter 3

Kael

I stared in disbelief as the Marshal strode across the blood-spattered sand, the last rays of sunset painting his pale skin gold. *The bastard*. The Beast had been about to win and my mission salvaged, but he'd ruined it. Just like he'd destroyed everything else in my life.

The other nobles who'd fought loped after him like a pack of wolves, trying to match his long strides. He didn't seem to notice them, his gaze intent on one thing.

Me.

Had he recognized me? It had been years since he'd seen me, Teodosija only sending me on missions when she knew I wouldn't face him, but he might remember. *Ydonja knows I thought about our last meeting every day.* I straightened my back, uncomfortable with how my new breasts strained the fabric—I looked like one of those water-fat courtesans that I'd once derided—preparing for violence. If he attacked, I'd steal his sword. I'd done it once before, I could do it again.

He surged onto the platform, dominating the space, and drawing all eyes to him. His dark hair billowed behind him and he wore the bone and leather armor favored by the Empire's military elite, supposedly made from the bones of our fallen gods. Black kohl was smeared around his eyes to protect them from the sun's glare, just like the desert dwellers painted theirs. My stomach churned with hatred as our eyes met for a split second before I forced mine to the ground beneath my feet. I took a shuddering breath, trying to ignore the need to kill him for what he'd done.

Aella whimpered next to me, her face pale with dread at being so close to the Marshal. We all knew who the slave catcher was.

"It'll be alright," I whispered. "I'll find you. I swear."

He stepped forward and Carita gave him a practiced smile, gesturing for him to come closer and inspect her wares like a vendor at the market.

"Prince Theron, congratulations on your victory."

A voice boomed through the arena, declaring him the winner once again, and the crowd erupted, a mixture of cheering and jeers as the rest of the nobility was announced.

"Carita," he said, nodding to her and finally tearing his gaze away from me. I watched him out of the corner of my eye, not wanting him to notice me again.

"As the victor of the games, you have the first choice of our flowers."

Gross. Why not just call us sex slaves and be done with it?

The nobles had gathered around Carita and the concubines, eagerly eyeing us, their voices low as they made crude comments about our bodies.

"Look at the tits on that one," an elf snickered, pointing to me.

"I want a Kyrie Remnant. They squawk when they come," another said, garnering a big laugh from the others.

My stomach twisted with disgust. They treated us like animals. I'd forgotten what it felt like after living in the desert for the last five years. Teodosija had warned me that the Marshal was off limits, but I hadn't realized how hard it would be to ignore the women beside me as they were mistreated. Part of me had a fool's hope that I could kill the Beast before any of them were hurt, bringing them with me back into our hideout. But there was no way I would be able to save all of them now and the realization hollowed my chest.

Aella trembled next to me, her eyes wide and filled with tears that refused to fall. I interwove my fingers with hers and she gripped my hand tight, her knuckles turning white. I couldn't even try to comfort her. Anything I said would be a lie.

I edged in front of her as the nobles jostled each other, leering at us. I didn't want them to see her, as useless as the gesture was.

Carita stepped forward and silenced them with a sharp look. "Prince Theron, if you please."

He moved closer, and I made the mistake of looking up. His gaze locked on me and I froze, my heart thudding against my ribcage. I knew that expression. It was the same one he'd given me in the canyon. The same predatory glare that had been on his face as he cut off Haemir's hand.

Theron stepped toward me, his head tilted as he looked down into my eyes. His bronze stare was intense yet unreadable and something stirred inside of me I refused to acknowledge. My pulse fluttered wildly, but I didn't look away even though I knew hatred filled my gaze.

His expression hardened, and he nodded curtly to Carita, who smiled, her teeth sharp in the twilight.

"The Desert Lily is yours." She announced, clapping her hands together in delight as Theron motioned for me to step forward. I squeezed Aella's hand before gently disentangling our fingers, feeling like a monster for abandoning her. Carita snapped her fingers at a servant and a young girl hurried to her, carrying a silk sack.

"For your safety, your highness. This will prevent her from harming you." Carita handed the Marshal a strange object, and I realized with horror that it was an electrum torque collar with an onyx stone; a beautiful necklace that proclaimed me to be owned by another.

My body shivered as he stepped closer, his body heat radiating off him in waves, and my mind raced with thoughts I shouldn't be having about him; he smelled like leather and citrus and something else indescribable, something that made my skin flush with warmth despite myself.

I closed my eyes for a moment, almost forgetting what we were here for before opening them again when I felt cold metal against my throat. His fingers trailed against my throat as he clasped the torque and I forced myself to remain still, not to move away and break the trance of his touch. His eyes flooded black as they held mine, the collar on my neck heating as he marked me as his.

I turned my eyes away from his as he stepped back, my skin still pulsing as the power activated. The crowd erupted into cheers and a voice inside me whispered that I'd made a terrible mistake.

"Come."

"She will later," the noble behind him snickered, and turned to glare at them. They were sick, twisted beings. I couldn't wait to rid Adraedor of all of them.

I held my head high as I followed the Marshal, my mind racing as he led me past the gathered Elves. A hand squeezed my ass, and I smacked it hard without thinking.

"Remnant bitch—" The Elf began when Theron turned, his expression thunderous. He grabbed the male by the throat, lifting him to his toes despite the weight of his armor.

"Touch what's mine again and you'll lose your fingers." He growled, dropping him. The other Elf wilted under his glare. I almost missed it as Aella, her face so pale she looked as if she was about to faint, was chosen by Rhazien.

Shit. Shit. Shit.

"My lord, wait a moment," Carita called, hurrying over. "Her clitoral piercing hasn't been activated yet. You'll need to heal it and set your intention for her desire."

He studied her for a beat before nodding. "Thank you for informing me."

How didn't he know? Surely, he had a massive harem. He'd been here long enough to accrue one. I cast a backward glance, locking stares with a scared Aella as he took me away. I couldn't just leave her... What should I do? Try to kill him first and then go for the Beast? I'd never make it. The best warriors the empire offered surrounded me. One of them would likely wound me, if not slaughter me outright, and I wouldn't be able to complete my mission. I didn't have a choice. Silently, I sent a prayer up to Ydonja, promising that I'd come for Aella once I'd escaped the Marshal and killed his brother.

I just had to play along for a few hours until I could slip away and kill the Beast. I'd survived worse; I could do this.

Probably.

The Marshal eyed me as I followed him through the colosseum, as if he wasn't sure what he was doing and was angry with himself for it.

"What's your name?" He demanded, his voice hard as he surveyed me.

Yeah, right. "Lily."

The corner of his mouth tipped up. "Sure it is."

He led me to a vast darkened room, the only light coming from a distant doorway, and gestured towards a giant spider creature that crouched over a bundle of webbing. The spider's legs made soft shuffling sounds as it walked, the chitinous plates on its belly clanking against each other as it approached him.

My breath caught in my throat as I stared at the vanira, its dark eyes watching me hungrily as he grinned, patting her on the side before saddling the wretched creature.

"Climb up," he commanded, stepping closer. His body was mere inches away from mine, our arms almost touching. His breath ghosted over my skin and my body hummed as our eyes connected.

"No way," I said, keeping my voice steady despite the fear coursing through my veins as I eyed its menacing form.

"Vaernix won't hurt you. I've raised her since the day she left her mother's brood sack."

"That means nothing to me," I protested, accidentally backing up into him as I tried to move away. He pressed his body close to my back as his lips brushed my ear.

"It *means* that I take care of what's mine." His large hands gripped my waist as he lifted me, heedless of the fact that I wore nothing under the scrap of fabric and my newly bare sex was on display and sat me atop the saddle.

"I'm not yours," I growled. I couldn't help it. Teodosija would want me to play along and be the wilting flower he expected, but I refused. All I wanted was to rip the sword from his waist and drive it into his stomach again. It was obvious that he didn't recognize me. I'd have the element of surprise on my side.

"You. Are. Mine." He ground out, his eyes never leaving mine. "I won you."

"You can't own a person."

"Look around you. Everyone here is owned by someone else. Accept it. That's how you stay alive." His gaze shuttered as he turned away and I let out a breath as if I'd been released. I'd once believed the same as he, keeping my head down to survive and enduring hideous things without comment. Until I learned that there were fates worse than death. Now I did whatever it took, regardless of the risk. The vanira shifted, and I stifled a shriek.

"Don't be afraid," he said as he slipped into the saddle behind me, his hard armor sharp on my back. "She won't bite."

His arms caged me in as he grabbed the reins, pulling them tight, and the vanira set off. I gripped at the saddle horn, a shiver racing up my spine as we started forward. The beast was graceful, its massive legs moving in smooth strides as it followed his commands. The rough hairs pricked the sensitive skin of my thighs, but I was too afraid to move and relieve the discomfort.

His breath was warm on my neck and for a moment I forgot about how much I hated him, how much this terrified me. His hands were gentle as he tightened the harness and it sent a shiver through me.

The spider shuddered, threatening to throw us off balance, and Theron steadied me, his large hand spread over my bare stomach. The trip to the castle took mere minutes atop the massive beast, and soon we were entering the sand-filled courtyard and dismounting. Vaernix chittered as the Marshal spoke to her in Elvish, telling her to go rest. An attendant led the vanira away, and I stared up at the enormous black ziggurat.

Before the Godsfall, the sons of Atar and Kearis had been like brothers, with Atar's favorite mountain forge in Kearis' territory, long before it had been named Cavantha. The Elves had built the castle and the original parts of the city with the strong basalt and obsidian from the range to shield themselves from the sand wyrms and desert storms and live amongst the Kyrie safely.

It was clear in the design that some occupants had once flown, the massive black structure filled with outdoor patios on each level for the night dwelling elves to enjoy once the sun went down having landing platforms.

I turned to find Theron watching me as I surveyed the castle, his eyes intent on my reaction. Glaring at him, I moved to study the fortifications rather than marveling at the splendor.

"Come on."

He attempted to grab my hand, but I pulled away, instead letting him lead me away from the courtyard and toward a side entrance. We had spies in the palace, but none who would help us get inside. I cataloged everything as he guided me up a back stair to his apartment, counting how many stairs were on each level and how many floors we passed. He opened the door to reveal an enormous suite with a massive patio shadowed by sheer curtains hanging from the ceiling. The wind caught the cloth, and it billowed like sails on a ship, the spicily scented braziers burning as night descended and Ydonja's stars shone.

His suite was a mix of dark and light. The walls were painted a warm cream color, and the floors were of black stone. Accents of red and iron gray—Axidor colors—dotted the space, from throw pillows to metal bookcases holding tomes about creatures before the Godsfall.

Maps of Maeoris covered the walls, but something else caught my attention. A bath bubbled in the corner, large enough to hold two people with space to spare, steam drifting upward. Anger filled me once more, imagining the slaves dying of dehydration while these water-fat bastards lorded it over all of us. The room was silent except for the distant clanging of the foundry and the wind whistling in from the open balcony doors.

I glanced up to find him staring at me, as if at a loss of what to do now that he had me in his den and I had the distinct impression that he hadn't thought this through.

"Where's your harem?" I asked, glancing around. I needed to know how many people I'd need to avoid to escape.

He shook his head. "I don't have one."

I made a non-committal noise in the back of my throat.

"Come here." He told me and I gritted my teeth, forcing my feet to move forward. I could do this. I'd let him fuck me and then I could complete my mission. Then Teodosija's plan could truly begin. After what had happened when I'd first arrived in Adraedor as a child, my relationship with sex had always been... difficult. With my lovers, I'd never felt fulfilled. But I didn't expect to enjoy this. It might even be easier than usual.

I lifted my chin as I met his eye, not bothering to disguise my hatred as I untied the fabric, letting the silk slip from my body until I stood naked before him.

"Is this what you want?"

He sucked in a breath, his eyes heating as they roved my curves before he stepped closer. His rough hand drifted down my stomach and I stayed motionless as my skin prickled. He cupped my sex possessively, and I gasped as one of his fingers dipped between my folds to rest on my new piercing. Heat flooded my core, the pain receding as he activated the metal and I glared at him.

"Drier than the Restless Sands." He smirked as he backed away, leaving me standing bare before him. "I don't fuck unwilling women. I don't need to." He turned, walking to the bath where he stripped off his armor, tossing it on a large pillow.

My clit throbbed, and anger wound through my veins. Of course, he didn't. Why would he when he could force any woman to beg for his cock with just a little magic? And how long until I was begging him to take me?

Chapter 4

Theron

I watched the angry concubine as she tied on the scrap of cloth they'd given her as a dress, stripping off the rest of my clothing for my bath. I still wasn't sure what had compelled me to choose her, but I didn't regret it.

As she dressed, I couldn't help but study her; the artful curves of her body and proud shoulders, the way her long muscles flexed under her skin. She was strong—not some soft-bodied, trained courtesan—most likely a slave from the mines. My heart beat faster as my gaze traveled to her breasts, pierced with electrum rings that glinted against her pale pink nipples in the candlelight. Her lengthy silver hair glimmered like a halo around her face, outlining those green eyes that seemed so familiar to me.

Though the wrath that appeared to consume her was clear on her features, I found myself captivated by it almost as much as her beauty. I wondered if she felt any other emotion besides rage and contempt for us all—did compassion or kindness ever flicker in those emerald depths? Did she ever feel something towards us beyond loathing? Did I want her to?

I'd only healed her clitoral piercing without setting any arousal intention, not desiring a mewling sex kitten like

Rhazien, his harem trailing him like a pack in heat. If I ever fucked her, it would be because she wanted me to. My cock pulsed at the thought and the concubine's eyes widened as I stepped into the bath, the water rising around my legs.

The heat of her gaze trailed all over my skin, her eyes following every plane of my body and locking on my cock, causing it to harden further.

"What are you looking at?" I asked, a smirk playing across my lips.

"Nothing," she spat, anger coating her features once more.

I let out a soft chuckle, motioning for her to approach the bath. "Come here, *Sia*," I said, my voice low and husky.

She hesitated for a moment before stalking closer. "That's not my name."

I shrugged and sank into the hot water, groaning as my muscles relaxed. "Neither is 'Lily.'" She glared at me, her full lips pursing. Something was refreshing about her open hatred. So different from the false faces in court. "Aren't you going to ask me what it means?" I prodded.

"No." She crossed her arms, pushing her ample breasts together and looking down in surprise before adjusting her stance. Carita must have made significant enhancements.

"It's our word for the desert blossom, Areca." It was a highly sought-after plant, though harvesting it had perils. A sharp-toothed little creature mimicked the flower with its tail and you could never be sure if you were about to lose your fingers or pick a bloom.

"The drug?" She wrinkled her nose, and I leaned back in the water, spreading my arms over the rim of the tub.

"Indeed." Fitting, as I already seemed addicted to her reactions. I wanted to goad her, just to see what she'd do next. "The soap is here."

She narrowed her eyes at me, her voice smoky and dark as her stare. "I thought you don't touch unwilling women?"

"I don't. You'll be touching me." I said, relishing the look of loathing she shot my way as her hand drifted to the collar I'd put around her throat, claiming her as mine. "And yes, that will prevent you from drowning me."

"How thoughtful." She growled brfore picking up the cloth, and roughly running it over my skin.

"Slower," I commanded, relaxing further into the bath.

"Asshole," she muttered under her breath, her ministrations slowing even though they remained just as violent. I grinned, enjoying the way she yanked my hair and how resistant she was to me. She was a challenge, and I was determined to win.

The door to my chamber burst open and Raenisa strode in, her features twisted into a mask of worry.

"Stop playing grab ass with your concubine," she said in Elvish, handing me a robe that matched my House's colors. "Your mother is looking for you."

I groaned, pushing myself out of the bath and grabbing a towel for my hair. Raenisa didn't react to my nudity, though her attention lingered on Lily's breasts, fully visible through the white fabric. Possessiveness filled me and I stepped in front of her, blocking Raenisa's view of her body.

"Did she say why?"

She rolled her eyes and flopped onto the couch, kicking her boots onto the table. "Why do you think, idiot? What the hell were you thinking beating Rhazien?"

I only thought I had to win the woman behind me, and not about the political ramifications at all. "Fuck."

"Yep." She popped her lips before grabbing one of the desert peaches from the bowl and taking a bite. She chewed thoughtfully, her eyes studying me. "You can't keep throwing your weight around like that and expect it to end well."

Raenisa was not a warrior born and bred, but out of necessity. Out of the high houses, only two eligible females weren't related by blood to my brother and I. Raenisa and the She-snake, Tannethe, the Empress's niece and sister to Theodas. When Rhazien had tried courting her, Raenisa had come to me with a proposition. She would join my army under the guise that we were getting closer and avoiding the marriage market together. Since she had zero interest in anyone with a cock and I'd planned on never returning to court, it'd seemed perfect. That we'd become close friends had been an accident, though one I was thankful for. Unfortunately, now the court has been brought to us.

"Yeah, yeah," I said, pulling on some clothes.

With her black hair streaked with blood-red and copper eyes, she cut an intimidating figure. Her curves were deceptively lethal as hidden beneath them were muscles carved from hard-won battles and training. She wore a gold-colored jacket with scarlet enameled fire ants along the shoulders in honor of her House's crest.

"You know I'm right. This is our chance to get out of this Atar-forsaken desert. Don't fuck it up."

I sighed. "I hear you, Rae, I wasn't thinking."

"We both know it was your cock leading the way." She leaned around me to look at my concubine. "She is a pretty thing. What kind of Remnant is she?"

"Ask her yourself," I said, buttoning my black breeches and looking over my shoulder at Lily where she glared at Raenisa. I switched from Elvish to the common tongue. "Lily, this is Raenisa, my second-in-command."

"Lily, eh? They're really leaning into that flower business." She said, studying her before I blocked her again. "What are you then? Probably a Wraith Remnant given the hair, huh?"

Lily didn't respond, instead turning to me as I slipped on a black shirt, buttoning it quickly. "Where are you going?"

"To a meeting. Raenisa will stay here and keep an eye on you."

"I will?" She raised her brows, taking another bite of her fruit.

"Yes." I tossed her a bag of coins. "Order her some clothes, will you? And food and shoes. Whatever a woman needs."

"You don't plan on keeping her, do you?" Raenisa asked in alarm, and I nodded. "Are you sure that's wise?"

"Not at all." I grinned, "But the damage is already done. Might as well get some enjoyment out of it."

"Theron—" She began, and I cut her off.

"See you soon." I stalked to the door before turning around once more. "And keep your eyes on her face and off her tits," I added in Elvish, making Raenisa scowl.

I strode into the sultry night air, gripping my sword tightly as I made my way toward my mother's suite on the floor above mine.

My heart pounded in my chest as I walked up the steps to the grand entrance, second only to the Emperor's rooms. Two tall elves dressed in black stood guard on either side of the door, their eyes never leaving me as I approached. They nodded respectfully when they recognized me and opened the doors without a word.

My mother, Nyana Carxidor, was waiting for me in her chambers, a man-made cavern lined with gold and ivory furniture and draped in silken fabrics. A large chandelier hung from above, casting its shimmering light across everything below. She stared at me, her eyes a golden match to the Emperor's, but somehow even more malicious. Her black hair was pulled back in a bun at the nape of her neck, accentuating her sharp features. She exuded an aura of power, one that filled the room when she entered it.

She held out a goblet of sweet wine to me as I drew near her and I took it without question, though I didn't drink. If she thought it would benefit her or Rhazien, she would poison me in an instant.

We stood there in silence for a few moments before she spoke. "I suppose you're happy that you've humiliated your brother." She paused, waiting to watch my reaction. A minor victory, goading her to speak first.

I kept my face blank, something I'd learned young after she'd sent Rhazien to steal me from my father. "Rhazien isn't capable of feeling humiliation; only different degrees of narcissism."

The corner of her mouth lifted. Fuck, she was happy that I'd taken the bait.

"Clever," she said, sipping from her goblet. It seems that you have some talent for a man who professes he doesn't wish to be Varzorn's heir.

"I don't give a shit about being the heir," I growled. "I just want to leave this fucking desert."

She chuckled and shook her head. "And here I thought raising my children would make me proud. You always were so stubborn, Theron. Your father ruined you." She took another sip of her wine and gestured for me to sit down on the divan opposite her. I did so grudgingly, though I still kept my posture erect in case she attacked me. "Adraedor is full of opportunities to grow your wealth and power. You had only to seize them. But now you need not bother. Rhazien will be Varzorn's choice."

"Then my actions don't matter."

"Oh, they do," she said, her words laced with icy venom. "I'm working to make sure it is Rhazien who ascends the throne. And you're going to help me."

I snorted in disgust. I was well aware of what she was trying to do; use me as leverage against Rhazien, who had been favored by the emperor since his birth. They had always given him preferential treatment while they cast me aside like some worthless servant. But if there was one thing I knew about my mother, it was that she did nothing without a plan. They called her 'The Weaver' for a reason. That ability was why she pursued my father initially. The Axidor words, 'The Eye that Looks Ahead,' had won her over before she'd even met the man. Had she paid more attention, she would have seen how ill-suited they'd been from the start. My father, Larion Axidor, had been a master tactician, yes, but didn't have the same ruthless ambition as her. She wanted something from me and I had no intention of giving it to her unless it benefited me in the long run.

"So that's why you summoned me here? To threaten me into helping your beloved son become Varzorn's heir?"

"It is not a threat," she replied coldly. "It is an ultimatum and an offer. If you help me, I'll get you reinstated into the Niothe."

She watched me for a moment longer before adding in a softer tone of voice. "You are my son, Theron, and I love you no matter how much we may disagree."

I snorted. "That almost sounded sincere, mother. Unfortunately, I'm not a child to fall for your lies anymore." Her soft expression melted away, revealing her icy features once more. "So, what do you want from me?" I asked finally, folding my arms across my chest.

She smirked, clearly pleased by my willingness to cooperate. "First, I need you to watch your cousins. They're a dangerous lot, and they would do anything to take the throne away from Rhazien if they could. You mustn't let them gain an advantage over him."

She paused, her expression calculating. "Second, I want you to get close to Tannethe."

"The She-snake? I don't think so."

"Allying with the Vennorins is the best move." She argued.

"Why? Because the Empress is a Vennorin? She hasn't produced an heir and we all know that Varzorn only chose her for the bride's purse."

"Why do you think she hasn't birthed a child?" She lifted a delicate brow, and I realized what she meant, rage filling me. If she hadn't prevented the empress from conceiving, then she wouldn't have—I shoved the thought away, determined to stay present. My mother would kill me if she saw an opportunity. She'd always treated Raura Vennorin as a friend and ally, but Nyana would stop at nothing to get what she wanted. "We have their bride-price without sharing power. The Sarro children have a viable claim, twice related to the royal line. Not to mention the Amyntas brothers with their prior claim. The

Vennorins aren't related by blood and will need us for legitimacy. They're the least likely to betray us."

Of course, she'd put that in her calculations above her children's happiness.

"It doesn't matter, regardless. I have Raenisa." I pointed out.

Her smile could cut. "We both know that the Taelyr girl isn't interested in marrying a man. That's why Rhazien pursued her in the first place. He wanted the alliance without giving up his harem. She's going to have offers during this visit as well."

Dread weighed heavily on my stomach. It seemed our ruse hadn't worked at all. We'd just been insignificant enough for it not to matter until now.

"Fine." I stood, stepping away from the chaise. "I'll help you watch out for any other potential heirs in the competition, but don't expect me to be interested in Tannethe. Rhazien can have her."

I sat my wine on the table next to the vase of scorpion weed without drinking and turned as the doorman announced the empress. The dread in my middle turned to stone as she walked into the room.

Raura Carxidor was just as I remembered her—long auburn hair, piercing silver eyes, and a sly grin that promised all sorts of temptations. She wore a deep blue gown with a low-cut neckline that highlighted her curves and her Vennorin parentage. When she saw me, she beamed, her face alight with pleasure.

"Theron," she said in a husky voice. "I was hoping to see you here."

I didn't respond, too angry and disgusted to speak.

Instead, I bowed in acknowledgment of the empress before turning on my heel and marching away without another word.

"There's a ball tomorrow night. Be there." My mother called after me, but I didn't turn around.

I wanted nothing more than to get back to my suite where I could be alone with my entertaining concubine and forget everything that happened tonight.

Chapter 5

Kael

I glared at the woman across from me, debating if I should kill her or not. The stupid collar wouldn't stop me this time. My stomach still felt queasy from when I attempted to kill the Marshal in the bath. I could think about it in the abstract, but when I'd grabbed him by the hair, intent on pushing his head underwater, it felt like something had taken hold of my guts and yanked them through the floor. But I'd been able to hurt him, pulling his hair... I'd need to test the limits because I needed to kill him. Each moment in his company only made me want to drive my sword through his heart even more.

"Sooo..." Raenisa drawled, "I guess I should call someone?" I didn't respond, only staring her down until she made a face. "Alright." She stood and went to the door, speaking to a servant in the hall.

I searched the room for a weapon. There had to be a knife around here somewhere. If I caught her off guard, I could take her down, regardless of the armor. But there was no time; Raenisa returned with a scarred female Kyrie Remnant behind her holding a platter of food. Another servant followed with a basket filled with fruits, cheeses, and pieces of bread.

The smells of the spread reached me, and my stomach growled in response. I stepped away from the bedroom door, glancing over at Raenisa as I did so. She observed me as we both settled into our chairs while the servants set up their offerings on the table between us.

I nodded to her and the Kyrie Remnant's scarred face lit up with a wry smile that didn't reach her right eye; her skin twisted in a mass of scars partially obscuring an orb covered in a milky film. Unlike Teodosija and the other Kyrie Remnants that lived in the desert, she didn't wear her hair in braids, instead letting her curls bounce around her head, the same color as her ochre skin. There was an energy to her that radiated warmth and hospitality, something I didn't associate with the austere castle, and especially the Elves.

"Greetings, my lady," she chirped as she placed the platter of food on the table. "I'm Mirijana, at your service." It was surreal, her attitude so light and friendly in such a tense atmosphere. Raenisa smiled tightly at her and nodded in acknowledgment before returning to our staring contest. "You must be the Lily that everyone is talking about."

I cleared my throat. "Um, that's me." Shit. I'd become more high profile than I'd wanted.

Mirijana took no notice as she set out our meal—humming under her breath as she moved around the living room, setting out plates for each of us with even more water. I'd eaten more in the last few hours than I normally did in days. And more than a slave might in a week.

Raenisa motioned for me to eat first. "Go for it."

Yeah, right. "I'm not hungry."

"Then I can call Kadir to do a fitting." Mirijana beamed. "Lady Taelyr said the Lord Marshal wants you to have a full wardrobe." She breezed out of the room, her sweet voice tinkling like a bell as she called for more help. Raenisa dunked a chunk of bread in a cheesy dip, groaning as she took a bite.

"You should try this," she said around a mouthful of food, not bothering to close her mouth. "Theron wanted me to feed you."

"I don't give a fuck what the Marshal wants."

She barked out a laugh. "Aren't concubines supposed to be charming?"

"In my experience they are," a man said from the doorway, another one of the Harvestmen. The big red-haired one that reminded me of a Kyrie with his hawklike gaze. I'd almost killed him once when he'd been scouting to find our hideouts. He looked different from when I'd found his perch, lying motionless on a cliff in the Black Highlands for hours as he watched us. He was cleaner, and better fed, but just as dangerous; I should have finished him when I had the chance. But Haemir had been there and his priority was always saving who we could, not vengeance, and he'd called me off.

"Zerek!" Raenisa hollered with an affable grin, sprawling on the cushions like she owned the place. "Come and eat. Theron is speaking with his mother and wants us to entertain his trophy."

"Better call for more wine than. He'll need it after crossing fangs with the Weaver." He leaned forward to grab a hank of roasted ferolope wrapped in a desert palm leaf.

"You know that's right." She laughed, her expression falling when another elf joined them. He was tall and lean as a blade, the sides of his head shaved, the black length of his hair trailing down his shoulders. He stepped lightly, almost like a cactus cat threading the dunes. I recognized him; the careful male, always hanging back a little from the rest of the group when scouting, and the one I'd encountered most on raids.

"Herrath," she greeted him coldly, her previous good humor melting away.

"Raenisa, Zerek." He sat, his posture perfect and at odds with the other Harvestmen's ease. I eyed them, trying to figure out why their demeanors had changed.

"What are you doing here? Shouldn't you be with the other snakes?" Zerek remarked, running a hand through his messy red waves.

"I'm not a Vennorin." He scowled as if they'd had this conversation often.

"Might as well be," Zerek muttered, and I looked back and forth between them, intrigued despite myself.

"I'd rather be here," Herrath said, sitting up straighter as Mirijana returned.

"I talked to Kadir, and he's going to be bringing up a bunch of choices, especially in the Axidor colors." She beamed at me.

Joy. Then I could be another piece of furniture.

"I don't need much." I'd be leaving soon, not that they knew that.

"Theron said a full wardrobe," Raenisa called, and I scowled at her.

"Anyone else think it's strange that Theron claimed a concubine?" Herrath asked, leaning forward and grabbing a handful of roasted seeds. "He's never done that before."

All their eyes turned to me, and cold shivers ran down my spine. The combination of malice, indifference, and appraisal washed over me and I had to resist the urge to curl up in a ball.

Fuck, this was bad.

"Not that I care what you think, but it is weird," Zerek said, tossing a berry into the air and catching it in his mouth. "What do you think happened? Did Theo knick him with his sword and he's acting in a half-drugged stupor?"

Raenisa snorted. "What else was he supposed to do?"

"Lose?" Herrath shrugged.

"And give Rhazien the opening to kill him?" Zerek shook his head, grabbing more food. "This was the right play. I just wish he'd picked one that didn't glare so much."

"Hopefully, he'll tire of her soon."

I narrowed my eyes at him and Mirijana smiled uncomfortably. "Miss, why don't you come into the bedroom and we can discuss your options before Kadir arrives?"

I stood, happy to leave the Harvestmen to their meal. The bastards. Any time a slave escaped, they were the ones scooping them out of the sand and dragging them back to be punished by the Beast. It was strange seeing them as just people and not fearsome spider-mounted warriors, scouring the Red Wilds for our hideouts. Stranger still to be treated as a prized possession, rather than chattel.

The Marshal's room was the complete opposite of the oppressive atmosphere outside. It was like a cocoon made of warmth, silken sheets, and pillows on a massive bed topped with a bedspread that featured a wyrm done in deep reds and iron accents. Shelves lined one wall, filled with books and pictures of mythical beasts. Thick luxurious rugs covered the floor, giving it a cozy feel even with its expansive size. A fire crackled in the hearth off to the side, providing gentle heat to ward off any chills from the night air.

The walls were adorned with large tapestries depicting fantastical creatures and another that looked like a diagram of an ancient sand wyrm, its wings outspread and labeled in Elvish. It wasn't anything I expected.

"Let's just take a look in the harem en suite and see if there's anything in there to work with," Mirijana said, opening the door to a connected room. "Oh. Well, this complicates things." The room was empty, only a sparring mat spread across the massive space. I frowned. No windows in here either. Would the Beast sleep somewhere similar? I'd need to be welcomed in to infiltrate a bedroom like this.

"So, how long have you worked here?" I asked, casually flashing her the rebel hand sign to see how she'd react.

"Three years," she replied with a smile, oblivious to the signal I'd sent. I didn't think she was one of ours, but I had to check.

"And you like it?" I pressed, looking for a collar or piercings and not finding any.

"It's not too bad working for the Lord Marshal. I spend half the day in the kitchens and the rest of the day reading. The Marshal doesn't need much."

"Hmm."

The door opened, and a figure stepped through. He was slight, with glowing pink hair and olive skin. His eyes were piercingly blue and two iridescent scales marked his right cheek. He wore a long black cloak draped over a simple white shirt, breeches, and boots. In his hands he carried a bundle of fabric, an array of colors flashing in the firelight.

"Good evening," he said without inflection, "I am Kadir." He bowed slightly and flashed us both a perfunctory smile, though it lacked warmth. His voice had an exotic lilt to it I didn't recognize, and I worried that the empire had spread even further than I realized. "Let me see what I'm working with."

He stepped closer and looked me over, his eyes studying the details of my face and body. He ran a hand through my silver hair, testing its length and texture. His gaze moved up and down my figure in clinical detail, with no lust or admiration in it; he assessed me objectively like a piece of merchandise. He murmured to himself as he pulled out a selection of lingerie from the bundle he'd brought in with him.

"This will do for now," he said with a nod as he fingered a blood-red sheer nightgown hemmed in fluffy feathers. He held it up against me, assessing how it would fit on my body before handing it over. "Put this on."

I frowned at the scrap of fabric. "I'm not wearing this."

"Why not?"

"Because I'm not a pastry?"

He ran his eyes over me again. "How do you like your clothes to make you feel?"

I shrugged. "Covered?"

"Protected? That's too easy. If you could wear anything, what would you like to convey? How would you want people to see you?" He asked, his aqua gaze boring into mine.

"Powerful," I answered, raising my chin. I thought back to the moment I'd killed Rafe, the human foreman that had assaulted me when I worked in the mines. Watching him crumple in front of me was what it took for me to realize that I couldn't hide anymore. It was the first time I believed I could change things.

A true smile spread across his face. "That I can work with. Try this." He handed me a delicate piece made of black sheer silk with a beaded design that had been shaped into tiny wyrm scales along the front. The fabric glinted in the firelight, shimmering like liquid metal. He helped me into it and carefully arranged my hair around my shoulders as I stared into the mirror. "It's exquisite."

My posture shifted as the lingerie clung to me, exuding an aura of strength that had been missing before. Since Carita had changed my body, I hadn't felt... right. I kept forgetting that my breasts were larger and was surprised when they bounced or got in the way. And my skin was so thin, with no protective callouses anymore. But seeing myself now, wearing these clothes and with this body, it felt like a different type of armor. Like it wasn't truly *me*. I could do anything and it wouldn't really be me doing it.

I looked up at Kadir, who nodded in approval. "Now that," he murmured, "is what power looks like." Kadir gestured for me to spin. "We can start."

The next ten minutes were a blur as he measured every part of me, making notes of which fabrics he liked as he held them beside my face, other times frowning and tossing it away onto the floor, only for Mirijana to chastise him good-naturedly.

A figure stood in the doorway and I turned to find Herrath standing there, watching us with dark eyes.

"Anything I can help you with, Lord Tavador?" Mirijana said, her voice trembling.

My head whipped around and I looked between them, attempting to discern what had made the normally cheerful servant seem afraid. I edged closer to her, ready to intervene if necessary. I didn't know why the others didn't like him, but if he frightened Mirijana, then he was the one to watch.

"Could I speak to Lily for a moment?" He tore his eyes away from her to nod at me.

"Of course, my lord. I think we're done here." Kadir said as he gathered up his fabrics, flashing me the rebel signal for 'danger' so quickly I almost missed it. My heart leapt. I wasn't alone here. *Thank Sithos.* Everything else had gone wrong, but I had an ally. I could salvage this.

Mirijana followed him from the room, glancing between us before leaving.

"What do you want?" I asked, crossing my arms over my chest and covering my straining breasts, looking down at them in a new light. Armor. Just more protection.

Herrath eyed me with disdain. "I don't trust you," he said, his deep voice sending a chill down my spine. So he was smarter than the others. He stepped closer, looming over me like a storm cloud ready to strike. "I'm warning you now," he continued, his eyes flashing dangerously. "Don't fuck with Theron or I'll kill you."

I glared at him. "I don't think the Lord Marshal will be happy if you destroy his property."

"Do we understand each other?" His voice was low and threatening.

I hesitated, my breath stuttering as I stared at the pulsing vein in his throat that I wanted to slit open. This bastard threatened me? I held my breath, swallowing my bloodlust before nodding. I had to play along if I hoped to complete this mission. The door opened, Theron stalking inside and I let out a slow breath. Herrath turned toward him with a smile, inquiring after his mother and leaving me standing in the room wondering what the fuck was going on.

Chapter 6

Kael

The Marshal's eyes drifted over me as he spoke with Herrath, who remained deferential despite Theron's cool demeanor. What was the point of having a warrior you didn't trust to stay so close to you? I crossed my arms over the black lingerie Kadir had given me. The bodice fitted tight, pushing my new breasts up and accenting my slim curves. Tiny panties matched, the fabric covering hardly any of my ass cheeks.

"Where are the clothes the tailor brought?" Theron asked, glancing at Herrath, who looked at me with polite interest as if he hadn't just been threatening to kill me two minutes ago. I'd be more offended if I hadn't tried to murder him multiple times. Call it even.

I gestured to the pile of lingerie, revealing my breasts. "You're looking at it."

His expression turned hungry before he glanced at Herrath as if just remembering his presence. He stalked into the other room, grabbed the robe that he'd been wearing earlier, and tossed it to me. I caught it against my chest.

"Put this on," he growled, and I glared back at him as I shrugged into it, ignoring how his scent enveloped me, my eyes going heavy-lidded. Leather and citrus. I scowled when I realized my piercing must be activating. Shit.

"I'm not going to say 'thank you.'"

"Didn't expect you to."

"How is it you chose the surliest concubine in the city?" Zerek called with a laugh. "I swear I've been attacked by scopscions nicer than her."

"The servant said you have nothing set up for a harem and she'll be by later to talk about it," Raenisa told him, drinking her wine and making a surprised face at the glass before taking another sip.

"Her name is Mirijana," Herrath murmured, his long fingers gripping a glass of wine.

"What did your mother want?" Raenisa asked, taking a bite of one of the honeyed pastries, a crystalline bee molded on top.

"For me to stop showing up Rhazien." He grumbled, sitting and piling a plate high. "Come here, *Sia*," he demanded, motioning for me to sit on the couch next to him.

"Why?"

I glared at him, and the room quieted as they watched our interaction. Nerves pricked my stomach, but I didn't back down.

"Because I want you to." He grinned lazily, his bronze eyes taking in my clenched fists with amusement.

"I'm not your pet," I growled.

He smirked. "That's where you're wrong."

"Well, this is fucking weird," Raenisa said. "Why don't you save the flirting for after we leave?" I scowled, and he looked away. "What else did the Weaver want?"

"For me to support Rhazien to become the heir in exchange for a return to the Niothe."

Zerek rolled his eyes. "We've heard that before."

"Exactly," Theron groaned when he took the first bite of braised pelatar, a rabbit-like creature that roamed the dunes. "Fuck, I'm starving."

"So, what are we going to do?" Raenisa asked.

"We'll focus on finding Striker and his rebels. Avoid the court as much as possible," the Marshal began, and I tried to stifle a laugh. They'd been searching for me for five years, and still didn't know that 'Striker' was a woman.

My chortle drew their attention back to me, and Herrath frowned when he caught me smirking. He opened his mouth as if he wanted to say something, but then closed it again when Raenisa frowned at him.

"I'll go scouting," Zerek announced, standing up. "We have had no luck in the south. I'm thinking they're north by Sailtown."

Nope. Wrong direction, idiot.

"Good. Be back by tomorrow night. We have to make an appearance at one other event, at least."

"Not going to happen," Zerek announced cheerfully. "We both know I can't be in the same room as my brother."

Theron grunted in agreement. "Fine. Just make sure you return in a few days."

"I'll go too," Raenisa said and Theron shook his head.

"Nyana made some... comments about our situation."

My ears perked up. What situation?

"What did she say?"

"We're both back on the market."

The female warrior groaned, pinching the bridge of her nose. "Fuck."

"Yeah."

"Well, I'm going to need more to drink." She stood up. "Come on, let's go drown our sorrows." Zerek and Herrath rose as well. "Not you." She pointed at Herrath, who rolled his eyes.

"A pleasure, as always, Raenisa."

As the group disbanded, I stayed seated on the couch, watching as Herrath finished his wine, his eyes flickering over to me before he left with a respectful nod to the Marshal.

"You're not coming north with me," Zerek laughed as they headed for the door, stretching and rolling his shoulders as they walked out.

Raenisa's voice drifted back to us. "We'll see if you're still saying that after five drinks."

He chuckled, stopping at the door with Raenisa, who glanced over her shoulder.

"Your concubine didn't eat, by the way."

I scowled at her back as she strode into the hall, leaving me alone with the Marshal.

Theron turned to me, his face a mask of frustration. "You didn't eat?"

"What does it matter?"

"Because you're mine. And I take care of what belongs to me."

"I don't belong to you," I growled.

He stepped closer, his voice low and dangerous. "Oh, but you do. And I'll make sure you know it."

He picked up a piece of the braised pelatar and brought it to my lips without a word. I stared at him for a moment, trying to decide if this was some sort of trick or test, but his face remained stoic.

"Open for me."

"No."

He took a small bite of the meat, gesturing grandly to show me it wasn't poisoned.

"See? It's safe." His eyes were heavy-lidded as he studied my mouth, waiting for me to move. He was a patient hunter, but I knew that already. I reluctantly opened my mouth, allowing him to slip the morsel inside.

I hadn't realized how hungry I was until the savory flavor hit my tongue and my stomach growled in appreciation. My teeth brushed his fingers and a soft groan escaped him.

"Do that again and I'll bite you," I warned.

A smile tipped up the corner of his mouth. "Don't tempt me."

I snorted, and he continued feeding me pieces of soft bread smothered in honey, sweet berries dusted with sugar, and tart citrus fruits sprinkled with salt until I was content and full.

Theron watched me as he fed me and though he had not yet said it aloud, there was something in his gaze that told me he meant every word of his earlier declaration: that I belonged to him now.

"You're very stubborn," he said warmly, brushing a lock of hair behind my ear.

I jerked away from his hand, eyeing him with distrust.

"I'm not yours."

"We'll see about that." His eyes flooded black until the whites were covered in darkness.

My heart pounded in my chest as I leaned back, feeling as if danger was lurking unseen around me like a predator in the night.

"What are you doing?" I demanded, scrambling up. "What magic are you casting?"

He blinked, his eyes flickering back to his usual dark bronze. "I wasn't doing any magic."

"Don't lie to me. Your eyes changed color."

"Ah." He gave me an embarrassed shrug. "It's a sign of powerful emotions. Svartál have eyes that switch colors when we are experiencing intense emotion. They only change when we are using our magic because it takes more mental fortitude to set an intention in stone or metal."

He paused and stepped closer, his gaze steady on mine as if he was waiting for something.

"How does your magic work? What spells can you cast?" I asked, curious. It wasn't like the Elves in the mines took a break from whipping us to explain the intricacies of their power.

"A secret for a secret. Tell me your name." He said, throwing his arm over the sofa and settling in. For him, this was the middle of the day, though they'd woken early to take advantage of the sunlight to host their gladiator games. I'd been up for almost twenty-four hours and a yawn escaped me as I answered.

"Absolutely not."

He grinned, apparently relishing the challenge.

"Fine. A secret for a favor."

I raised a brow. "What kind of favor?"

"Not that. I'm not going to fuck you until you beg me to."

"Never going to happen."

"Then you have nothing to be afraid of."

"I'm never scared."

"Must be nice," he muttered before going back to the subject. "What do you know about my kind?"

"That you're colonizing assholes who stole our gods and immortality from us?"

"All true." He agreed, grabbing a goblet of water. "We believed we were stronger than even the gods and we were right."

I glared at him. "Prick."

"Assuredly." He took a sip. "My kind, the Svartál, isn't the only kind of elf. Atar also made the Sálfar, our light cousins."

"Where are they?" I asked, interested despite myself.

"Dead. Way before my time. Our history says there was a disagreement between us during the Godsfall and the Svartál killed them all. But not much else is known."

"Not surprising." I leaned further into the cushions. "What does that have to do with your magic?"

"Because after we turned on them, Atar cursed us and the Svartál couldn't access the celestial metals anymore. Only the earthborn metals, like gold, silver, and the like, are within our reach now."

Huh. It would explain why they couldn't build massive monoliths like this castle anymore.

"What does gold do?"

He smiled as if pleased I was talking to him without prodding. "Adds strength. Other metals and stones have unique properties, but they all affect the body. Unlike the celestial metals which influence the world outside of us. Now we have to rely on old speaking stones because we can't make them anymore."

That was a solid piece of intel. If we could destroy their speaking stones, it would hobble their military.

"What about the rest? Silver, copper—"

He cut me off. "Nope. Time for the favor first."

I narrowed my eyes on him. "What do you want?"

"For you to take a drink." He held the goblet to my lips, and my heart started beating wildly in my chest. In the desert, a man giving water to a woman by hand was part of our marriage ceremony. It was his pledge that she would always drink first and the symbol that bound them. My cheeks flushed as I fought to stay calm. There was no way he knew about that. This was just more power plays with him. Forcing me to be docile like you'd train an animal by feeding it by hand. It meant nothing.

I leaned closer, letting him press the metal against my lower lip and tipping it up. The desire in his eyes made it hard for me to focus on anything else as I drank, his gaze never leaving mine.

"Happy now?" I asked, my voice tight.

"Ecstatic."

I stood abruptly, determined to not let his manipulations get under my skin again.

"I'm tired. I'm going to bed."

"Want company?" He called, a laugh in his voice.

I paused at the door, turning to look at him. "You know I'm going to escape, right?" I threw back, my tone challenging.

He raised an eyebrow. "Good luck with that," he said, his words dripping with amusement.

The dismissive asshole. How dare he think he could control me like some kind of pet? My thoughts drifted back to the way his fingers had brushed against my lips and the heat in his eyes as I had drunk from his goblet, which only fueled my anger.

Without waiting for a reply, I marched into his bedroom, my heart pounding with wrath and frustration. But despite my bravado, I couldn't shake the feeling that he was right. I was trapped, and I didn't know how to get out. I stripped the blankets from the mattress. Dragging them with me into the sparring room, I set up a makeshift bed on the mat and settled in for the night. I collapsed onto the pile of bedding, exhausted from the day's events. As I closed my eyes, images of Theron's intense gaze filled my mind. His lips on mine, his hands on my skin. I shook my head, trying to push the thoughts away. He was my enemy, and my brain needed to remember that, no matter what his magic tried to tell me.

Sleep never came easily to me, and tonight was no different. I was still awake when the door creaked open, and through slitted eyes, I saw him standing there watching me, his outline stark in the firelight. I drifted off while gazing at him, my body no longer able to remain awake as I tumbled into a dreamless dark.

Chapter 7

Theron

I tied on my belt, slipping my short sword into the scabbard. Striker, the bastard, had stolen its twin years ago when he'd escaped in a mass slave revolt. I still had the other sword's sheath, waiting for its return. One of these days, I'd finally kill him and reclaim it.

"What do you think, my lord? Kadir thought coordinating with your armor would be best." I turned to find Mirijana gesturing to my irascible concubine as she strode through the door. My cock pulsed as I took her in. She wore a tiny red top that was little more than strings, with a ribcage fashioned from gold over the fabric. A series of looping threads with jingling adornments dangled from the rib bones, matching the golden bone bangles on her wrists. A scarlet skirt hung low on her hips, made of only a narrow panel of fabric in the front and back, with her muscular legs exposed.

I strolled over to her, running a finger down the golden sternum as she narrowed her eyes at me. It was solid underneath the veneer. It would deflect a blade. "This is good quality. Send the tailor a gift on my behalf. Be generous."

"Of course, my lord."

Lily glared, raising her hand to touch her hair that was held in place with a claw of gilded finger bones and sharp sticks. Soft cosmetics darkened her pale lashes, making her green eyes blaze. Kadir had gone all out, enhancing her dangerous beauty. "Why is this necessary?"

I smoothed my black dress shirt, considering pulling on my bone armor. Part of the reason I wore it was to show that I didn't need the magical enhancements they did to be the best. Going unadorned would only increase that assumption.

"Because you're accompanying me to the ball tonight as my guest."

She stared at me, her mouth falling open. "Why?"

"For you to entertain me, of course." Her sneer made me chuckle. I didn't know what madness had possessed me to claim her, but I didn't regret it. I hadn't laughed so much in years.

"Come on, *Sia.*"

She sighed. "Let's get this over with."

I led her down the grand stairwell, our feet echoing against the polished flagstone. The castle was built into the side of a mountain and part of the walls was unfinished stone, giving it an austere yet inviting atmosphere.

As we descended, her shoulders drew higher in apprehension; I had no doubts she was regretting coming with me. We passed through a wide archway and entered the crowded ballroom.

The halls were adorned with tapestries showing battles during the Godsfall in brilliant reds and golds, while oil lamps lit up every corner, giving it a soft ethereal glow that rivaled even the stars outside. The floor was a mosaic of marble tiles arranged in swirls and waves within circles that seemed almost alive. Each breath we took seemed to bring them to life as they shimmered in response. At one end of the room, there was an orchestra made up of Elven musicians playing gentle melodies on ancient instruments; the sound like liquid light. At the other, there was a raised platform covered with velvety fabrics and pillows where guests could rest during interludes between dances and conversations.

"Prince Theron Axidor and…" The announcer trailed off as he stared, at a loss for words. All eyes turned to us as I swept her into the ballroom, the courtiers erupting into whispers.

Lily glared at me and I hid a smile, taking in the court in full regalia for the first time in years. Atar's balls, I hated it.

"You've lost your mind." Raenisa hissed, stalking up to me in a yellow dress that showcased her muscular frame. "You brought your concubine?"

"Why not? Nyana made it clear that she wanted me to get close to the She-snake. This—" I slung an arm around Lily's shoulders that she immediately stepped out of, shooting a glare my way "—is a buffer." I clenched my hand, my fingertips itching to touch her soft skin again.

"I don't know if I'm happy or not that you're directing some of her poison away from me." Raenisa pondered, her mouth pursed in a thoughtful moue. "Then again, now it's abundantly clear to everyone that I'm available."

"Sorry, Rae." I snagged a custard tart topped with milkweed thistle from a passing waiter. "We only have to get through the next week."

"And then what?" She glowered at me. "You brushed away your mother's offer to get out of Adraedor, but I don't get what the plan is anymore."

Herrath joined us, wearing the Tavador colors of silver and emerald, and catching Raenisa's comment. "We hold the line and see what the emperor asks of us."

She scowled at him. "We're not all paragons of perfect sons, Herrath. Just because you're alright sitting and waiting for someone to tell you what to do doesn't mean that I am."

"That's because you haven't looked ahead," I said, pulling Lily to my side once more. She ignored me, instead studying the room as if eying the best escape routes.

"I swear to Atar if you quote your family words to me one more time..."

I chuckled. "Think about it, Rae. Of the factions, there are only a few contenders for the throne. And any choice gets us out of here."

"Just explain it, fuckhead."

"First, there is the Carxidor, Vennorin, Tavador, and Lazan alliance."

"You forgot Gairis," Herrath put in.

"And Findis, the rat bastards," Raenisa added, setting her empty glass on a waiter's passing tray.

Herrath shot her a cool look. His mother was Lord Findis' first-born daughter.

I waved it off. "Rhazien has the strongest claim since he's the eldest born of a Carxidor bloodline and there's no way I'll be chosen. My mother allied with Raura long ago, binding the Vennorins to the throne financially, but not by blood, since the empress hadn't conceived. That's why Nyana needs Tannethe with Rhazien or me. Black Theo and his siblings aren't a threat, but they don't realize it. Regardless, if it was Rhazien or Theodas, neither one of them would want me in charge of Adraedor and their cash flow. That's giving me too much power. Much better to send me overseas to Iophith, where I'm not a visible threat, and install someone they trust."

Herrath gave a nod as if he'd thought of this as well. No doubt he had as the only son of the Tavador line. They were one of the oldest noble houses but had always had trouble conceiving, and with the lack of marriage alliances and dwindling capital, their political influence had waned. Now they only had one heir to pin all their hopes on.

"What about the others? The Sarro cousins and Zerek and his brother, Xavier, have a claim."

"The Sarros have the next strongest claim after Rhazien and I since they're related to the throne twice through the Sarros and Ceadors. But the Young Bear is too hot-headed, Varzorn would never choose her and the youngest is too sweet to be taken seriously."

"Their brother Xadrian is an option." Herrath pointed out.

I nodded. "The Darkstar is a wild card."

"Did you hear that he's been adding Heliot onto his surname?" Raenisa made a face. "One stripe of silver hair and he's suddenly leaning into his Sálfar heritage." Raenisa took a sip, then held the glass to her forehead. "Ambrosia."

"The emperor would never go for it." Herrath shook his head. "It doesn't matter that he can use celestial metals—"

"Barely," Raenisa muttered.

"Varzorn hates the Sálfar."

"Regardless," I cut in. "The Sarro, Ceador and Amyntas alliance." Herrath opened his mouth, and I held up a hand. "I'm not listing the minor houses again. They're going to push for the Sarros on the throne since they have the best chance. They're

Varzorn's cousins for all that they're generations younger. Zerek and Xavier are only related once, three generations back, and aren't blood-related to the Sarros, so they can intermarry. And if any of them take power, they would put their siblings in charge here and we'll be out."

"And House Rorel and Cairis would support you, but they'll believe that's off the table..." Herrath said.

A smile spread across Raenisa's face. "So we're leaving?"

"Unless you're married off..."

She shook her head. "Not going to happen."

"No? What if Varzorn chooses Caelia and the Young Bear needs a bride?"

"Well, then sacrifices will have to be made."

Of course, that would change her mind. I chuckled, my fingers tracing a circle on Lily's spine and causing her to scowl at me, but I couldn't keep my hands off of her. "Our priority is finding Striker. I'm not leaving the desert without my sword."

Lily made a choking sound, and I grabbed a glass from the tray nearest me and handed it to her. "Here, *Sia*. Drink."

She took it, drinking deep between coughs until she could breathe normally once more.

"Theron!"

I whipped around to see Varzora Rorel and her brother, Osiel, rushing toward me. A genuine smile spread across my face, and I opened my arms for Varzora to jump into them.

"Zora! Oz! What are you doing here?" I asked, letting go of Varzora to embrace Osiel as well, holding them both tight. When my father had fled Athain and my mother, we'd gone to stay with his family and the twins had become practically siblings to me, but it had been years since I had seen them last.

Varzorn had punished their family for harboring us, and they never came to court unless ordered to attend.

Varzora was a bubbly and charismatic girl with hair ranging from black to red at the tips. She was short for an elf, with bright onyx eyes that lit up when she laughed. Osiel, on the other hand, was tall and lean with shoulder-length black hair and round glasses. His topaz-colored eyes were serious, but he had a kind heart behind them. Osiel was also incredibly studious—always reading or doing something to gain more knowledge.

"We heard you were here." Varzora panted, her face flushed from running across the room to get to me. "Are you alright? Everyone's talking about your fight with Rhazien."

"I'm fine," I said, smiling at their concern for me. "Where's Aunt Lyta?"

"Mom couldn't come," Varzora chirped. "But she sent a care package. I have it in our villa."

My heart tugged uncomfortably. Every time I received a package from Aunt Lyta, it included a little gift that had once been my father's or something from their childhood. How would she react knowing that I'd lost one of the Axidor swords? Thank Atar that Osiel always had his head in the clouds and Varzora was too excitable to notice I only wore one sword or I'd be in trouble.

"I look forward to it."

"And to answer your question, obviously we wanted to see you." Zora squeaked.

"And your library." Osiel put in, pushing his spectacles up his nose. He could have used a piercing and fixed his eyesight in a minute, but he said that he liked how the glasses felt on his face.

Varzora rolled her eyes. "And Oz wants to read the histories that are kept here. He's studying the Godsfall."

"There are several inconsistencies I want to figure out." Osiel began, his face lighting up as it did every time he talked about his research and I basked in the glow of nostalgia. The years we'd lived together had been the best of my life. Until my father was killed and I was forced to live in a cage... I shook off the memories, glancing at Lily in surprise when she scoffed. Osiel blinked as if he'd just noticed she was there. A ridiculous notion given her appearance. It surprised me that anyone present could look away from her. The desire to throw a tablecloth over her to keep their hungry eyes off her luscious body warred with my enjoyment of the insufferable courtier's reactions as I paraded her around.

"What?" I asked, my brows furrowing.

"Nothing."

She tried to decline, but I motioned for her to continue. "No. What were you going to say?" I prodded, staring down at her.

"The victors write history, and you Elves are liars. It's no wonder things don't add up." She said, looking around us as if searching for a weapon. "Remnants have histories we pass down that are nothing like yours."

Osiel tilted his head. "Are you saying I should ask the Remnants for information?"

That wouldn't work out well. Varzorn always ordered me to burn libraries when razing a city. Anything they knew would be passed down orally.

She looked at him in surprise that he was speaking to her politely. Osiel was like that, though. He believed everyone had knowledge to offer if you were clever enough to find it. We joked that the Rikkert blood must have run thicker in him.

"We have our own stories of when our gods were slaughtered," Lily explained. "You could compare them with your information as a starting point. Where else would you be able to speak to so many Remnants from all over Maeoris?"

"I think that's the first time I've heard your concubine speak without growling." Raenisa joked, and Lily shot her a caustic glare.

"You're a concubine?" Zora asked, her eyes widening. "Why did you become a concubine? What's it like when—"

"Zora…" Oz warned, and she stopped talking to peer at her twin.

"What? Was that rude?"

He leaned in close to whisper in her ear, shooting Lily an apologetic grimace.

"What? No slaves where you live?" Lily questioned, sending them an acidic glare. One that Oz matched when he caught my eye and I knew that he'd be giving me an earful later.

Zora shook her head. "No. Sorry for—" she waved a hand as her cheeks reddened. "—all that."

The concubine softened, lifting her chin in acknowledgment of her apology.

Oz's expression darkened, and I turned around to see Theodas Vennorin approaching, flanked by his brothers, Tykas, and Trevyr. Theodas was the oldest, and he carried himself as such. His face was hard, with cold, blue eyes that could turn ruthless in an instant. Tykas was huge and strong, like an ox, while Trevyr was the opposite of both of them. He was sleek and clever with a sharp tongue and knives always on him, fastidious to the point of fussiness, especially with the silver eye that replaced the one he'd lost. Tykas, despite being the strongest, was the odd man out of the family. The one the others bossed around and forced to do their dirty work.

"Theodas," I said as he stopped next to me. "Look at you, already walking about. Last I saw you, you looked ready to piss yourself."

"Charming as always, Theron." Theodas' voice dripped with sarcasm. "Maybe if you focused less on your wit, you'd still be Lord Marshal."

My jaw clenched, and I dug my nails into my palm to prevent myself from lashing out.

"Well," I drawled, trying to keep my tone steady. "At least I'm not the one who follows commands like a mindless lapdog."

Theodas' expression darkened as he stepped closer to me. "If you think I'm merely following orders," he growled. "Then you don't know the first thing about amassing power."

"Not surprising, given his upbringing." Trevyr chimed in, picking a non-existent piece of lint from his sleeve. "Can't expect good breeding when you're raised among pig slop."

Oz tilted his head, studying the second oldest Vennorin. "Does he think that raising livestock on a country estate is some sort of insult? I'd heard that the Vennorins weren't too bright, but seeing it in person—" He clucked his tongue as his twin hid a grin behind her hand. I couldn't tell if he was being purposely obtuse or not, and neither could Trevyr.

Tykas remained silent, a flush creeping up his neck as he looked over the gathered nobility, as if desperate to be anywhere else. He kept sneaking peeks at Zora and glancing away just as quickly. I stepped back from Lily and nearer to my cousin, my expression darkening.

"What do you want, Theo?" I drawled, taking a sip of my summer wine.

"I wanted to thank you, of course." A viperish smile spread across his face. "Defeating Rhazien in his own competition—" He shook out his shoulders in a faux shiver. "Incredible. Made our bout insignificant in comparison."

Raenisa sneered. "Plenty of time for a rematch."

"Less than you think." Trevyr snickered, his silver eye spinning to land on Lily for a long moment.

"I should go. The emperor is expecting me." Theodas said, straightening his shirt. "Thanks again for knocking your brother out of the running, Theron."

I scowled after him to find Trevyr staring at Herrath. "Aren't you coming?"

He shook his head. "I'm where I'm supposed to be." Of course, he was spying on me as he had been for years.

Trevyr raised a brow over his silver eye and turned, drifting into the crowd after his brother. Tykas opened his mouth once, as if to apologize for his siblings' behavior, but snapped it closed, following them into the throng, his massive shoulders slumping.

"Well, that was annoying," Raenisa quipped, draining the last of her glass. "At least we didn't have to deal with the She-snake."

A throat cleared, and I turned to find Tannethe standing behind me. Fuck.

"For Ydonja's sake." Raenisa flinched, almost dropping her drink.

"Good to see you too, Raenisa," Tannethe said, drawing closer. The She-snake was an apt nickname for her. Her long, straight black hair cascaded down her back, bejeweled with tiny silver pins that glittered in the night air. Her golden eyes twinkled with mischief as she winked at me, a sensual smile curling over her lips. I could practically feel the waves of lust radiating from her as she slithered nearer, trying to entice me into playing her game of power and seduction.

"It's a pleasure to see you again, Theron." She murmured, gazing at me with an intensity that made me want to draw my sword. She looked like she wanted to swallow me whole.

"Tannethe," I said, debating how to respond. Nyana wanted me to court her, but the last thing I wanted was to invite the snake back to my bed. Not that she wasn't beautiful—she was. But her perfectly coiffed and pampered appearance couldn't compare to the feral beauty of the concubine beside me. "Are you looking for Rhazien? He was at the head table." I tightened my arm around Lily's waist, pulling her close, and for once, she didn't fight me, instead glancing between us with rapt attention.

"I was searching for you." She purred. "It's been years since we've seen each other. Remember the last time? In Athain?"

I'd been drunk on the anniversary of my father's death and she'd come to my suite. I'd left right after I'd come, stumbling to the vanira cave to sleep beside Vaernix. Even then I knew better than to be vulnerable near the She-snake.

"Not really," I said and Raenisa snorted.

Tannethe shot her a venomous look before smiling. "Then you'll need a reminder. I'm game whenever you are." She ran a finger down my chest before turning and slinking away after her brothers.

"Not that it wasn't hilarious," Raenisa started. "But is it wise to snub her after what Nyana said?"

I shook my head. "It doesn't matter, remember? Our focus is on finding Striker."

Lily stiffened beside me, and I spun to find Rhazien behind me.

"I may have some information for you then, brother." He grinned. "For the right price, of course."

Chapter 8

Kael

I fought to keep my expression neutral as the Beast leaned closer, the scent of Areca smoke overwhelming. My hand itched for my weapon. I could kill him right now, take his head off in one fell swipe with my blade. But I didn't have my beloved sword and it would be suicide. I was supposed to get out clean, if possible.

"What do you want in exchange?" Theron asked, his tone nonchalant. I'd have believed it if he wasn't gripping my waist tight, his fingers digging in below my golden ribcage.

"Isn't it obvious? For you to be in the desert and stop fucking up my plans."

"By that logic, you'd lie to me and send me on a wild chase to keep me in the sands longer." The new elf, the one he called 'Oz,' nodded in agreement.

"Do you think Striker is only a poor reflection on you?" Rhazien said. "I've been ramping up patrols for the last four months to catch him before this visit for a reason."

It *had* been worse recently, making it almost impossible to sneak people out. I hadn't realized it coincided with an event.

"What do you know?" Theron asked, his thumb tracing my bare skin absentmindedly. A shiver worked its way through me, a pulse of heat low in my stomach. Rage followed quickly after. His fucking piercing was messing with my head. It didn't seem to work when he wasn't near me, but when he was, I was drawn to him. My body came alive in ways that it never had before.

"You sent Zerek in the wrong direction. They're not in Sailtown."

Shit.

"We've been all over the south. We can't find them."

"I have an informant that says they have an established camp in the Red Wilds."

Fuck, fuck, fuck. We had two camps, one in the wilds and another through the Bone Gap. Somehow, they'd found the first.

"Where exactly?" Raenisa asked, squinting at him. Herrath looked like he wanted to melt into the floor, his eyes cast away from the pair of brothers. Interesting.

"Dance with me and I'll tell you." Rhazien offered his hand, palm up, to Raenisa.

"Not happening." She growled, looking at him as if it were a viper ready to strike. "I need to use the bathroom. Excuse me."

"Take Lily with you," Theron said, giving me a push toward her.

"What?" No. I wanted to hear if they knew where our base was and who the informant was.

"Come on," Raenisa grabbed my wrist, tugging me away with her to the back of the ballroom.

We made our way to the bathrooms, set deep into the side of the mountain. Intricate carvings with reliefs of wild creatures and Thanja, the goddess of nature, and Atar's wife, tending to them, covered the walls. The floor was composed of colorful tiles that formed a mosaic of the night sky that glittered in the dim light from the small lanterns that hung from sconces on every wall. Marble countertops gleamed beneath gold-rimmed mirrors that reflected us as we walked by. Sleek golden faucets adorned stone sinks, water pouring out in a steady stream before collecting in carved basins at the bottom. Liters of water cascaded down into nothingness while my people suffered with only drops to drink back in the slave quarter. Disgusting.

Raenisa splashed water on her face, pressing a towel to it and groaning. "Ydonja's tits, this week can't end soon enough."

I said nothing, just watching her for a moment. She reminded me of Orya's sister, Roza, fierce with zero tolerance for bullshit, but not nearly as bitchy as the Sirin Remnant. If she'd been a slave, we might have been friends.

"You all seem pretty obsessed with Striker. I heard he was just a myth." I leaned against the sink, feigning nonchalance as I picked at my skirt.

"Nope. He's very much real. He killed our best friend, Calyx, and almost took out Theron on the same night he stole his sword. We've been trying to find him for years."

I made a non-committal noise in my throat. I didn't remember killing a Harvestman, but it could have happened. "You can go ahead. I'll meet you in a minute." After I snuck out of the party and into Rhazien's suite.

"Yeah, right. I might think Theron's an idiot for keeping you, but I'm not going to let him down by letting you run off."

I sneered, ready to lay into her when Tannethe strode inside, her expression twisting into a sinister smile when she saw us.

"What a pleasant surprise to see the two of you here together," Tannethe hissed. "I didn't know Theron's playthings were friends."

"Plaything? Hardly," Raenisa made a face. "Try second-in-command, bitch."

"Oh, is that the new term for it now?" The She-snake asked with a sly grin. "Regardless of the name, everyone knows he owns you, just like that little concubine." She flicked a finger at me.

My back straightened, and my head rose. "No one owns me."

She laughed like I was being naïve. "You're a slave. That's your entire purpose."

I kept my gaze on her steady, refusing to let this woman scare me. I spotted two rings that could be used for poison, but nothing else under her slinky gold dress. Kadir had given me both protection and weapons in my outfit. I could kill her if it came to it.

"Better to be forced into service than willingly submit." My fingers drifted over my electrum collar for a moment. "You're being traded for a crown. One you won't even wear. And you're out here dying to spread your legs for him? Worrying about a slave? Pathetic."

Raenisa burst into laughter as Tannethe's porcelain skin reddened, her lovely features twisting into an ugly mask.

"How dare you speak to me like that?" She advanced on me, her hand raised to strike. Raenisa stepped in front of me as I reached to pull out the needles concealed in my hair.

"Leave, Tannethe. Before you really fuck up."

"I won the last time we sparred." She said, her lips flattened in a scowl.

"Before they trained me in the Niothe." Raenisa reminded her. "Don't tempt me."

"I won't forget this." The She-snake hissed, turning on a sharp heel and walking out.

"'I won't forget this,'" Raenisa mocked the empty doorway. "Speaking to a Taelyr about holding a grudge? The power-hungry snakes."

I stared at her, fighting the desire to laugh. She was one of my sworn enemies, the oppressors of my people. A slave-catcher. It was strange seeing her as a normal person... In another life, she might have been a fellow rebel. Someone I'd enjoy being on watch with because she always had a joke at hand. I shook my head. This wasn't my fight. I had one mission—to kill the Beast and get out. These confusing feelings wouldn't be a problem after that.

"Well, that was entertaining." A rasping female voice sounded from behind me. There was more room in this bathroom? Sithos' icy balls. This was wasteful.

"Caelia!" Raenisa said brightly, her hand flying to her hair. "Um. How are you?" The same female warrior from yesterday started forward, her short hair a mess of spikes and curls. She didn't wear a dress, instead favoring a green and gold brocade vest and fawn-colored breeches with tall boots.

"You mean after that bitch's brother poisoned me? I'm fine. Xadrian figured it out quickly. In time for me to see Theron win this one here." She came forward, her gaze lingering on my curves in blatant perusal. I glared back at her, uninterested. "I would have picked her too. Like a woman with a smart mouth." She gave me an inviting smile, and I scowled at her.

Her laugh was like a crow's caw, with an edge of human glee. "Don't worry, flower. I'll keep my hands to myself."

Raenisa bit her lip. "Want to go grab a table? Theron will find us."

"So you're not pretending to court him anymore?" Caelia said, raising a brow.

"Apparently that didn't convince anyone," Raenisa grumbled.

"Only the people who don't know you." She grinned and Raenisa blushed, biting her lower lip. "Come on."

Caelia led us to a table off to the side near where the food was laid. I glanced around, looking for Theron before realizing what I was doing. It didn't matter where he was. The longer he was away, the better for my stupid piercing.

We sat at the empty table, and I toyed with the white linens. A servant came, bringing three glasses and a jug of iced water with him. My mouth dried as I saw the moisture beading on the sides.

"May I serve you, my lady?" He asked Caelia, who waved him on.

"Don't stand on formality because of me. I'm starving."

"Of course." He nodded, filling up each of our goblets. "Would you like any wine or ale?"

I tuned them out as a strange awareness came over me. It was almost as if something was tickling at the edge of my senses. I turned to find a man I didn't recognize staring at me as he sauntered over to our table, the eerie feeling intensifying.

"Xadrian." Caelia grinned at him. "Perfect timing. We're about to have our first course."

This must be the wildcard Theron had discussed. The Darkstar. He had olive skin like a Sirin Remnant, not the same pale complexion as most Elves. His hair waved to his shoulders and was black except for a streak of white in the front. His eyes were the deepest earthy brown, and he had a beauty mark on his cheek, somehow pulling all my attention to him. He moved gracefully as if he was a panther stalking its prey.

He said nothing, but I felt a strange awareness as he slipped into the chair beside me. The feeling intensified when Xadrian's gaze met mine and our eyes locked together.

"Caelia, Raenisa. Care to introduce me to your enchanting friend?"

"That's Theron's concubine," Raenisa said flippantly, and I glowered at her. I had a name. Not that she knew it, but still.

"Interesting." He eyed me again, his gaze tracing my face as if trying to recognize me. I glanced away and tried to focus on my food. He continued to watch me intently as if he were attempting to decipher my every thought. He toyed with a silvery necklace at odds with the green and gold both he and his sister wore, and my eyes darted to it.

"And what's your name?" He asked, leaning closer to me. "Unless you want me to refer to you as Theron's concubine all night."

"Lily."

He smirked. "Nice to meet you."

"Your pendant is beautiful," I commented, struggling for something kind to say. It kept drawing my attention, flashing like a silver fish in a stream. "Where did you get it?"

He smiled, his full lips curving into a grin that sent a shiver down my spine. "It's a family heirloom passed through the generations of the Heliot line." His accent differed slightly from everyone else's here. Interesting.

He seemed to watch my every move with a certain intensity that made me feel wary and flustered at the same time.

"What kind of metal is it? Silver?" I asked. He shook his head, and he reached up to tuck away a loose strand of hair behind my ear, his fingers brushing my cheek.

"No, it's—"

"Lily, there you are." Theron placed his hands on my bare shoulders, the rough texture of his palms rasping my skin and sending a shiver of arousal through me. "You and Raenisa disappeared." He raised a brow at his second-in-command, who stifled a wince.

Caelia laughed. "You were right, Rae. He found us and in less than five minutes."

Raenisa chuckled, glancing at him as if to see how angry he was about our disappearance. "Join us, Theron. We're just settling in."

"Your concubine is most entertaining." Caelia praised as if complimenting his outfit. "You should have heard her tear into Tannethe."

"Beautiful with a sharp tongue?" Xadrian pressed a hand over his heart. "I'm lost."

I frowned at him as Theron's hands spasmed on my shoulders, but his tone was still light. "We're returning to our suite. I have an early morning. As do you, Rae." He shot her a pointed look.

Xadrian shrugged and gave Theron a knowing smile before turning back to me. "We'll have to continue this conversation some other time."

I nodded, and the Marshal scowled.

Xadrian's lips quirked into a smirk and he took a sip from his goblet, not bothering to hide the amusement in his eyes.

"If you'll excuse us," Theron said, giving Xadrian an icy glare and tugging me away. The peculiar awareness that had been teasing at the edge of my senses dissipated as we moved toward the door, leaving me feeling both relieved and disappointed.

He grabbed my hand and laced our fingers together before briskly leading me across the room. We reached his chambers, and he shut the doors behind us, pushing me against them and making me gasp.

His hands were on either side of my face as he leaned closer to murmur against my ear.

"Stay away from Xadrian," he demanded, his voice low and menacing.

I rolled my eyes. "We were just talking."

"I don't want you speaking to him," he said, his body pressing against mine until all my awareness focused on where we touched. "He's dangerous."

I snorted. "And you're not?"

He narrowed his eyes at me, not answering the question. "He can look all he wants, but if he puts his hands on you again. I'll kill him. Understand?"

I glared up at him as he fixed the piece of hair that Xadrian had tried to tuck away.

"I'm not a bone for you sharp-eared dogs to fight over," I growled.

"Of course not, *Sia*. Because you're already mine." He murmured, running his nose over my cheek before pulling away. My heart pounded in my chest, wetness slicking between my thighs.

"I haven't begged yet." I reminded him.

"But you will." He grinned at me, one side of his mouth tipping higher.

I swallowed, worry filling me. How much longer until my piercing proved him right? I shuddered at the thought and he stepped away, letting me go.

"Go to sleep. I'll send someone to fetch you in the morning."

Chapter 9

Theron

I turned over in bed, stirring again and tangled in the sheet, unable to sleep long. A whimper drifted from the training room and I wiped the grit from my eyes, realizing what had woken me. I slid out of bed, pulling on a pair of loose breeches before padding over to the door. Another whine of distress came, and I yanked it open, ready to destroy whoever made Lily sound like that.

She lay in the furthest corner of the room as she had before, wrapped in the blankets she'd stolen from my bed. She whimpered again, the sound so at odds with her normal assertive demeanor that a pang hit my gut.

I hurried over, scooping her up out of the corner and into my arms. She was light in my arms; her fierce personality made her seem larger. Her long silver hair cascaded across my arm like liquid moonlight as I cradled her against me. She snuggled into me in her sleep, sighing contentedly and seeking my warmth even in her dreams.

I carried her back to my bedroom, the fire still burning low in the hearth, laying her down before crawling onto the mattress beside her and pulling her against me. I wrapped my arms around her, keeping her close as she nestled deeper into my embrace, her face tucked into my neck.

It felt... right having her in my bed. I'd never slept with a woman before, not wanting to be vulnerable at rest. But feeling the soft puffs of her breath against my skin lulled me back to my dreams.

When morning came, Lily still slept peacefully beside me. I brushed a kiss against her hair, not examining why I felt the compulsion to do so, before carefully untangling myself from our embrace and grabbing the clothes I'd need for today's hunt. Hesitating in the doorway, I left the door cracked so she wouldn't wake up in darkness. I didn't want to leave her.

The door to my suite opened, and Herrath stepped inside. He didn't appear as if he'd just woken up; his clothes were pressed, each hair in place as usual as he tugged on his armor.

"Zerek still hasn't returned, but Raenisa is waiting for us with the vaniras."

I nodded, expecting as much. Zerek would avoid his family as much as possible. "How hung over is she?"

A faint smile pulled at his lips. "Horribly."

"I warned her." He chuckled, and I had to remind myself that he wasn't my friend or my soldier. He was a spy foisted on me by my mother and the empress. Herrath had betrayed me before and would do it again in an instant. I pulled on the rest of my clothes, spreading kohl around my eyes to protect against the sun's glare. We would be out longer than usual on this hunt and would need to carry extra water.

"Go on ahead, I have to find my attendant and tell her to keep an eye on Lily today."

"I'll do it." He blurted out. "You go first and I'll join you."

I eyed him for a moment before nodding. "Are you sure you don't want to spend time with your family?"

He cast his gaze down, shifting as if uncomfortable. "I'd rather finish the mission."

"Alright then." I wasn't sure why he didn't want to see them, but I wouldn't question having an extra set of eyes. "See you on the sand then." I glanced back once into my room where my concubine still slept before leaving, Herrath following behind me as he straightened his armor and called for Mirijana.

Twenty minutes later we were on the sand mounted on our vaniras, the black grit blowing in the morning wind. The sun had almost risen, lighting up the desert in a brilliant golden glow. The rolling dunes beneath the spiders' feet were nearly magical, the sand shifting with the slightest breath of wind until something else caught my eye. A hint of movement at the edge of my vision that looked like a massive shadow slithering across the dunes. I blinked, and it was gone. A trick of the light, no doubt.

There hadn't been wyrms since the Godsfall, with Thanja's fantastical creatures dying with her. But they'd once lived here, causing sand storms with their immense wings and terrorizing anyone who dared to cross into their domain. It was said that you could still see them in the storms, riding the winds before diving back into the sand and swimming through it like water, but I'd never seen proof of it.

"Atar's sweaty balls. I already drained half of my canteen." Raenisa complained, her long hair tied up in a greasy tail as she fanned herself.

I tossed her the extra one I'd packed for her, expecting this. Raenisa might mock me for taking my family's words to heart, but it'd kept me alive through the dark years after I'd been forced back into my mother's clutches. And it prevented her from getting sunstroke at least once a month. "Was she worth it?"

"Caelia?" She sighed, her expression turning dreamy despite the dark circles under her eyes. "We just talked most of the night."

"And drank," Herrath said, directing his spider mount beside mine. She glared at him, but he ignored her, instead pointing toward the Red Wilds. "We spend most of our time scouring the highlands, but there are tons of places for them to hide. If we go overland straight to the Red Wilds, we can reach the place Rhazien told us about faster."

I nodded, eager to finish this and return. Not just to my concubine, I reminded myself. But to face Zora and Oz without feeling guilty that I'd lost one of the family swords. This was my chance to find Striker and get revenge for Calyx's death. To leave this desert, once and for all.

"Let's go."

Raenisa groaned as we started moving, her eyes flooding black as she touched her electrum earring. She sat straighter, no longer hunching in discomfort as the magic took hold, healing her hangover. The wind blew hot and dry around us, carrying the scent of sun-baked rock and creosote. Even though it was still early, the heat was oppressive and sweat beaded on my forehead almost immediately.

Vaernix moved quickly, happy to scuttle over the dunes and stretch her many legs.

The sun was high when we arrived at the Red Wilds, marveling at the massive mesas that towered ahead of us. They were dark red, a stark contrast against the sky and sand around them. Raenisa whistled low in admiration as we came closer, taking in the endless expanse of rock formations. Rattleweeds rolled past, larger than any I'd ever seen before.

"I've heard the slaves talk about this place," Herrath said, gesturing to a cluster of stones toward the east. "The Kyrie have stories about some of these formations. I think that one is supposed to be Kearis and Cetena's courtship, with the smaller one representing Sithos' birth."

"Gods, you're boring," Raenisa complained, stretching her back and arms as she readied for a potential fight. It had been her routine since the beginning of her training, her musical background influencing her fighting style.

He shot her an impassive look as he scanned the range, and an idea hit me.

"Are any of them for Vetia or the Inferi?" I hadn't forgotten the man who said he'd help me years ago, only to betray us. Haemir, one of the rebel leaders, was an Inferi Remnant. It stood to reason that those stories of his goddess would draw him.

Herrath considered for a beat before pointing further west. "That cluster there of the three pillars and the smaller stone in front? That could be Vetia and her triad."

Vetia was unique amongst the gods. She wasn't like Rhaedos, forever searching for a mate that he never found or even her parents in a couple. Supposedly she and Sithos tried to be together, forming a chain of volcanoes in the Molten Sea with their violent lovemaking before she left him, instead shifting to her smaller form to take three lovers as her triad. It had passed on to her descendants, with Inferi females being stronger in magic, and gathering their own triads of doting males.

I'd once found the idea interesting in the abstract, but having claimed Lily... I growled low in my throat at the thought of sharing her. I'd kill any man who touched her. "Theron?" Herrath questioned.

"Good enough for me," I replied, shaking off the anger that had gripped me. I caught his pleased smile as he hurried ahead, leading the way.

"Let's scout it out before going any further," Herrath called back as he looked around warily. There were stories about these mesas being home to fierce creatures like scopscions and rebels alike, but there was something else here too. An awareness that made the fine hairs on the back of my neck stand up. We were being watched.

I pointed to a narrow break in the rocks below the cluster of pillars. "There. It's a natural choke point. They'd be able to pick us off without our numbers overwhelming them."

Raenisa cocked her head. "Then how do we breach it?"

An animal call I'd never heard before echoed across the plains and sent a chill down my spine despite the heat. It sounded like an eagle's call combined with something else... a wolf's howl, perhaps?

"Fuck. They've spotted us."

Herrath cursed under his breath as he drew his sword and signaled for us to retreat into the dunes. "We don't have enough men for a full assault."

"We don't need one. Just to draw out Striker. He's always at the head of each raid. If we attack, he'll come."

I caught Raenisa's dubious look as I pushed Vaernix forward, her legs traversing the rocky terrain with ease. This was why we'd domesticated the beasts in the first place, to carry us over our jagged mountain ranges in Athain.

I took a deep breath and steeled my nerves before pushing ahead, ready for whatever might come our way. We raced through the boulders, dodging rocks and leaping over crevices until we came to a narrow opening that led into darkness.

Without hesitation, I rode in and a flurry of arrows struck my chest before being deflected by my armor. Screaming rebels scattered from Vaernix's path, having never seen a vanira up close before, but others attacked us with swords and spears, their faces determined. They wore makeshift armor made of bones, their eyes black hollows in the low light from their face paint.

I twisted and turned to avoid their attacks, my sword clashing with theirs as we fought. The sound of metal striking metal filled my ears as I focused on taking out my opponents one by one. Raenisa battled alongside me, her long hair flying behind her as she spun and kicked her enemies. Herrath was a few feet away, fending off attacks from several rebels at once, but he seemed to hold his own.

"Run! We'll hold them off!" A young male Wraith Remnant shouted. I searched for Striker as I batted away a spear, taking off the arm of a rebel with it as the man screamed. Striker was a sinewy youth that wore clothing and a hood that hid his skin and face during raids. Any of these men could be him.

"Look for my sword!"

Raenisa and Herrath fought alongside me, their weapons clashing against our enemies' with ferocity. The smell of fresh blood and sweat filled the air as we pushed our attackers further into the darkness. I swung my sword with ease, knocking aside their attacks and striking back with deadly precision. Raenisa fought beside me, her movements fluid and graceful as she twirled her staff, eliminating anyone who came near. Herrath was quick to follow, his spider mount crawling up the sides of the mesa to take out any archers who tried to shoot at us from above.

"They're escaping!" Herrath shouted, a streak of blood painting his cheek.

"Capture one! We need to interrogate them!" I leaped from my vanira, grabbing a male Kyrie Remnant when a whip wrapped around my wrist, tearing my hand away and letting my captive escape. My eyes widened as a young Inferi Remnant ran out of the shadows, tall horns curling from his head and fiery eyes blazing as he yanked on the whip, pulling me off my feet. My first thought was that he looked like a younger Haemir, with the same firm chin and nose.

I scrambled to my feet, trying to dodge his strikes. Was this him? Haemir's son? His whip caught my chin, opening the skin and I growled, advancing on him. He may be talented, but I was a warrior full-grown and battle-tested with the might of Atar on my side. The whelp didn't stand a chance.

The Remnant was about to strike when a loud battle cry sounded from behind us. A magenta-haired rebel threw herself at me, but Herrath intercepted her. The Inferi Remnant glanced at her, giving me the opportunity I needed. With a quick feint, I sliced through his whip with my sword and tackled him to the ground, pinning him beneath me.

"Roza, run!" He screamed as a grunt sounded behind me, Raenisa grappling with the girl until she pinned her and Herrath sprinted off after another fleeing rebel.

The Remnant struggled against my grip, his hands beating furiously against my armor, shredding his skin as he cursed me.

"Where's Striker?" I demanded, pressing my forearm against his throat.

The Remnant's face twisted in a sneer as he spat at me. "I don't know what you're talking about," he said, his voice dripping with hatred.

I could feel my patience slipping away, and I pressed the blade of my sword against the pulse fluttering in his neck. "You will tell me where he is or I will cut your throat."

My threat didn't seem to have an effect on him, and the Remnant snarled, refusing to back down. His eyes blazed with anger and defiance, but I could see fear in them as well. He knew I was serious, and I would not stop until I got what I wanted, even if it meant killing him.

I pressed his head harder against the ground, his horns scraping against the stone. "WHERE. IS. HE."

"You'll never find him," he said through gritted teeth, refusing to answer my question.

My grip tightened on his throat as my blade dug into his skin. "Where is Striker?"

"Fuck you," he growled. Raenisa shouted as the Sirin Remnant rolled out of her grasp and kicked her before jumping on the girl once more, straddling her before beginning to bind her hands.

"Ydonja's tits, they're wily." She panted as the Remnant cursed her, saying some things that gave even Raenisa pause and I knew she was memorizing them to use on me later. She knotted the rope before gagging the girl with another length.

Herrath approached, a female Fae Remnant in his possession, already bound and walking docile before him.

"Not if you're fast." He sent her a cutting smile she didn't return, instead raising her hand in a lewd gesture. "There aren't any left. The rest have fled somewhere else in the caverns."

I glanced down at the Inferi Remnant, who glared at me. "We're taking our prisoners back to Adraedor for more questioning," I announced, holding his gaze, and watched as a spark of fear lit in the depth of his eyes. He knew what that meant, and he knew there was no escape. Not for any of us.

Chapter 10

Kael

I woke slowly, Theron's citrus and leather scent thick in my nose. Wait. The Marshal? My eyes flew open when I realized I slept on a soft bed and not on the floor in the sparring room.

I glanced around the room, taking in the rich tapestries and ornate furnishings. I was in his bedroom. This time, there was no escaping my circumstances; I hadn't just used him to sneak into the castle but had been invited into his bed. My cheeks burned with embarrassment and shame as I got up to leave.

A sudden movement drew my attention to the door, and I tensed, ready to defend myself. But instead of an attacker, a servant entered the bedroom. Her ochre skin glowed in the morning light, and her curly hair framed her face like a halo. Mirijana, the same Kyrie Remnant as before. She breezed in, giving me a knowing look when she saw me standing there in my lingerie.

"Good morning, Lady Lily," she chirped with a slight bow of her head. Her eyes were soft and kind, making it easier for me to relax despite the uncomfortable situation.

"Morning," I mumbled, tugging at my hem. "Where's the Marshal?"

"Out scouting. He asked me to keep you company today." She beamed at me. My frustration grew as I realized Theron had plans for me that did not involve sneaking around the castle and reconnoitering as I'd planned on doing the moment he left me alone. I gritted my teeth and tried to hide my annoyance.

"Come, let's get you dressed," Mirijana said, gesturing to several dresses and gowns laid out on the bed. The fabrics were luxurious and finely crafted. I had worn nothing like them before and some part of me wanted to feel their softness against my skin, even though it felt like a betrayal to my fellow rebels.

"I don't need to dress up," I barked, trying to cover up my embarrassment with anger. "He's not even here to see me."

But Mirijana just smiled again, her expression gentle but firm. "Humor me," she said with a wink. After bathing and grumbling about the amount of wasted water, she helped me into a gown; an emerald green dress with a delicate lace bodice that clung to my curves. She pulled an ivory comb through my hair as well, styling it in an intricate braid that cascaded down my spine like a waterfall.

Finally, she stepped back and examined her handiwork with satisfaction before turning to face me again. "There," she breathed, her eyes glowing with admiration as adjusted a strand of my hair.

She hadn't dressed me as a concubine, but as a lady of a high house, similar to what the other women had worn the night before. It made me uneasy, like a bird trapped in a gilded cage. I was used to desert sand scraping my skin, not the luxury of this palace.

"Are you sure this is for me?" I asked, fingering the delicate sleeve. Outlines of lilies and skulls in the same green thread formed a subtle pattern that I ran my fingers over.

"Of course. Kadir sent them for you."

My suspicion vanished. I was pretty certain the tailor was a rebel as well and must have designed these for me, knowing I'd blend in more if I wasn't half-naked all the time. Maybe I'd have a chance of losing Mirijana and skulking about the castle after all.

She grinned at me, her skin barely moving on the scarred part of her face. I grimaced, my lips contorting into a scowl despite her sunny disposition. What had they done to the poor girl?

"You seem chipper for a servant," I drawled. "But if you're not happy here, I've heard there are ways to get people out of here if they need help."

Mirijana's smile faltered for a moment, but then she shrugged, undeterred. "Oh, I've heard of them," she said, twirling a strand of her curly hair around her finger. "But things are so much better now that I work here. I used to be in the mines..." Her fingers went to her unseeing eye, drifting over the shiny knots of scars. "But that's over. And the Marshal takes care of his servants."

I scoffed, rolling my eyes. "Lucky you," I muttered under my breath.

Mirijana's smile faltered, and a hint of sadness touched her gaze. "It's not luck, Lady Lily. It's—" She cut herself off, glancing away. "Anyway, let's not talk about that."

I eyed her before backing off. "Well, I'm sure it's lovely to work here. Would you mind giving me a tour so I can get a lay of the land?"

Mirijana smiled brightly again and nodded. "Of course," she said. Taking my hand and tucking into her elbow, as if I was a fine lady, she started leading me down the corridor.

"Lead the way."

She grinned again, her eyes brightening with excitement. "You're going to love it," she promised, and I couldn't help but wonder what Theron had saved her from to merit this kind of loyalty.

"This is The Castle of the Three Suns," she began, gesturing to the intricate stone walls, which were carved with figures of wyrms and five-pointed stars. "It holds a long history within its halls. It was built by three of the oldest Salfár houses, though only our records of the Daelors remain."

I snorted. That wasn't surprising. Everyone knew the Scourge of the Gods, Eiran Daelor. The elf that had convinced Atar to craft Endbringer, the sword capable of killing a god, after Kearis insulted him. Not that he'd lived to see his dream realized. During the Godsfall, Tiordan Carxidor had come to power and Daelor had vanished. In Haechall, the fae said that Daelor was still alive and kept prisoner, but I didn't believe it. What usurper would keep the rightful king alive? I hadn't been aware that he had been a Salfár though, and I still was uncertain what the differences were.

"Interesting," I responded, trying to keep my tone friendly, even if I wasn't sure how well I was succeeding. She led me down a wide hall, lined with portraits of generations of governors and their families, before leading us to the Martial Gallery. It was an immense room filled with all manner of weapons and armor from days gone by.

A large tiara caught my eye - shining like white gold with intricate carvings of leaves that sparkled in the light. As I drew closer, I could almost feel an eerie power emanating from the tiara. It seemed... alive—as if it were calling out to me. I couldn't stop myself from reaching out and brushing my fingertips against its smooth surface. It was smooth as silk beneath my skin, and a strange warmth seeped into my veins. It was beautiful—too beautiful for words—and it seemed to draw me in like a moth to a flame. Mirijana noticed me staring at it.

"It was once worn by Eiran Daelor's queen consort. She was said to be exquisite." I imagined a stone-faced elf adorned with this tiara as she helped decimate entire populations with her genocidal husband.

"Sure."

It was clear that Mirijana felt indebted to the Elves after they pulled her from the mines, but her hero-worship was making me want to slap her. I needed to lose her, and fast.

Placing my hands on my middle, I made a face. "My stomach is growling. I forgot to have breakfast."

"A thousand apologies, my lady," Mirijana said, her eyes flying open. "I shouldn't have rushed you out the door."

I waved it off. "Could you bring me something from the kitchens? It doesn't have to be large."

She shook her head. "I'll grab you a tray. Come on."

"I'll just meet you back at the suite," I said, patting my stomach. "I'm not feeling well."

Her eyes widened, and she squeaked. "Of course. I'll get you some tea to settle your stomach as well. Go straight down these stairs two levels and turn right to get back to the Marshal's rooms. I'll see you in a moment."

I nodded and set off down the hallway. As soon as I rounded the corner, out of sight from Mirijana, I started trotting towards my destination—the Beast's set of rooms. I had to move fast—if anyone caught me in the corridors; I didn't know if I could talk my way out of it. Thank Ydonja for the dress; at least I wouldn't have my ass and tits on display and attracting attention.

The halls seemed to stretch on forever as the castle creaked and moaned around me like a living thing as the desert sun heated the stone. Every time a door opened or closed, my heart almost beat out of my chest—but thankfully, no one ever found me along my way. After what felt like hours of winding around the austere castle but had likely only been minutes, I discovered the Beast's suite. On the opposite side of the castle to Theron's, it appeared to be a mirror image of it.

The room was fit for a king, with velvet couches and gilded furniture. The walls were adorned with rich tapestries and paintings of naked women mid-coitus. At the far end of the suite, a massive patio overlooked the courtyard below, complete with outdoor tubs to take in the starry night sky in comfort. The patio was golden and shimmered in the light of several braziers that lined its edges. Black silken fabric hung from above to shield those bathing from the sun's harsh rays. It was an oasis amidst all this desolation, a place where one could forget their worries—at least temporarily. And I hated that a monster enjoyed it every day.

An ornate hookah sat on top of a nearby table, its elegant stem encrusted with jewels and shining against its black lacquer base, the scent of Areca smoke drifting from it. Arrangements of datura flowers hung from the ceiling, adding vibrant color to the otherwise neutral tones of beige and gold that permeated throughout. A luxurious carpet stretched into the living space, where almost a dozen women lounged.

My heart sank as I realized that this was the Beast's harem, and they were all staring at me. I scanned their faces, searching for Aella, but the woman was nowhere to be found. I cursed under my breath as Zija, the lead concubine I recognized from the colosseum, stood and approached me with an air of authority. She was a beautiful Inferi Remnant, with dark hair, bronze skin, and twisting horns adorning her head. Her features drew back in mild disgust as she surveyed me before dropping into a curtsey.

"Hello, my lady, what can I—" Her deferential attitude dropped the moment she realized I wasn't one of the Elven nobles. "What are you doing here?" Zija demanded, crossing her arms over impressive breasts that were only covered by a smattering of beads.

"I'm—"

"Nevermind," she spat, turning away and giving me a dismissive wave of her wrist that caused her harem-mates to laugh. I noticed that they all had similar horns to Zija's—not uncommon among Inferi—but also that some of them had wings, too. Clearly, the Beast preferred his women to be of a certain race and nature. "Your presence here is unwelcome. Leave."

"Gladly." I turned to walk out when sharp nails dug into my wrist as she grabbed me. "Wait a minute. I recognize you. You're Prince Theron's concubine. The one he keeps parading around."

I raised a brow. "Is that right?"

She sneered at me, stepping into my space. "He might think it's entertaining to dress you up like a lady, but we all know where your place truly is." She pressed a finger on the tip of my nose, pushing me back. "In the trash."

Before I could react, the door opened and Mirijana hurried in. Her eyes darted around until they fell on me. She seemed relieved to find me, her shoulders dropping as a smile lit up her face.

"Oh, there you are, my lady! Did you get lost on the way back to your room?"

At Mirijana's interruption, Zija let go of my wrist and stepped away from me with a smirk. "I see. She's simple," she stage whispered to her harem-mates who tittered, before turning her attention back to me. "You should be more careful where you wander."

Mirijana grabbed my arm and pulled me away from Zija. "Yes, yes she will," she promised before spinning to face Zija again with a deep bow of apology. "I apologize for any trouble we have caused you, miss."

Zija pursed her lips as if irritated Mirijana hadn't called her 'my lady' as well, before waving her hand in dismissal. "Go," she spat before turning her back on us.

Mirijana ushered me out, her fingers tightly gripping my arm as we left the Beast's harem behind. I let out a relieved breath as we rounded a corner, trying to shake off the chill of Zija's words and the sight of the Beast's women.

"Thank goodness that's over," Mirijana said.

I bit my lip, anger still boiling inside me. "That woman was a piece of work."

"Yes, she is," Mirijana agreed, casting a nervous glance behind us. "I don't know why they let her stay here. She's unbearable."

"The Governor must have a strange set of preferences," I replied, still angry at the way Zija had treated me.

"Indeed." Mirijana chuckled and shook her head. "Come now, let's get back to your suite before the Marshal returns."

I blew out a frustrated breath, my mind already racing as I tried to figure out a new plan.

Chapter II

Theron

I went into my suite as the sun was setting, exhausted but pleased after capturing three rebels for questioning. We'd never been able to catch any in the wild before, only ones already in the city, and they knew nothing about the rebel hideouts. Lily looked up from where she was seated as I entered, her expression shuttering as we made eye contact. She wore a lovely green gown that intensified her eyes even more. They reminded me of the pines on my father's estate, the towering trees creaking like an old door as they swayed in the breeze.

"Lord Marshal," Mirijana stood and curtseyed. "How was your hunt?"

"Successful." Lily stiffened, her eyes darting around as if she wanted to run. Interesting.

"Would you like a meal sent up? I can prepare one." Mirijana started clearing away the tea set on the low table.

"In an hour," I said, unhooking my chest plate and tossing it in the corner. Mirijana immediately picked it up and set it on the stand and I winced as Lily shot me a disgusted look. I'd made a habit of throwing my things all over, confident that they'd make it to the right place, but I normally didn't have to watch the servants clean them. I removed the rest of my armor, putting it on the correct rack as Mirijana left to prepare a meal.

"Come on." I grabbed a pair of robes, tossing them over my shoulder. Lily narrowed her eyes on me.

"Where?"

"You'll see."

"Pass." She crossed her arms and looked out the window as if studying the pink and coral sky. The corner of my mouth tugged up, keen on a challenge. I crept closer, and she glowered at me, her lovely face even more gorgeous when twisted in hate.

Leaning over her, I put one arm on each side of her, boxing her in.

"You're coming with me, *Sia,*" I murmured, edging nearer as she stiffened. "You can walk with me or I'll throw you over my shoulder and carry you." I ran my nose over her cheek, and she shivered. "I think you know which one I'd prefer."

She glared at me and pushed me back, her small hands firm against my chest. "Fine." She snarled, and I chuckled.

"I knew you'd see it my way." I grinned and grabbed her hand, pulling her out of the room.

We descended a series of servant stairs—I didn't feel like seeing anyone from the court if they'd woken early—and hallways until we emerged in an underground cavern. The air was damp and cold, with a hint of earthy soil. Lily gasped as we stepped into the space, her eyes wide as she took it in.

The massive chamber was illuminated by glowing plants and stones that dotted the walls, giving off a soft light that made everything seem ethereal. The water stretched out before us, cool and inviting, reflecting the lights above like stars twinkling in the night sky.

"We imported the plants from Athain. We cultivate them in the hollow mountains to provide light for us. They only grow in humid areas though, so we can only use them in this room," I explained, wanting to share a small piece of my homeland with her.

"You bastards," Lily said, her hands balled at her sides.

I turned to her in surprise, not expecting such a vehement reaction.

"You let slaves die of dehydration while you hoard all this water for yourselves!" She hissed, throwing her arm out and gesturing to the expansive grotto.

I opened my mouth to argue, but I didn't have a response. We'd done nothing to provide relief for the people suffering in the desert, instead choosing to use water to control the population.

"What would you have me do?" I said, my anger growing as shame heated my neck.

Lily looked up at me, her eyes blazing with defiance and wrath. "You could start by giving them some of your precious water."

"I've tried that before," I growled. "You know how they repaid me? By killing one of my best friends."

"So you let them all die? Let the desert and the mines suck everything out of them until they are withered husks to be tossed away like trash?" She threw her arms wide. "When you have all of this! There is no honor in you Elves. You wage warfare against people that you *know* can't stand against you since your people stole their magic and immortality, all the while lauding how incredible you are to each other. You sharp-eared assholes."

Her eyes were narrow slits of hate as she raged at me and I ran a hand through my hair, frustrated.

Because she was right.

"Even if I wanted to change Adraedor, I couldn't." I edged closer to her, and she stared up at me defiantly, despite my invading her space. "You think that you're the only person here that's trapped? We are all stuck in a web of another's making. I've just learned how to live with it."

"There are worse things than death, you coward."

A growl built in my chest as dark memories crowded my mind, images of dark blood bubbling on my father's lips as he told me to run. "Oh, I know. I've lived them. What do you think I'm trying to avoid?"

Her chest heaved as she glared at me, before tearing her eyes away and stepping back. She clasped her arms, peering over the water, and I sighed.

"It's just the way it is," I said, though the words tasted like ash on my tongue. "I can't change it."

She nodded, and I felt a twinge of guilt. Despite her anger, she still didn't understand how hard it was for me to be here. Attempts on my life at every turn. How the sight of Rhazien ignited a flood of memories that threatened to drown me. The constant need to protect everyone from him, even at my expense. How I was subject to my uncle's whims, with only a false semblance of freedom, when I followed his orders exactly. I hated it, but there was nothing else I could do.

I tugged at my shirt and she watched me as I stripped off all of my clothing, hot and sweaty from spending the day scouring the desert. Her eyes raked over me, widening as she took in my body and my cock pulsed as her gaze landed on it.

She glanced away, red creeping onto her pale cheeks. Saying nothing more, I stepped into the water, sighing with pleasure as the liquid soothed my tense muscles.

"What would it take to get you in here with me?"

"Nothing you have." She responded, turning her back on me.

"How about another trade? A secret for a favor?"

She turned to me, eying me. "How would I know you were telling the truth?"

I smiled. She'd taken the bait. "Don't you think you could tell?"

Without any hesitation, she crossed the chamber, kicking off her shoes next to the chair I'd thrown our things on.

Her hands went to the buttons of her dress and I bit my lip, forcing myself to stay still as she undid it. The fabric hung loosely off of her shoulders, revealing the smooth line of her back and the curve of her hips.

My eyes trailed over her body as she pulled away all of her clothes, reveling in its beauty. Her skin was pale as snow, with a smattering of freckles on her chest and down to her stomach. The silver strands of her hair glimmered in the dim light like Ydonja's stars against a night sky and I wanted nothing more than to touch it, to feel its softness against my skin. Every part of her was curvaceous perfection, and I grew intensely aroused by the sight before me.

"Atar almighty," I murmured in Elvish, and she tossed a glower over her shoulder at me.

Her clothing lay discarded on the ground as she slipped into the pool, no trace of shyness or modesty visible on her face as she moved closer to me. The water lapped against her body like a hungry lover, and my desire surged up within me before I tamped it back down again. Not until she begged.

Ripples radiated outwards as she slowly submerged herself up to her shoulders in the cool liquid.

My breath caught as I watched her revel in the blissful pleasure of water against her skin. She closed her eyes and tilted back her head until only half of her face emerged from beneath the surface, basking in its embrace as if she were worshiping a god. Her long hair swirled around her and I knew then why Kearis had fallen in love with Cetena, the water only adding to her ethereal beauty.

"How do you know how to swim?" I asked in Elvish, and she rolled her eyes.

"I'm asking the questions." She responded in the same language, her brusque attitude in place before her mouth fell open as she realized what she'd done.

Caught her.

I grinned, moving closer. "I'd wondered if you understood my tongue. Your glares always seemed well-timed."

"Clever." She dead-panned and I chuckled. "Where did you go today?" She continued in Elvish, her accent lilting in a way that made my cock throb.

"Into the Red Wilds," I answered without elaborating, determined to make her rack up as many questions as possible. For all her talk about honor, I'd push her to repay me in kind.

"They're pretty large..." she said, letting the question dangle for me to finish.

"Hmm." I stifled a laugh at her expression as I avoided her trap. My mother was the most conniving woman on the planet. She couldn't think that I'd fall for that.

"What did you find?"

"The rebel base." She didn't react, as if she'd already guessed, and a niggling suspicion began in the back of my mind.

"What happened?" She demanded, moving close to me in the water. My erection brushed her stomach, and she gasped, taking a step away from me.

"Ah, ah," I said, my gaze tracing her face. Her cheeks were more flushed than usual, her breath coming in little puffs. She was as affected by me as I was by her. "That's two questions. Answer one of mine or do me another favor."

She gave me a withering glance. "Ask."

"What's your name?" She opened her mouth, and I cut her off. "Your real name. Not anymore of this 'Lily' business."

She sighed, frustrated. "Kael. Short for Kaella," she answered. "That counts as two answers."

"*Kael,*" I murmured, looking into her eyes. "It suits you better." She looked away again and cleared her throat, irritated with how much she had revealed to me in this short amount of time.

"What happened after you found the rebel stronghold?" She gave me a pointed look that told me it was my turn to answer questions now.

I laughed softly as I pushed back my wet hair and thought back on what had occurred after I'd discovered the rebel base. "Well," I began, conscious of how close we stood in the water and how much closer we could get if either of us were so inclined. "They tried to flee, and we stopped them. I ended up capturing three. One of them is the leader's son." I said casually, watching her reactions.

She didn't react, instead making a non-committal noise in her throat as she turned away from me, going underwater.

"No Striker, I presume?" She asked after surfacing.

"Is that a question?" I swam closer, circling her once more. "Because I'll need payment."

"No." She looked at me with disdain. "What will happen to them?"

"They're to be interrogated," I answered carefully. I watched her, looking for a sign that she was part of the rebels, but there was nothing there. She remained still and silent, waiting for me to continue. "And then Rhazien will execute them for treason."

She nodded but didn't react.

"My turn," I said, swimming up close to her once more until I could make out the beads of water on her spiky lashes. "Why do you care what happens to them?"

She stared at me for a long moment, so long that I didn't think she'd respond. "Because they're like me, trapped in a prison of another's making." She stepped into my space, uncaring that her breasts grazed my ribs and my cock pressed against her stomach. "The real question is, why don't you?"

The moment hung between us, my lack of significance painfully clear. I wanted to pull her closer, to feel her skin against mine and kiss her until her rage blazed into passion, so I could ignore what she was attempting to make me face.

But I couldn't.

Instead, before I could do something foolish, she moved away and waded to the edge of the pool. My gaze followed her as she stepped out onto the stone, water dripping from every inch of her nude body as if she were a goddess stepping forth from a lake. Her curves were emphasized by the rivulets of water that skipped down over each one, making me want her even more than before.

I shook my head to clear it of such thoughts and told myself to focus on the task at hand—capturing Striker—but no matter how hard I tried, my gaze still returned to Kael's figure as she dried herself off with a white towel that had been left for swimmers. She didn't look at me as I emerged from the water this time, and I had the strangest sensation that I'd let her down somehow. We didn't speak again as we made our way back to my suite. Mirijana had food waiting, but my stomach was hollow.

"Stay with Kael," I told Mirijana, who looked around in confusion before she realized I was referring to the silver-haired concubine glowering at me once more.

"Oh! Are you leaving again, Lord Marshal?"

I jerked my chin in assent. "I have some rebels to interrogate."

Kael scowled at me, her expression dark as I turned and fled from her presence, and the confusing feelings she inspired in me.

Chapter 12

Kael

I paced the suite, still waiting for Theron to return. It had been hours; the moons drifting across Ydonja's stars as Rhaedos' moon forever chased the mate he'd never found. Where was Theron? Was Gavril still alive? He had to be, right? Theron had said that Rhazien would execute them, no doubt making a big show of it to the slaves. I could save my brother if I could figure out where Theron was holding them. My gaze stopped on Mirijana, whose eyes kept fluttering closed despite resting her chin in her palm.

"Mirijana," I began, keeping my voice light. "How much longer do you think Theron will be?"

She yawned, pressing the back of her hand against her mouth. "Not too long, my lady. It's almost dawn."

The sun had yet to make it over the mountains, the range so tall that it shaded Adraedor in darkness longer than the rest of the world each day. Time was running out if I was going to save Gavril.

"Is the dungeon far away? Is that what's taking him so long?" My whiny voice was foreign to my own ears, but it worked on her.

"Not far at all. It's by the royal guard's barracks." She patted my hand with a weary smile. "He'll be back soon."

I pressed my lips together, my mind whirring. We'd passed the barracks on the way in from the Colosseum. It was close to where those wretched vanira were stabled. "Perhaps I'll just take a nap then and wait."

"Of course," she made to rise, and I gestured for her to stay seated. "Don't worry, I can get it."

I grabbed the blanket on the chair, passing it to her before grabbing one myself.

"Thank you," she shot me a relieved smile and a twinge of guilt hit me. If they caught me, Mirijana would be punished, possibly even executed. But if I did nothing, Gavril and whoever else they'd captured would be killed. I hardened my resolve. Haemir and I had both lost too much already. I refused to lose more family.

I feigned sleep, my heart pounding in my chest as Mirijana's snores filled the room. When I was sure she was deeply asleep, I crept to the door and cracked it. The hall was empty; my bare feet made no sound on the cold stone floor as I raced down the servant stairs and out into the courtyard where we'd come in.

The chill of early morning air stung against my skin beneath the sheer nightgown that hung from my body like a thin veil with a deep scarlet robe draped over it. My hair was tousled around me and I hoped it was enough of a disguise that if anyone saw me, they wouldn't recognize me as a concubine, but as possibly a visiting noble.

With every step, I felt like time was slipping away from me. In the distance, I could hear voices coming from within the guard station and feel eyes upon me as though some unseen force were already catching up to me. But no matter how afraid I was, I kept moving.

The wind whipped through the city, carrying sand with a cacophony as if it was warning me, but I pushed the strange notion away. I had to get in there. Haemir couldn't survive another loss.

I approached the guard station slowly, my hands shaking and my heart racing. The door was slightly ajar, giving me just enough space to slip through without creating too much noise. When I stepped inside, the guard turned his attention toward me and yelled in surprise before laughing.

"Are you lost?"

I pasted on a polite smile, biting my lip as I approached. "I'm sorry, I was separated from my—" I launched myself at him, scrambling onto his back and wrapping my forearm around his throat.

He wheezed, trying to tear my arm away, his fingers digging painfully into my skin, but I squeezed tighter, cutting off his blood flow. He slammed my back against the wall and I groaned but didn't let go. There was no way I could hold on long enough to strangle him. I had to make him pass out. His attacks became more and more feeble as I held on, my muscles straining as he crashed to his knees and I rode him to the floor, where he finally went limp.

"Fuck," I whispered, shaking out my arms as I stood over him. Checking his pockets, I found a knife and grinned when I realized it was made of earthborn iron. *Someone didn't trust his compatriots.* Earthborn iron stifled their gifts, preventing Elves from healing. Some were so sensitive to it that just touching it would burn their skin. I wrapped my hand around the leather handle, testing the weight of the blade. Perfectly balanced. Very nice.

The guard stirred, and I stabbed him without thinking, my knife slipping between his ribs and finding his heart. I didn't enjoy killing an unarmed man, but I would do anything to protect my family. Wiping the blood off my hand onto his shirt, I left before anyone else saw me, darting past the barracks and into a dark alleyway where no one seemed to have noticed my presence at all. Taking a deep breath, I slumped against the wall behind me in relief as I surveyed my surroundings.

Chittering came from a cave entrance and I shuddered. That was the stable, which meant that the entrance over there was probably the dungeon.

I spotted a figure exiting the door as I watched; Theron, and he was followed by another man in a cloak. The Harvestman that had threatened to kill me, Herrath. My gut twisted with anger as I crouched in the shadows.

"Tough son of a bitch," Herrath said. His voice held no hint of emotion or empathy; it was cold and calculating, just like in the bedroom when he'd threatened me.

Theron grunted. "I have to talk to Rhazien. We need more time."

They'd tortured my brother. I wanted nothing more than to kill him right here and now, but that would only guarantee Gavril's death when my collar prevented me from finishing the job.

I watched them leave and silently crept through the door, quickly dispatching the guard inside with my knife and pulling the key ring out of his pocket. The dungeon itself was a wretched sight to behold. The air was dank and smelled of sweat, urine, and blood. Low moans echoed against the stone walls as I passed by each occupied cell, and in the dead of night, there seemed no hope for any of them. Torches and stained patches of dried blood lined the floor, revealing more horrors than I cared to witness.

I breathed through my mouth as I made my way down into the depths of the dungeon. Dark shapes writhed in cells even farther below, their screams muffled by the thick walls so none could hear them but me. There were some Elves who were chained up with iron manacles that burned their skin and kept them from using their powers; others were just left to rot in isolated cells with only rats for company.

It was enough to make me sick to my stomach, but I kept going, determined to find my brother. After almost vomiting, I found him in a small cell at the end of the row, Roza and Cithara with him.

He smiled when he saw me, his fiery eyes attempting to widen despite their terrible swelling. It was a wonder he could see at all. Blood matted his dark curls around his horns, though thankfully they were both still intact.

"Kael? Thank Vetia, you're still alive." He stood up, reaching his hands through the bars and grasping my hands. I squeezed them, checking to see if all his fingers were there.

"I could say the same," I choked out, my voice thick with emotion as I reached into my pocket and pulled out the ring of keys. Tears blurred my vision as I freed them, my brother sweeping me into a tight embrace.

A sob escaped me as he held me. He might be two years younger than me, but he'd been my light in the darkness as children. When I'd come to the desert, a frightened ten-year-old packed into a slave wagon, the dregs of the slave quarter had found me. An orphan with no protection? They took me easily, no matter how hard I fought. I don't remember those months—my mind blocked them out—but I remembered when Haemir saved me. He'd broken in, swinging his great hammer into one of my captor's chest, collapsing it with a wet crunch, before roaring and killing the rest until he'd painted the room red. I'd been terrified when he took me back to their barracks, thinking I'd traded one captivity for another until Gavril started flitting around me like a bright little butterfly, obviously happy and better fed than any other kids I'd seen here.

I pulled away, inspecting his face and making him wince. "Stop being a baby and let me see."

"Stop it, Kael." He dodged my hands. "Come on, we have to get out of here before they return. "

Roza, a Sirin Remnant with magenta hair that despised me almost as much as I disliked her, sneered at me. "What happened to your tits?"

"Oh, fuck off. Roza."

"I think they look nice," Cithara put in. She was a new recruit, a Fae Remnant with mismatched eyes that I'd never seen separated from her sister.

"See. The fae said it, so it must be true." I said, shooting a glare at Roza as Cithara picked at her sleeve, apparently unaware that the conversation had continued.

"Enough of this. We need to go. Now." Gavril said, tugging me toward the door.

"I can't."

He stopped, turning to stare at me incredulously. "Are you insane? The entire court is here. Teodosija had already called off the mission, but you snuck out before she could tell you." He narrowed his eyes on me. "Thanks for that, by the way. Dad is pissed."

I flinched. "Look. I've already infiltrated the castle. I'm so close to killing the Beast and I've been gathering intel, too. "

Roza crossed her muscular arms, flipping her shorn hair to the side. "Like what?"

"Like the fact that they can't make any more speaking stones. If we can break them, we'll hinder their communications, making it harder for them to expand."

Cithara nodded. "Teodosija and Haemir can use that."

"What my dad needs is his daughter," Gavril said, grabbing my hand once again. "Come on, Kael. It's too dangerous. You don't have any backup."

"I have help. The tailor, Kadir, is one of us." I shook my head. "I'm staying. I can do this. I swear it. Theron keeps me close, I can—"

"Theron?" His features twisted. "You mean the Marshal?"

Heat flooded my cheeks. When had I started thinking of him as Theron and not the Marshal? Maybe when I woke up in his bed…

"That doesn't matter. What matters is that I'm so close to completing this mission." He shook his head, ready to argue more when I cut him off. "We don't have time for this. Someone is going to come any second." Pulling him into another embrace, words spilled out of me. "I have an ally. I'll send you updates, alright?"

He nodded reluctantly. "You better, or I'm coming in for you. I don't care that the emperor is here."

I rolled my eyes. "Just tell dad I'm alright. And that I'm sorry."

"I'll tell him the first part, but the second one is all you."

"Enough of this," Roza growled. "We're leaving."

I pulled Gavril into a quick hug, desperate to soak up as much affection as possible before he left. "Skirt around the guard station and go up the mountain a bit and you should make it out with no one seeing you. They all go to bed at dawn and will be lazy."

"More intel," Cithara murmured as Roza scowled, stalking out into the early morning, the Fae Remnant following behind her.

"Be safe." Gavril shot me one last look before running after them. His easy jog soothed most of my worries about his torture. He'd heal from all of it.

I blew out a breath before leaving the dungeon. Their shadows melted into the remaining pools of darkness as I hurried back to the castle. I needed to return to the suite before the Marshal or I'd be back in one of those cells myself.

I was almost there, just a few steps away from the entrance when a figure stepped out from the shadows. Xadrian emerged from the darkness, his wavy dark hair so mussed his pale streak was barely visible. His beauty mark danced on his cheek as he regarded me with a smirk.

"We meet again." He said, his voice smooth and measured as if he met concubines in darkened courtyards all the time. For all I knew, he did. "What were you doing out here in the middle of the night?"

My heart lurched into my throat, but I kept my voice level. "Just out for some air."

He stepped closer, and I had to force myself not to step back. "Alone?"

I nodded, unable to find words amidst my sudden fear he would give me away. After all, why was he here? Was he also looking for someone?

He cocked an eyebrow at me. "Theron should be more careful with his possessions."

"I am not his property." I snapped, my better judgment fleeing in the face of my anger.

"Is that right? Then where are you hurrying off to?"

I scowled at him. "None of your business."

He laughed, low and intimate in the darkness. A bright ring glinted on his finger as he grasped my hand, his skin warm against mine.

"Come with me," he murmured, his voice dark and seductive. "Let's find out how much you don't belong to him."

I recoiled from Xadrian's grasp, feeling a spark of power between us. A deafening boom sounded as a jagged rock close by split into two pieces, and I seized the opportunity to escape. Sprinting across the grounds, I didn't look back until I reached the castle entrance, Xadrian's laughter echoing in my ears.

I raced up the stairs, my heart thumping in my chest. Cautiously opening the door to our suite, I slipped in, Mirijana's snores providing some comfort that the Marshal hadn't returned. Running into the bedroom, I shoved the knife beneath the mattress and yanked off my clothes. The sound of male voices had me scrambling into bed as Theron walked in. I fought to keep my breathing even as he stared at me before he shut the door gently. I let out a shuddering breath, my heartbeat pounding in my ears like a hammer in the foundry. Fuck, that was close. I listened to him moving around the suite until the clinking dishes lulled me to sleep.

Chapter 13

Theron

I glanced at Kael, but her face was set in hard lines that hadn't shifted since we'd woken. If I'd thought our conversation in the lagoon had helped us understand one another more, I was sorely mistaken. She was even more distant than before, not even treating me to her sharp words or glances, instead keeping her attention locked outside the carriage window. It reminded me of those months after my mother had let me out of the cage, withholding the smallest bits of affection to keep my behavior in line.

I took a deep breath and tried again. "What do you think of the city?"

Kael didn't answer, and I followed her gaze out the window to where gilded spires glinted in the hazy lantern glow. The original section of the city was said to be a wonder of Maeoris, but Kael seemed unimpressed by its splendor. For someone who had spent most of her time outside its walls, it should have been awe-inspiring. But then again, had she spent her life in the slave quarter? I'd assumed that she had, but I'd never asked. I knew next to nothing about the woman I'd claimed as my own. Only the unwavering certainty that she was mine.

The noble district was stunningly crafted, showcasing the talents of his forebears in abundance. Its winding streets were framed by tall black stone walls, the sharp corners of obsidian cladding glinting in the moonlight like stars scattered across the sky. Statues and mosaics lined every street corner, brightening up the darkness with their beauty. Elven artisans had built this district from nothing but sand and rock, creating a unique desert city of dark hues and intricate designs.

The few plants that grew here seemed to thrive despite the lack of water, sending their vines to encase buildings and statues alike in a pale green embrace. The air was heavy with spices, both sweet and savory, mingling with exotic perfumes to create an almost dizzying atmosphere and a crowd shouted as a man blew fire from his mouth in a cloud. Everything about it was designed for beauty—no expense had been spared to ensure its opulence. A stark contrast to the rest of the city. We had built the addition with speed in mind, lacking any soul in its red stones.

Kael just stared out at it all wordlessly, her expression curious, but her lips pressed together in a thin line. I almost felt guilty for disrupting the silence between us and wished I had said nothing.

Then she spoke up in a soft voice, "It's strange how this place can be so beautiful yet so hollow." She turned to look at me with those intense green eyes; they seemed to hold something deeper than words could express. "Why do you keep bothering me?" She asked, her tone weary.

"Do I need a reason to speak to you?"

Her eyes flashed, and relief flickered through me. I preferred her fire over her ice. "Most people have a point to their conversations."

"Where are you from?"

She lifted a delicate shoulder, and my gaze flicked to her dress, a bold blood-red sheath that clung to her curves and left precious little to the imagination. "It doesn't matter."

"Humor me."

She glared at me, and my cock throbbed. It wasn't on board with the plan to wait. "I'm not your entertainment."

"Do you want to be?" I murmured, sliding closer to her. She trembled, goosebumps running down her arm before she shot me a nasty look. As if it was my fault that her body reacted to me. It was only fair. She should be as obsessed with me as I was with her.

"I'm from Haechall." She said, her voice hard.

I froze, not wanting to frighten her back into silence, even though worry threaded through me. I'd decimated Haechall on Varzorn's orders. It was a wasteland now. "Have you been in Adraedor long?"

"What's long for me is nothing for you." She turned those eyes on me once more, pinning me to my seat. "If I tell you I've been here for more than a decade, what does that mean to you? That's a blink to an immortal. To me, it could be a third of my life. Slaves don't last in the desert."

"I'm not that old," I muttered even as dread filled me. The Fall of Caurium had been fifteen years ago. "I'm only two hundred and seventeen. That's young for my kind."

Her eyes widened in disbelief, and her mouth twisted in a mirthless smirk. She shook her head and let out a low, hollow chuckle before turning away.

The carriage came to a halt, and I stepped out, holding my hand for her to exit. She grimaced at the harnessed vanira, taking care to step away from it as we walked toward the stone entrance. The outdoor amphitheater was bedecked in imperial colors: red, black, and gold ribbons cascaded down from the ceiling of the stage, billowing in the midnight breeze. Flaming torches lined the walls, casting a warm glow across the sandstone and colorful mosaic tiles that depicted the city's history, images of Kearis and Atar building together. People bustled around us, their faces illuminated by the firelight as they searched for their seats.

"Come on." She didn't fight me as I tucked her arm into my elbow, guiding her to the front of the amphitheater, ignoring the section that the Emperor had claimed, my mother and Rhazien by his side. Tannethe stood next to her, a seductive grin on her face as she beckoned for me to join her, but I pointedly looked away. Nyana gave me a disapproving glare before we moved to take our seats, angry at my blatant refusal of her demands.

We sat, surrounded by the various Thain Noble Houses and their scheming members vying to claim the throne for themselves. The Vennorins were almost too obvious in their plotting; a family of vipers with too much money and not enough connections. House Sarro had old blood but lacked popularity among the nobility. And then there was House Taelyr and Cairis; enemies who had recently become lovers that seemed to be winning over hearts of all persuasions with their displays of devotion, not that Raenisa was interested in spending time with her newly married cousin.

There was a sense of excitement in the air as people waited eagerly for some entertainment; musicians tuning their instruments offstage and the scent of fried dough drifting around us. I heard a familiar laugh and looked over my shoulder to see

Raenisa sitting with Caelia Sarro; her smile was radiant as the older woman whispered something in her ear. Herrath didn't seem to be in attendance, and Zerek still hadn't returned.

"What is this? A play?" Kael asked, crossing her arms over her chest.

I shook my head, glancing away from the stage to watch her glower at the assemblage. "It's a dance, *Sia*. The story of Kearis and Cetena's courtship."

"Seems like poor taste to make a show about gods you murdered," Kael muttered under her breath and I swallowed a laugh.

The audience grew quiet as a pair of scantily clad performers emerged from backstage and began to weave their way up the spider silk ribbons suspended in the air.

"Kearis flies high above the seas and sees Cetena in the waves, her tail as strong as his wings, and knows that she's his," I whispered, my lips brushing the shell of her ear and causing her to shiver. They moved swiftly, almost lovingly, as they pulled themselves up and wrapped around each other as the music began before swinging apart in a wide arc across the stage. Scented smoke drifted over the floor, swirling as the ribbons swayed.

"Cetena leads Kearis on a chase, her tempests turning the sea into a roiling mass. But that doesn't dissuade him. He has to have her." The first performer twirled sensually around the second, her body entangling with his as their eyes connected. He smiled down at her before swooping in for a kiss; one leaving them both breathless. A prominent bulge in the male's thin breeches left no doubt to the veracity of their performance. Kael gasped beside me, her hand gripping my arm tightly as she watched the dance continue, spellbound.

Kael's breath came in shallow pants and I felt her trembling against my side; her flushed cheeks were hidden beneath a curtain of silver waves and her lips slightly parted in excitement.

"Cetena journeys to the depths of the ocean, sure that the Lord of the Skies wouldn't dare follow her. What man would give up power for love?" I murmured, letting the scent of her hair fill my nose.

The two performers continued to swirl around each other in the air, their bodies meeting in suggestive poses that they held a touch too long, grinding against one another. They laughed as they teased each other, pulling off what little clothing they'd started with until they were bare, with only the silks to shield their nudity. It was as if they were unaware of the audience, only thinking of the other as they erotically intertwined within their silk cocoon high above us all.

"Kearis follows her to the heart of the ocean, ready to spend eternity in the sea if it meant they could be together. Cetena sees his love is true and they return to the surface, where Kearis spreads his wings, bringing her into the sky with him."

The woman gasped as the male entered her, spearing her glistening folds for all to see. Kael's breath stuttered, and I found myself watching her instead of the erotic exhibition. The way she pressed her thighs together as she squirmed, her white teeth stark against her lower lip as she bit it, how her fierce eyes softened with arousal. The performer above couldn't hold a candle to the concubine beside me.

"They join and Kearis welcomes the sea into his territory, so they never need to be parted again." It was supposedly how the Salt Wastes to the west had been created.

Her gaze followed the graceful movements of the dancers as their coupling grew more frenzied. A gasp escaped her as the woman climaxed, her body spasming as the male groaned, emptying himself into her. The audience roared in appreciation as the two of them held onto each other at opposite ends of a vertical sheet, twirling around it before releasing themselves into a dramatic fall from the sky.

Kael's breathing was ragged and her eyes dazed as she watched them land safely on the stage before taking a bow. I watched her, unable to look away from her flushed cheeks and trembling lips.

"That was... not a dance." She murmured and a low laugh escaped me.

"Wasn't it?"

I looked up to see Xadrian staring at her as well, his eyes locked on her mouth. Possessiveness rose in me and I stood, blocking his view of her.

"We've made our appearance. Let's go back to the palace." I growled, my irritation with Xadrian roughening my voice.

She took a steadying breath, not meeting my eye. "Fine."

Taking her hand in mine, I led her away from the spectacle, my thumb caressing her skin in circles. Our return to the castle was a blur, with all my attention riveted on Kael as she got a hold of herself, her pink cheeks cooling to her normal pale pearlescent complexion.

The tension between us was palpable as we entered what I already thought of as *our* suite, the air thick with unspoken words. I could feel Kael's gaze on me as I walked ahead to light the candles. In the warm glow, she removed her earrings and took down her hair; soft waves cascading over her proud shoulders invitingly, a sight so domestic that it made my chest ache.

She climbed into bed without saying a word, her movements stiff even though we were both wearing night clothes. I half expected her to drag the bedding back into the sparring room. Maybe she enjoyed sharing a bed as much as I did. We lay side by side, neither of us daring to move or speak lest we break the fragile peace that hung between us like a whisper.

Kael turned her back toward me and I felt as if I'd been released from our standoff. I closed my eyes, settling onto my pillow as my thoughts drifted. Every one of them filled with her flashing eyes. I started to drift off as she shifted position, a faint moan slipping from her lips. My eyes flew open as the blanket moved and she sucked in a quiet breath as she pleasured herself. She was almost silent, only the smallest noises escaping her. My cock went rock hard in an instant, my sac tightening to the point of pain.

My pulse raced as I rolled closer to her, the scent of lilies filling my senses as I placed a gentle hand on her waist.

Kael stilled, sucking in a breath as I skimmed my fingertips over her silk-clad stomach. Hesitant but not pushing me away, either. My hand wandered lower, caressing her curves before finding its way between her legs, where I replaced her hand with mine. I pushed her panties to the side, revealing her slick folds as I traced the seam of her cunt. She gasped softly as I brushed against her pierced clit; goosebumps rising with each touch as I began pleasuring her with soft circular motions of my fingers.

"Yes, *Sia*," I murmured, dragging my teeth over her shoulder as I ground my erection against her hip, dipping a finger into her wet heat and groaning. I didn't need to use my magic for her to be desperate for me. Gods, I couldn't wait to feel this pretty cunt clenched around my cock.

"Don't talk. I still hate you." She growled, and I laughed, leaning in to nip and suck her neck.

"Hate me all you want. This cunt is still mine."

"Shut up."

Kael shuddered next to me, sighing in pleasure as she moved into each stroke before arching against them when I sped up. I leaned down, sucking the tip of her breast through the fabric, and she shouted, bucking against my hand.

"Gods, I can't—"

I pulled her nightdress down, bearing her pierced breasts and taking her nipple into my mouth. Her moan turned to an incoherent shriek as I flicked her piercing with my tongue. She reached down to clutch my cock, her hand moving in time with mine as I thrust into her palm. Her walls tightened around my fingers; her moans growing louder and louder until she came with a shout.

"Gods, *Sia*." I groaned, my cock jerking in her grip as I watched her come. She tore her tortured eyes away from mine, burying her face into my chest even as she ground against me.

"*Fuck you. Fuck you. Fuck you*," she repeated and I caught her as she melted in pleasure, holding her tight to me as I let myself go. I buried my face in her hair, reveling in the warmth of her body as I spilled my seed between us, all over her stomach and palm.

Kael stiffened beside me, angry once more, and I sighed, getting up to get a towel to wipe the mess off her skin. But no soap. I wanted her to wear my scent; a secret reminder that I owned her body, and she belonged to *me*.

Snuggling back into bed with her, I wrapped an arm around her waist and pulled her close. She remained stiff in my embrace; unyielding before she sighed, and I chuckled. Pride that she'd submitted to me filled me and I kissed her neck, my heart pulsing when she melted into me, giving in to our connection without words.

Chapter 14

Kael

I woke up still tangled in Theron's arms, his heavy cock pressed into the small of my back as he cupped my breast in his sleep. Self-loathing coursed through me, my cheeks burning as the night came crashing back over me. How easily I had let him guide me into pleasure despite knowing what he'd done. His hands were powerful, yet gentle and precise as he teased and tormented my body until I was begging for more, tipping me over the edge of blissful oblivion, something I'd never allowed another man to do.

It had to be the piercing. His magic drove me to wantonness, with only the need to climax in my mind. A mix of shame and rage swirled within me, my stomach roiling. The piercing was the only reason he had such mastery over my body. Right? I wanted to lash out at him for everything he'd done—for manipulating me into such an untenable position and destroying any hope I'd had of escaping unscathed from this game we were playing.

I shifted, trying to move away from the warmth of his body without waking him. But when I glanced over my shoulder, I stilled as my gaze settled on him in sleep. His face was softer now, all signs of his hard exterior softened by slumber. His sharp nose and taut jawline had relaxed, now that he wasn't frowning, with only the slightest hint of stubble covering his cheeks. Even his arms folded around me protectively, as if shielding me from harm, were gentler than when conscious.

My heart caught in my throat as his soft lips parted with each breath, a small curl hinting at a smile in the corner of his mouth despite being asleep. There it was again; this strange pull towards him I couldn't explain or fight, no matter how much I wanted to deny it. In sleep, he looked like a warrior who could conquer any foe, yet... vulnerable. And I hated him even more for it.

His eyes were still closed, but he must have felt my stare because they slowly cracked open to meet mine. We stared at each other in a silent war of wills, and I shivered, wanting nothing more than to grab my pilfered knife and carve out his dark heart. But I was unwilling to leave the comfort of his arms to retrieve it.

The realization galvanized me and I jumped up from the bed, not wanting Theron to see how much he affected me, but it was too late; his gaze followed mine, and we locked eyes again.

"Kael?"

He stood and walked closer to me, a small smirk tugging at his lips. I trembled as he reached out for my hand, his soft touch like lightning through my veins. He pulled me to him and cupped my face in his hands, his breath warm against my skin.

"Don't be ashamed," he breathed. "You felt something too. Why deny it?" My heart thumped painfully in my chest and I looked away, but Theron tilted up my chin so our eyes met again.

"Tell me you don't want me and I'll stop. You have all the power, *Sia*." His words were honeyed promises that couldn't hide the trap they were.

I opened my mouth to tell him he was wrong, but the words wouldn't come. My hesitation seemed only to spur him on and he leaned in further, his nose brushing against mine delicately as if testing the waters before taking things further.

I spun away from him as Raenisa ran in, worry etched on her face. "The rebels escaped."

"All of them?" He asked, running a hand through his greasy hair and swearing when she nodded. I turned my back on him as if searching for my robe to hide my vicious glee. Those assholes wouldn't be touching my brother again.

"Fuck. Rhazien is going to be pissed." He said, pinching the bridge of his nose.

"I heard him raging at the guards." She leaned against the doorframe as she looked between us with open curiosity. "Apparently, he had an execution planned as a treat for Varzorn that he already told the emperor about."

The sick, sharp-eared bastards.

"For Atar's sake," Theron scowled. "This week can't end soon enough."

Shit.

The clock was ticking, and I still needed time to kill the Beast. I took a breath, trying to push down the anxiety that had settled deep in my stomach. It was an arduous task, with Theron's piercing gaze still following me around the room as I pretended to consider clothing. His eyes stayed on me, a predator stalking its prey, and I couldn't help but wonder what thoughts ran through his mind.

The red-haired Harvestman, Zerek, strode into the suite, his usual charm and wit noticeably absent. Dust rose from his clothes as he plopped down on the couch, his preternaturally beautiful face etched in grime. "Sorry to disappoint you, but I didn't find anything in Sailtown."

"To be expected. We found them in the Red Wilds."

He took his feet off the table. "You did? Did you get the sword?"

"No Striker." Raenisa scowled. "And we only had them for all of eighteen hours. They escaped."

Zerek's mouth hung open. "I'm gone for two days and you fall apart. See, this is why I should be second in command."

"Oh, fuck off," Raenisa said, rolling her eyes before they began bickering.

Theron wasn't distracted by the exchange, his attention still following me as I tried to keep my expression neutral.

Herrath entered the room stiffly, his eyes flooded black. "Lord Marshal," he began formally, and Theron frowned. "Your mother and Emperor Varzorn request your attendance at the execution block in the slave quarter."

Raenisa waved him off. "The rebels escaped. That's not happening."

"I assure you it is. Nyana informed me only minutes ago."

I tensed, my stomach tying itself into impossible knots. Had they recaptured Gavril and the others? *Fuck, fuck, fuck.*

Panic rose in my chest, grasping and threatening to suffocate me, but I forced it down, willing myself not to react. I couldn't let my emotions get the best of me, not now, not when Gavril needed me most.

"What game are they playing?" Zerek growled, his fists clenched. "I don't like this."

Theron's expression darkened. "Me either, but I have to go. I don't have a choice."

Raenisa spoke up, her voice calm but firm despite her obvious hangover. "We need to be prepared for anything. Varzorn is cunning. There's a reason his name was added to the invitation."

"So I wouldn't refuse," Theron murmured, pursing his lips before turning to me, his eyes searching my face. "Kael, stay in the suite. It's not safe for you out there."

"Kael?" Raenisa wrinkled her nose. "I liked Lily better."

I ignored her as I met Theron's eye once more. I had to go; the thought of leaving my brother and the other rebels to face their fate alone was unbearable. "Why? Don't want me to see what your people do?"

He ran a hand down his face. "Gods, does everything have to be a fight with you?" He growled. "Fine. Come. But I'm trying to spare you."

I nodded, relief washing over me as I dressed, my mind racing with worry and plans to save the rebels from Rhazien's grasp. We rushed out the door and down to the vanira stable, eager to get there as quickly as possible. Even the thought of riding on the giant spiders didn't deter me—I just wanted to reach our destination.

As we rode through the city into the slave quarter, the squalor and poverty that surrounded us struck me. It was so different from the opulence of the palace and the barrenness of the desert. I saw a young girl running through the alleys, and my heart lurched. I knew what it was like to live alone on the streets at that age.

We arrived at the pavilion in the deserted marketplace where Rhazien had made his display of power. An immense crowd had gathered, tension and fear in the air like a tangible presence. Where were they? I scanned the sea of people. How was I ever going to get them out of here? Theron pushed to the front, and I trailed in his footsteps, for once grateful for his size as the crowd made way for him and I got a glimpse of the stage. Relief filled me, so overwhelming that I almost fell to my knees, followed by guilt so thick I tasted it on my tongue like copper.

It wasn't Gavril or anyone I knew on the execution block. It was three slaves - two men and a woman - being presented to Rhazien's court as rebels who were guilty of treason against him. But they weren't anyone I'd ever seen before. My stomach lurched with sickness and anger as I realized what was happening.

Rhazien was going to execute them, and he didn't care that they were innocent. It was all a ploy to maintain his hold on power.

Theron stepped forward, pushing through the crowd until he reached Rhazien's courtiers.

"What's going on?" He demanded, his voice hard.

"Theron," Varzorn called, and I watched as the Marshal's shoulders straightened as a man and woman approached him and he dipped his head in greeting.

"Your majesty. Mother."

The pair were both tall and imposing, with matching black hair and golden eyes that glittered dangerously in the light and marked them as siblings. There was an air of power and cunning around them—a dangerous combination that could easily be turned against him. These two had caused everything my people suffered. Killing Rhazien was nothing compared to taking out the emperor—

Theron's voice broke into my thoughts as he spoke with Varzorn. "What's going on here? These aren't the rebels."

The emperor sighed, looking weary as he gestured to the three slaves on stage. "Really Theron. I know they all look the same, but do try to keep up." A hint of a smile played about his lips and the hairs stood up on the back of my neck.

"These are rebels who have been caught attempting to overthrow Lord Rhazien's rule. He has ordered their execution." His mother said, her expression hard. "You did well catching them."

They stared at one another for a long moment and I sucked in a breath as the Beast sauntered forward, dressed in his metallic armor once more, sweat glittering on his shorn head.

"Yes, brother. Excellent work." Rhazien sneered, his lip lifted in half a snarl. "Come, let's speak."

Theron glanced back at me before turning his gaze to Raenisa. "Rae, take my concubine to the castle."

"And deprive her of the show?" The Weaver mocked, her cold eyes glinting in the sunlight as she inspected me, her expression one of mild disgust. "Go to the viewing platform, Lady Taelyr. Your brother is there as well, Zerek." She sniffed. "Though he dressed appropriately."

Raenisa didn't respond, only offering a curt bow and taking hold of my arm, dragging me to the box of other nobles as Zerek slunk behind me and Herrath looked like he wished he could melt in the desert sun. Theron joined his brother, his posture stiff, as if ready to run.

No one dared stand up against Rhazien in this place.

I couldn't just let this happen. Hoping to glimpse rebels among the sea of faces, I searched the throng, ready to step in and save these people. I couldn't just watch as they killed the poor quivering slaves.

There. Gavril stood in the crowd, a hood covering his distinctive horns.

Thank Ydonja, they were here. My heart leapt with joy at the sight of him, but it was short-lived as he shook his head, warning me not to interfere. My mouth fell open and his features twisted into regret. I couldn't catch my breath, my chest tight as my body reacted to something my mind refused to process. Roza stood beside him, tears running down her face as she silently watched the woman calling for mercy from the platform.

I wanted to cry too, to rail against this injustice, but I knew it wouldn't do any good. Nothing I said would stop this terrible act from taking place today; nothing could save these people now that they'd been caught in Rhazien's cruel trap.

But even if we couldn't save them today, I could still kill him and put an end to this vicious cycle of violence and oppression once and for all. My resolve hardened. Nothing, absolutely nothing, would stop me from killing this monster. I didn't care how I had to debase myself, as long as it ended with him dead at my feet.

As Rhazien made his way to the stage, my attention was drawn to Theron, who was being summoned by the ruthless governor himself.

"Oh shit," Raenisa murmured, "This is bad."

Herrath's hands gripped the railing beside me, his thin fingers like white tarantulas as he squeezed. A chill ran down my spine as Theron walked up to the execution block. What did Rhazien want with him?

As I watched in confusion, Rhazien approached Theron and whispered something in his ear. The words were too quiet for me to hear, but the way Theron's expression changed made it clear that whatever was said was not good.

My heart pounded in my chest as Rhazien turned to the crowd.

"Loyal subjects of our benevolent emperor," Rhazien began in a loud, clear voice. "Today, you bear witness to a demonstration of loyalty to our beloved Empire. Those who serve and obey shall be rewarded for their loyalty; those who betray us shall find themselves at the mercy of my justice." He paused, letting his words sink in as every eye in the crowd trained on him.

"Those who choose to go against me are few," he continued. "But they suffer unimaginable consequences. Betrayal is an unforgivable crime, and those foolish enough to attempt it will face a fate worse than death."

Rhazien's menacing stare swept across the crowd before landing on select faces on the viewing platform, his competitors as the emperor's heir, no doubt. A tremor ran through my body, the gravity of his warning pressing down on me.

Theron stepped back, a look of grim resignation on his face. He met my gaze briefly before turning away from me as if he couldn't bear to look at me anymore as his brother handed him an ax.

Chapter 15

Theron

I held the ax, its weight heavy in my hands, and looked down at the three slaves before me. They were dirty and ragged, their eyes filled with fear and hate. These weren't the rebels I'd caught. They were innocent.

Rhazien was forcing me to do this. Wanted me to execute these slaves in front of a sea of their peers as a show for the emperor. But not as an example of how he inspires terror in the populace. Nothing as simple as that. No, this was Rhazien showing Varzorn how he scares *me*. How he controls *me*. Stripping away the authority I'd won on the colosseum sands when I'd defeated him. What was one battle when the true test of power was forcing someone to do what you wanted? The other potential heirs watched, their expressions shrouded, knowing that it was just another way for Rhazien to torture me and illustrate his might.

I looked up at the platform, hoping to find some shred of comfort in the faces of my harvestmen, but all I saw was her. Kael, standing in the back with her white hair blowing in the wind. Her expression was unreadable as she watched me, just as she had stared down at me when I fought in the colosseum.

I closed my eyes, sending a prayer up to Atar, and took a deep breath before bringing the ax down quickly, putting each of the slaves out of their misery in one swift motion. It was a mercy that they would not suffer drawn-out torture and death at Rhazien's hands—I'd seen him make an entire day of it, painting himself red with blood in the blistering sun—but it still felt like an act of betrayal. The slaves' families wept as their loved ones were taken away forever; their cries echoed like ghosts through the air.

Rhazien's smirk was palpable from across the square as he savored his victory over me once again. Staring straight ahead, refusing to look at him or anyone else in the crowd, a roar filled my ears as I stepped down from the execution block, ignoring how a head rolled into the sand with a sickening thud.

My body was numb as I forced myself to walk to the viewing platform, my shoulders back as if unaffected. All this because Rhazien wanted to prove his dominance over me? I'd learned long ago that my family was made of senseless cruelty and blind ambition and there'd be no escape from them. But this was... it was the Fall of Caurium all over again.

Rhazien stood with his arms crossed, a smirk playing at the corner of his lips as he looked down at me. "You see, your majesty," he said, gesturing to the emperor, "loyalty is everything. Without it, a man is nothing." He turned his attention to me, his eyes gleaming with malice. "Wouldn't you agree, Theron?"

I clenched my jaw, gripping my fists at my sides. I knew what he was doing. He was trying to show our Varzorn that I was weak and that I lacked the loyalty necessary to lead. But I refused to give him the satisfaction, even if I didn't want to be the heir.

"I believe in loyalty," I said through gritted teeth, "but not blind obedience. A man should make his own choices."

Rhazien's smirk widened. "Ah, yes," he said, "the rebel prince. Always so eager to defy authority." He turned to Nyana, who stood beside Varzorn, watching the interaction with a cold detachment as she tapped her nails on the railing. "Isn't that right, Mother?"

She looked at me with the same hint of disdain that had always colored her gaze when it fell on me. I didn't know why she even bothered stealing me from my father. "Rhazien is the more loyal of my sons," she said. "He understands the importance of order and discipline."

I suppressed a growl, a surge of anger rising within me. It was always the same with her. Rhazien was the favorite, the one she doted on and praised, while I was left to fend for myself.

As if sensing and enjoying my frustration, Theodas let out a chuckle. "Looks like Theron's still struggling to win Mother's approval."

Caelia sneered at Rhazien. "Perhaps if you spent less time torturing your subjects and more time governing, you'd have more to show for your loyalty."

"And higher production," Raenisa muttered.

Rhazien turned to Caelia, his eyes narrowing. "I'll have you know that my governance is just fine," he said, his voice laced with venom. "But it's easy for someone like you to criticize from the sidelines, isn't it? Not much to do in Athain compared to Adraedor."

"Or on the front," Theodas put in, sharing a look with Rhazien, who grimaced at him.

I tuned out the rest of their bickering, my attention drawn to Xadrian, who was hovering near Kael once again. A surge of jealousy went through me as I saw him lean close, whispering something to her. She didn't seem to notice him. Her gaze locked on me, but it did little to ease the anger burning within me.

Varzorn cleared his throat, and I turned back to face him. "I've heard enough," he said, eyeing me with interest. "Theron has proven his loyalty and can be an asset to our realm." He looked at Rhazien, whose expression soured, and Theodas with a knowing grin. "Perhaps on the battlefield once more."

Rhazien smirked but said nothing further while Theodas' expression fell. Varzorn couldn't mean...? He held my gaze for a long moment before returning his attention to Nyana.

Caelia stepped beside me without turning her back on Rhazien, or Theodas as they hurried after the emperor.

"Make him pay," she whispered, her voice hard as she stared after them.

I nodded once. My eyes locked on Xadrian as he leaned close to Kael again and my anger surged inside me once more. Why wasn't Zerek or Herrath blocking him? Aracel Sarro, known as the 'Sweet Sarro,' rested her hand on Zerek's arm, her expression lively as they chatted.

I stepped forward, ready to pull Kael to my side, when I was intercepted by Raura, the empress. My heart sank as I recognized her fiery auburn hair cascading down her back. She was beautiful, of course. But it wasn't beauty that gave me joy. It was twisted, like a rose with poison thorns. The sight of her always made me feel sick to my stomach. Her eyes sparkled an unnatural shade of silver, and her lips curled in a cruel smirk.

She wore a deep burgundy gown that clung to her perfect body like a second skin, and she moved with grace and confidence as she stepped between me and Kael with one arm outstretched, blocking my path.

"Prince Theron," she said in a silky voice that sounded more like purring than words. "We didn't have a chance to talk last time."

I swallowed hard and forced myself to meet her gaze without flinching. "I have nothing to say to you." That was a lie. I had a chest full of things I wanted to scream at her, but I didn't have the time.

Her eyes narrowed, but she didn't press the issue. "Very well, but come find me later, won't you?" she said, trailing her fingertips down my arm before walking away. "I have an offer for you."

An eerie chill crawled up my spine as the warmth of her touch lingered where her fingers had been. I stumbled back, barely glimpsing Kael before I ran into Tannethe. She was draped in a shimmery gown that caught the light and exposed her curves, and she had a watchful glint in her eyes. Her voice was deep and sultry as she purred, "Theron, there you are. You didn't stay after the show last night for the party. I missed you."

She pretended to pout, and I stifled a wince. Atar help me, I couldn't stand any of this. The court, the games they played, and the way they used each other—I only wanted Kael, and to get back to our suite, where we could be alone.

"Rhazien can keep you company," I said, sidestepping around her. "Now, if you'll excuse me, I have to go."

I turned and finally reached Kael, pulling her to my side. "We're leaving," I growled, anger still simmering inside me as I glared at Xadrian who lifted a brow at my expression. Raenisa and the other Harvestmen made to follow me, but I waved them off. I wanted to be alone. Well, almost alone.

The only sound between us on the ride back to the palace was the soft rustling of the vanira's legs. Kael's rage radiated off of her like heat from the noonday sand. But I couldn't tell if it was because of what I'd just done or if it was because of what happened the night before.

When we arrived back at my suite, I dismissed Mirijana, not wanting a witness to my rage.

Kael remained quiet, her dark eyes filled with a mix of emotions that I had no desire to decipher as I paced around the room, my restless anger and self-loathing flowing off of me like smoke in a foundry. Kael glowered at me, her brows drawn together until I snapped and turned on her.

"What?" I demanded, my voice harsh as it cut through the air between us.

Kael wasted no time in unleashing her wrath on me. "How could you?"

I took a step towards her. "Do you think it's easy for me?" My hands balled into fists as I stared down at her. She didn't move away or say anything, she just stood there silently watching me with that same strange expression on her face. "Do you think this is what I want?" I spat, gesturing to the desert. "To kill innocent people, just so Rhazien can prove that I'm on his leash?"

"You could have done something." She cried, jabbing an accusing finger into my chest.

"Could I? What then? What could I have done?" I caged her in with my body, my hands against the wall. She lifted her chin but didn't speak, unable to find an answer, because we both knew the truth.

"I had no choice," I breathed. "You know how this court works."

"They're dead now because of you," Kael's voice was barely above a whisper, her voice shaking with rage. "You killed them."

"Yes!" I shouted. "Because if it wasn't their lives, it would have been yours! Or Raenisa or Zerek, or anyone else I might care about. That's how Varzorn works. He takes anything you love and uses it against you."

Kael didn't flinch in the face of my outburst, instead standing tall and staring straight back at me with resolve in her eyes. "Coward."

I stared at her, my chest heaving as we glared at one another before I turned, stalking into my sparring room, the anger inside me boiling over. I began throwing punches at the bag, imagining each hit was directed toward Rhazien or Varzorn, or anyone else who stood in my way.

Kael followed me to the doorway, her arms crossed over her chest. I didn't stop my attack, instead taking out the frustration of the past days on the leather bag in front of me. My fists flew faster and harder as my rage grew with each hit.

Kael watched me silently, her dark green eyes flickering in the dim light of the room as she took in my frenzied display. Her expression didn't change as my hands bled or when the skin sloughed off. I continued until I felt like all the anger had been taken out of me and replaced with a deep exhaustion that finally forced me to stop.

As Kael left the doorway, I slumped onto the floor, collapsing under the weight of my self-loathing.

Chapter 16

Kael

I watched as Theron swung his hands at the punching bag, throwing his fists as though he were fighting a demon, his muscles rippling as sweat slicked his skin. The bag's chain rattled. Each strike left a bloody print on the canvas, his movements jerky and painful, his eyes vacant. I hated him. I hated him for stealing my home from me. For my father's death. For Orya. My loathing was as insatiable as the desert, and not even an ocean of understanding could quench it.

But I knew he was right. There was nothing either of us could have done without forfeiting our own lives. The way he sacrificed those innocents… was it any different than the way I'd been willing to sacrifice whatever it took to save my brother?

My breath caught in my throat as he stepped away from the bag, bloodied and weary. Despite myself, a twinge of sympathy ran through me. What sort of life had he been living that he had to resort to hurting himself like this? What kind of man was he? He was as trapped as I. Neither of us could escape our fate.

He caught my gaze, his eyes filled with something I didn't want to name. My stomach twisted as I stared at the bloody flecks on his chin and neck. I couldn't stay in this room any longer, not with the weight of my confusing feelings bearing down on me. I had to get out of here. Not just in his suite. This entire castle. The city even. And to do that, I had to kill Rhazien. Then I'd get rid of my collar and deal with Theron.

Hurrying to the bed, I yanked out the knife I'd hidden, stuffing it in my pocket while Theron was still in the sparring room. I stormed out, my determination to end this game fueling my steps as I made my way through the castle. I wouldn't let him destroy me. Nothing had so far, and I wouldn't allow some broken prince to be the one to take me down. My shoes clicked on the polished stone as I hurried, unwilling to stay a moment longer.

"Kael?"

I froze, turning to find Mirijana staring at me. "Where are you going?" she asked, her eyes filled with concern as she glanced around.

I couldn't tell her the truth, not when my plan involved murder and revenge. "Just out for some air," I said, forcing a smile to my face that felt more like a grimace. "I'll be back soon."

"Oh, I'll come with you."

I tried to wave her off. "No need. I'm sure you're busy."

"Not at all. The Lord Marshal told me you're to be my priority."

"How..." Inconvenient. "Nice."

As I walked, she fell into step beside me and I couldn't shake the feeling that I was fooling no one, least of all myself.

Mirijana followed me, her footsteps as soft as a whisper.

"It can be overwhelming." Her usable eye was distant, lost in memories. "So much change, at once."

I nodded. I'd always struggled with change. It was never for the better. I gripped the knife through the fabric of my dress, still wrestling with the need to do something, anything, to get my mind off the bloody mess Theron had turned himself into. I eyed Mirijana, her water-fat body and lack of vision on one side. I could kill her and be on my way to killing Rhazien right now… I would kill her if it meant saving my brother or Haemir. What did that say about me? How different was I from Theron, really?

"You know what helps? Tea. Come on, I'll brew you some."

I reluctantly followed her as she led me to the kitchens, resigning myself to the fact that I wouldn't be leaving today. But happy to discover I that I valued innocent life enough to stay. It was the only reason I endured Theron; I told myself. What other reason could there be that I'd be willing to stay with a monster?

We entered the kitchen, its vastness filled with fragrant smells and bustling activity. The cooking area was big enough to accommodate a hundred chefs, with enough personnel to make food for all of them. Everywhere I looked cooks were scurrying about, creating delicious dishes from whatever ingredients they could get their hands on. A variety of unique aromas wafted in the air, and it didn't take long for my mouth to water.

On one side of the kitchen, there was a large oven, with several people tending the fire and stirring pots over it. On the other side, there was an area devoted to baking bread and pastries, as well as an array of fine cheeses and cured meats. In one corner, someone was hand-cranking an ice cream maker while others cut fruits and vegetables near a sink at the back wall. Everything seemed so organized; each cook had their own little space where they prepared specific dishes or took care of certain tasks... All this while half the city starved. I'd once thought that perhaps it wasn't just malice that made the Elves starve us. That it was logistics as well. The desert was never meant to support a population the size of Adraedor's and almost all our goods had to be shipped in. But this, this excess, this was proof that it was intentional. There was no way that the court would eat all of this. And I knew better than to expect handouts to go to the slave quarter.

Mirijana rummaged around on a shelf until she found what she was looking for—two teacups. She set them down on the island before moving to a timeworn cabinet tucked away in the corner. I watched her as she opened it, removing several tins of tea leaves before settling on one particular container; likely some kind of medicinal herb blend. She smiled when she saw me watching her and walked over to the stove, filling up an old kettle before setting it against the heat source.

The sound of bubbling water filled my ears as I waited for Mirijana to finish, my tiredness retreating as I took in the space.

Orya had worked here.

Memories of my best friend flooded my mind. Her face the first time she admitted she had a crush on Gavril, the way she used to snort when she laughed. The stark difference between Orya's gentle spirit and Mirijana's hardened exterior couldn't be more apparent. Orya had been a Sirin Remnant, too sweet for this harsh desert city. Mirijana was scarred and had seen too much, but still bubbled with joy.

Another sin to lay at Theron's feet. If he hadn't ambushed us in the escape, then Orya would still be alive. And Gavril wouldn't have become so hardened.

Everything went back to him.

"He's a complicated man," she said as if reading my thoughts. "The Lord Marshal."

I eyed her, unsure of what she was getting at. I hadn't thought that she and Theron were intimate before, but now I wondered.

"Were you his concubine?" I asked, ignoring the strange roaring in my ears that the idea caused.

"What? Gods, no." She laughed and then paused, shooting me a sheepish look. "No offense."

I raised a shoulder, leaning against the counter as the kettle whistled and she removed it, pouring water over the leaves in each cup. "None taken. Your tone seemed intimate."

She shook her head. "No. The Lord Marshal doesn't put his staff into uncomfortable positions like that. Unlike other members of the royal family." Her shoulders tensed and she turned her back on me to find some cream. "I'm just saying that he's a decent man. If you give him time, things will get easier."

"I watched him decapitate three innocent people earlier today." I snapped, unable to hold it in. "He's not a good man."

Her mouth closed abruptly before she breathed in deeply. "You haven't seen what I have. I'm sure he was doing what he had to survive."

"Like what?" I narrowed my eyes at her, crossing my arms.

"Well, Rhazien tries to kill him at least once a week, though he's slowed down recently."

"Excuse me?" My mind whirled. Why would the Beast keep him here if he wanted him dead? Unless that was the point.

"The Lord Marshal's brother sets traps for him all the time. I've found scorpions in his bed. Poison in the tub. Tainted logs in the fire." She waved a nonchalant hand. "You name it, Rhazien has attempted it."

"But why?"

"Because the Marshal has the next strongest claim on the throne, of course."

I shook my head. "No. I meant, why does he stay then? If his brother keeps trying to kill him?"

"He can't leave. He has to remain here until the emperor permits him, or they'll hunt him down as a defector, like his father."

What had happened to his father?

I pushed the question away and scoffed. "He's not trapped like us. He has power and influence. If he wanted to change things, he could."

Mirijana shook her head. "No, he couldn't. Not without consequences. Like being forced to stay in Adraedor, under the watchful eye of a brother determined to kill him."

I had no desire to hear it. I didn't want to feel any shred of sympathy for Theron. But the more Mirijana spoke, the more conflicted I became. Was he a victim, too? I clenched my teeth. No. He had options. He was taking the easy way out. The path that kept him comfortable. He was just as despicable as I'd always thought, because not only was he a bastard, he was a coward, too.

She must have seen the opinion on my face because she handed me my cup of tea with a sad smile.

"You don't know what it's like, Kael," she said, her eyes darkening with the memory. "The mines... they're a different kind of hell. They worked us to the bone, starved and beat us, with no hope of escape."

I listened, my heart heavy as I remembered. I knew exactly what she meant. Even five years later, I still had dreams of the mines, of the heat and the dark.

"But the Marshal," Mirijana said, her voice softening as she touched her sightless eye and the scar tissue around it. "He's not like the others. The Marshal doesn't see us as... as things to be used and thrown away. He saw me, a scared girl, and he took me in. Putting me to work in his household, gave me a chance to live with some dignity."

I looked down into my tea, unsure of what to say. I wanted to hate Theron, to blame him for everything that had happened, but hearing Mirijana's story made it difficult. He had saved her, had shown her compassion in a world that was so cruel. How many times had I wished for a rescue that would never come? Only Haemir had shown that kindness to me. And comparing Theron to the man that I respected above all others... No. Absolutely not.

"There was one time," Mirijana continued, her eyes distant as she recounted the memory. "I trusted the wrong people. I thought that they'd improve my life, but it was a trick."

My heart raced as I listened, a sick feeling in my stomach. I knew what it was like to be attacked, to be at the mercy of others.

"But the Marshal found me," Mirijana said, her eyes shining with unshed tears. "Fought them off, protected me. He didn't have to do that, Kael. He could have just let them do whatever they wanted. But he didn't. He saved my life."

I stared at her, my mind reeling with conflicting emotions. How could someone who had done such terrible things also be capable of such kindness? It made no sense to me.

Mirijana reached out and placed a hand on mine. "I know, Kael. It's difficult. But you have to remember, the Marshal is just a man. He's been given a situation that none of us would want. He's doing what he can to survive, just like we are."

"Some of us manage to do it without killing innocent people, though." I gritted out, pushing away the memory of driving my knife in between the guard's ribs. I'd wanted to escape my thoughts, not add to them.

She sighed, dabbing at her eyes with her sleeve. "I'm here anytime you want to talk. Alright?"

I nodded, and she gave me a soft smile, forgiving my stubbornness. I needed more help if I was going to do this mission and I couldn't find it with Mirijana.

"I'm ready to return now." I smoothed my hands down my skirt to keep them from shaking. "Can you send for Kadir? I think I'll need more clothing after all."

She beamed at me, taking my request as acceptance. "Of course. I'll take you back right now."

I gave her a faint smile. All the while, a plan began to form in the back of my head.

Chapter 17

Theron

I stared at my torn hands, the shame of what I had done staining them, and no amount of blood could wash them clean. Why did I let Rhazien use me like that? How could I have become the executioner of innocent people? I tried to take comfort in Varzorn's hint that I'd return to the Niothe, but it was still not enough, not with Kael's accusations ringing in my ears.

The thought of waging war on those who had no magic cut through me like a dagger. Who was I to decide someone else's fate? In a split second, I had to choose life or death for them—something they had no control over. The image of those rolling heads flashed through my mind once more. Even if they were Remnants, they deserved to live their lives free from torment and persecution. We weren't better than them for all the war we'd waged. We were arguably worse.

It wasn't fair—none of this was—but no matter how much I wished things were different, there was nothing I could do to change it. All I was able to do was wallow in my self-disgust and try to survive.

My body tensed as the door to my suite opened. Had Kael returned? Or Raenisa?

Herrath entered the room, the healing plate in his hand. He was the last person I wanted to see right now, but I couldn't muster the vitriol needed to toss him out.

"What are you doing here?" I asked, my voice hollow.

Herrath stepped closer and held out the plate. "I thought you might need this after what happened earlier."

Taking the metal disc, a pang of guilt for the way I had treated him in the past hit me. I pushed it away, reminding myself of Calyx. Herrath was not to be trusted. I placed the healing plate over my hand and called on my power, funneling it through the electrum and opal, focusing on healing myself. This act. This ability right here was our most important part of battle. To heal a trained warrior, even from the brink of death. The Remnants bred faster than we did, but while we had magic, there was nothing that could stop the Elves from dominating the world. It was only a matter of time.

"There's no shame in doing what your family asks of you," Herrath said, his voice calm. His complexion was more sallow than usual, exhaustion painting circles under his eyes that he didn't bother healing. A touch of bronze would have sorted him out, but he wasn't one to waste magic. Unlike Raenisa, who reached for a piercing at the slightest provocation.

My anger rose at his words. "There's plenty of shame in killing innocent people, Herrath. Don't justify it."

Herrath's expression hardened. "We have Houses to uphold, Theron. We can't just throw them away because you feel guilty."

"I *am* guilty," I said through gritted teeth. "And I'm disgusted with myself. And you, and everyone else, who supports this madness."

Herrath's eyes narrowed. "We're all living in a world of another's making. Understanding that, believing that, will keep you alive."

I shook my head. "I don't want to kill people for no reason. And I don't believe in using slaves as tools."

Herrath's voice grew icy. "You don't have to like it, but you have to follow orders. That's what it means to be a first-born son."

"And what about being the head of your house?" I shot back. "You're the last Tavador son. I'm the last Axidor. Doesn't that mean anything to you? Doesn't it mean we can make changes?"

A flicker of doubt passed through his eyes before Herrath's face twisted in anger. "You're just trying to absolve yourself of guilt, Theron. But you can't run away from what you've done. You have to live with it."

"I'm aware of that," I said, my voice barely above a whisper. "But it doesn't make it any easier."

Herrath's expression softened. "I know it's hard, Theron. But you have to be strong. Do what's necessary to protect your family and our people."

"Easy for you to say. You never stand up for yourself. Letting Raura boss you around like a bitch."

Herrath glared at me. "My family is doing what it takes to survive. Just like you did today."

I scoffed. "By marrying the snakes?"

"Yes," he hissed. "Because we're out of money and no one has pockets like a Vennorin, other than the royal house, which they also married into. We all do things we don't want to do."

"Spoken like a Tavador, 'We Remain.' With no mention of how you survive, or what's left of your conscience afterward."

He ran a hand over his face. "I didn't come in here to fight, Theron."

"Then why did you come?" I demanded. "We both know I don't trust you. Not after Calyx."

He winced, his eyes flooding black. "I never meant for that to happen. I don't have a choice, Theron. My mother and father live on a stipend provided by Raura. If I stop doing what she says, then my family loses everything. Why do you think they're so keen on me marrying? My bride will have to bring a hefty dowry to satisfy my mother." Bitterness dripped from each word. "Do you think your situation is unique? That you're the only one in the empire railing against what's asked of you, wishing life was different?" I didn't speak, and he continued. "You're not. But we all have an obligation to keep the peace and do what we can for the ones we cherish most." His voice trailed off in a whisper. "That's all we can do."

"Who are you trying to convince? Me or yourself?"

Herrath stepped away from me, his face unreadable. "I'm attempting to persuade you, Theron. You have to understand that sometimes it doesn't matter what we want or who we love—" His voice broke and he took a deep breath, steadying himself. "Just know that you're not alone."

I looked down at the healing plate in my hand, a surge of conflicting emotions warring within me. He was right in a way—we all had our struggles, our own battles to fight. But that didn't mean I had to accept this life of killing and oppression. There had to be a way to make a change, to break free from the cycle of violence. I couldn't just ignore my responsibilities as an Axidor. But I didn't want to merely accept the things I had done—what I had allowed to happen. I wanted to make it right. But I couldn't; not without sacrificing myself.

A strained silence settled between us. I was about to break it when the door swung open and Mirijana walked in with Kael following her. Herrath's eyes flew wide in surprise as if he hadn't expected to see them here. He recovered quickly, though, his face unreadable once more.

"Mirijana, Kael," he said, unable to control the flush that crept up his neck as he inclined his head to my servant and concubine.

Kael crossed her arms over her chest and gave him an icy stare. There was a palpable tension that hung between them for a few moments before she finally spoke, her voice low and controlled. "Any more advice for me?" She lifted a brow in challenge.

He glanced at me and Mirijana before shaking his head. "No, though what we discussed previously still stands." He excused himself a moment later, Mirijana watching him go with a nervous expression. As Herrath left the suite, his words echoed in my mind. He was right about one more thing; I wasn't alone. But it didn't bring me any comfort. It made things worse. If everyone was alright with what had happened today, then how could I ever hope to change anything?

"I'll go prepare a meal for you two, Lord Marshal," Mirijana said, following Herrath out, no doubt wanting to escape the tension that had descended the moment Kael and I locked eyes. The room was silent after she left. The pounding of my heart in my chest was the only sound I could hear. Kael didn't speak, her face stoic as ever.

"So, what did he say?" Kael asked, and I had the distinct impression that she didn't care for Herrath.

I finished healing my hands, setting aside the electrum plate. "He told me that sometimes you have to do things you regret to survive." I turned away from her, walking over to the armor rack on the wall and running a finger along one of the bones. "That it's all we can do.'"

Kael stepped closer, her emerald gaze devoid of emotion. "And what do you think? Do you believe him?"

I pursed my lips together, my heart heavy with guilt as I thought back to all the people I had killed in cold blood because of Varzorn's orders. Innocent people who had done nothing wrong but simply stood in his way. Like the three she watched me murder. I didn't want to imagine what would have happened to her, Rae, the others if I had refused. It was a weight that felt like it would never leave me, regardless of how much I tried to push it away.

"Yes," I murmured, still not facing her. "I do."

After a few moments of silence, Mirijana returned with a platter of delicacies and set it on the table, excusing herself with an awkward curtsey. We ate in silence, the only sound being that of our forks against the plates as we consumed our dinner. The room was cold, a desert wind bringing in a chill from the mountains, but there was something comforting about the intimate darkness as I watched Kael pick at her food. I wished she would rail at me more, do something other than stare at me with this icy disdain that reminded me of my childhood. When had her opinion begun to mean so much to me? We finished our meal, the air still heavy with unsaid words between us. I opened my mouth to break the silence, but no sentences formed, and it seemed that Kael was in the same predicament.

She stood, heading toward the bedroom. "You should get some rest. Mirijana said you're scheduled to fight in the colosseum tomorrow." She didn't meet my eye as she told me as if surprising herself with the kindness.

Atar's hammer, Rhazien couldn't stop fucking with me.

"I will in a moment."

She didn't respond, lifting her eyes to mine before heading into the bedroom on her own. I sighed, dropping my head into my hands. "Only a few more days and all this will be over," I whispered to myself, sending a prayer to Atar that it was true. Not that Atar answered prayers, though part of me had harbored a secret hope as a child that he'd hear me and come to slaughter Varzorn, Rhazien, my mother, and all the other Elves. But it had never came to pass. He'd disappeared during the Godsfall, the shame of the Elves' actions too much for him to bear. I understood now how he felt. If I could disappear and wander the world alone without having to face my kin ever again, I'd do it in an instant. I glanced at the bedroom door where Kael waited. Maybe not entirely alone.

I stood and went into the bed chamber, finding Kael already waiting for me in bed. Her eyes were like two slashes in the dark, glimmering with emotions that I couldn't decipher. Her hair shone in the moonlight, emphasizing her curves and making her look more gorgeous than ever. She pressed her lips together in a line as if she was trying to stop herself from arguing further. She may not have wanted me here, but I couldn't help it. I needed her beside me in bed once again. I didn't think I could sleep without her anymore.

I crawled into bed next to her, our bodies not touching but close enough that the warmth radiating off of her warmed me.

We both lay tensely until sleep finally took us away from each other's presence and we were lost in different dreams.

Chapter 18

Kael

The deafening roar of the colosseum filled my ears as Theron led me to the royal viewing box. Warriors clashed with monstrous creatures in the sand below, their weapons glinting in the sun and the scent of blood in the air. The Elven nobles of the high houses were out in full force, adorned in their finest attire, boasting their house colors. Confident in their grandeur, as if the gods had come back to life and were walking amongst us once more. I understood now why they'd waged war against the pantheon because I wanted to tear them apart.

Raenisa was already there, leaning against the rail and staring forlornly at Caelia. The Young Bear was studiously ignoring her as she spoke to a man I didn't recognize, his condescending tone causing her frown lines to deepen with each passing minute. He turned, and my mouth dropped open; his resemblance to Zerek was uncanny, with the same chiseled features, though his hair was a red so dark it looked like black cherry juice. This must be the brother he hated, Xavier. Varzorn and Nyana watched them like a pair of lobaros, their eyes lingering on the nobles on the edge of the pack, the ones they could pick off and use however they wished. The emperor wore a scarlet robe lined with gold, his armor made of white scales, and his crown of fiery diamonds. Both were beautiful and polished, but I wasn't fooled. They were just as deadly as the wolflike lizards that roamed the Black Highlands.

"Theron," Rhazien greeted his brother with an amused grin that didn't reach his eyes. For a moment, it was like I was staring at a skull thrown in a river, his body merely a shadow behind him before the image flickered away, replaced by the Beast's self-satisfied smile. "I look forward to seeing you on the sands today."

"It seems I'm your favorite performer this week." Theron drawled, feigning nonchalance as his fingers traced anxious circles on the bare skin of my waist.

"Just preparing for the future," Rhazien said and Theron narrowed his eyes, drawing me away without responding, though I felt a faint shudder run through him.

The clashing of metal against scales drew my attention, and I turned to the colosseum to see the Vennorin brothers clustered together, Theodas's gaze locked on Theron as Trevyr whispered something in his ear. Tykas, the lumbering one, looked up excitedly when each new lady arrived, only for his expression to fall once more and turn back to the fight. The air was thick with tension and posturing, their laughs just a touch too loud, their smiles too sharp.

Theron seemed to sense my unease and pulled me closer to him, his hand possessively resting on my waist. He smelled of leather and citrus, like a summer day on the battlefield. I couldn't help but feel a twinge of attraction that I tried to push away. Fucking piercing messing with my head. I'd had to sleep on my hands to avoid touching him, my body hungry for the pleasure he'd given me before.

As we approached the group, I caught snippets of their conversation—talk of alliances, marriages, and betrayals. The nobles were all vying for dominance, and the colosseum seemed to be the perfect backdrop for their power plays, the roar of the crowd covering up their whispers.

Raenisa caught my eye and gave me a small, sad smile as if she was just as uncomfortable as I was in this setting.

As Xavier continued to talk down to Caelia, Theron's grip on my waist tightened. I knew he was itching for a fight, and dread filled me at the thought of what might happen next.

Theron's hold on my middle intensified as Xadrian approached. His breath was hot against my ear as he whispered, "Stay close to me. I don't trust him."

I nodded, my heart racing as Xadrian sauntered up to us, his smug grin in place as usual, as if he found all of this posturing as ridiculous as I did. Theron stepped forward, his body blocking Xadrian's view of me.

"Xadrian."

"Theron," he drawled. "How lovely to see you again. And who could forget your charming concubine?"

I rolled my eyes as Theron's grip on me became even tighter. "Keep looking, Darkstar. This one is mine," he growled, the possessive note in his voice sending a shiver down my spine.

Xadrian raised an eyebrow, his gaze flicking between us. "Is that so? I didn't think she belonged to anyone."

Theron's jaw clenched as Xadrian sauntered off. I could feel his eyes on me as Theron pulled me even closer, his body radiating heat like a stone in the noonday sun.

I couldn't handle the tension any longer. "Excuse me," I muttered, slipping out of Theron's grasp and making my way to the bathroom. I let out a sigh as I left the pavilion, my shoulders relaxing. Gods, they were awful. Where was the restroom?

I ducked through a likely door before almost backpedaling. The room I entered was dimly lit, the scent of perfume and Areca smoke hanging heavy in the air. I was lost. Shit. The furniture was ornately carved, with silk and velvet cushions strewn about the space. Zija appeared in front of me, her lovely face contorted with anger.

"If it isn't the little plaything Theron's been flaunting around acting like she's a lady," she sneered. I glanced around the room; the other women wore only scraps of sheer cloth, nothing as sensual and elegant as the sky-blue dress I'd picked out today, still waiting for Kadir's visit.

I squared my shoulders, not about to let her intimidate me. "I'm not the one pretending to be the governor's queen and bossing everyone around as if my cunt is made of gold."

She bristled, her expression turning murderous as the other concubines tittered. "And yet he takes you everywhere. Even with the emperor here."

I raised a brow. "And that's my problem, how?"

I turned, ready to leave when I noticed someone in the back of the room. Aella, the Sirin Remnant I'd met on the day Theron chose me, was hunkered in the corner, her eyes wide with fear and a look of defeat on her face. Guilt sank heavily in my stomach when I realized I hadn't thought of her since I'd tried to steal into the Beast's suite.

"Aella?" I walked past Zija, ignoring her, as I took in the details of her appearance. Her hair was twisted into a series of intricate braids, with a simple, silvery dress clinging to her curves, so short that a slight breeze would reveal everything. She looked alright physically, but I knew how easily the Elves could fix that with their magic. Her hands trembled and tears pooled in her eyes.

"Aella," I whispered, my heart swelling with pity for her. "Are you alright?"

She shook her head, her voice barely a whisper. "No."

"Do you want to stay here?"

Before she could respond, Zija stepped in front of me, her black eyes blazing with fury. "You don't get to take her," she spat. "She belongs to Rhazien, even if she's worthless."

Aella whimpered, edging away from the fiery concubine, and rage began coursing through me.

"What did you do to her?" I demanded, stepping toward the statuesque Remnant. Her expression faltered for a moment at the look on my face before she sneered.

"Nothing that she didn't like." A twisted grin stretched her full lips.

"Like she had a choice." I threw back. "Come on, Aella." I held out my hand, as I had before when we stood in line together and waited. She stared at it for a long moment before slipping her small hand into mine. My mind whirled, unsure how I would help her, but I knew I couldn't leave her here. Not again.

"Let's go."

As I turned to leave, Zija grabbed my arm, her nails gouging my skin. "I told you she's staying here."

"Let go of me," I growled as she squeezed, her nails digging in deeper.

Raenisa appeared behind the power-hungry courtesan. "Back off, Zija," she commanded, her voice like steel. "I'd hate to see how Theron reacts to you damaging his concubine."

Zija backed off, letting go of my arm, and it throbbed.

"She's stealing one of Lord Rhazien's possessions." Her voice was sweet, but the expression she gave Raenisa… if I'd thought she disliked me, it was nothing compared to the rage she felt for the woman before me. What had Theron said? That Raenisa was courted by Rhazien before? No wonder.

"Her name is Aella," I said, sending Zija a venomous look. "And it's obvious that she's being mistreated."

Raenisa locked eyes with me before checking out Aella, her expression hardening when she took in her hunched shoulders and the way she flinched.

"Aw hells." She muttered before speaking louder. "Aella, do you want to leave?"

The Sirin Remnant nodded, her sea-colored eyes wet, and Raenisa sighed. "Alright, I'll keep her. Let's go."

"You can't just take her—" Zija started, but Raenisa cut her off.

"Tell Rhazien that I'm keeping his concubine. That he can consider it a… courting gift." Her expression twisted as if she could barely get the last words out.

Zija glared at her before dipping into an enraged curtsey. "Of course, my lady."

Raenisa sniffed, directing Aella and me out of the smoky room and into the hall. The Sirin Remnant kept her head down, unwilling to meet Raenisa's eye.

"Well, this is a mess. I was just lecturing Theron about having an inconvenient concubine and I went and adopted one. He's never going to let me live it down." She complained, scrubbing a hand over her face before brightening. "Wait. This is perfect. I can use her to make Caelia jealous."

"She's upset and needs rest," I argued and Raenisa rolled her eyes.

"She doesn't need to do anything, just stand there and be pretty. Unlike you with your mean glares all the time." She did an impression of me, crossing my arms and glowering. "I'm angry and I only have one facial expression."

I stifled an inane laugh. In another life, we might have been friends. The feeling struck me anew when Raenisa's eyes softened when she turned to Aella.

"I don't have any need of a concubine," she said, and the Sirin Remnant's shoulders slumped, no doubt expecting to be sent back to the Beast's harem. "But I could use a housekeeper. What kind of experience do you have managing a household?"

Tentative hope bloomed in Aella's eyes. "I worked keeping the books for my uncle's shop before he sold me to cover some bad debts."

Raenisa clucked her tongue. "He must be shit at dice." Aella managed a small nod and Raenisa eyed her thoughtfully.

"Honest to a fault is an excellent trait in a servant, I think." She clapped. "Well, if I'm not going to use her to make Caelia jealous, I might as well send her to my suite to get started."

I nodded, thankful that she'd been the one to suggest it. "Mirijana can help her."

"Great idea. I'll have Theron's servant teach you what to do for me, since I'm shit at running a household myself." Aella managed a small smile as Raenisa continued speaking, the haunted look she'd worn earlier receding. Raenisa flagged down a passing slave girl, tasking her with guiding her back to the castle.

I gave her a reassuring hug, whispering, "Serving in her house is better than serving in his bed. I'm sorry I can't do more." I'd have to figure out a way to get her out with me when I left. Fuck, just one more thing to take care of before I could kill the Beast.

She nodded when I released her, her eyes wide and wet, as if she couldn't quite believe she was free of the Beast's harem.

When she was out of earshot, I turned to Raenisa. "Thank you."

"So you can speak without growling." She laughed as my expression hardened and I glared at her. "Oh, don't pout, I'm just fucking with you." She snagged a tart off a passing tray as a waiter passed us. "Hiding from someone?"

"All of them."

"Can't blame you for that. The court is insufferable." She frowned at the red dress she wore, straightening the skirt. "They draw you in and take from you until there is nothing left."

I nodded, not knowing what to say. That's what it felt like to be one of their slaves. Strange to think they did the same thing to their own. Stranger still to have an actual conversation with Raenisa instead of having her talk around me like I was furniture.

Thankfully, Raenisa talked enough for both of us. "Come on, let's get back before Theron comes looking for you."

I scowled. "Can't have the princeling waiting."

Raenisa's expression hardened. "He's been through a lot. Theron's not like others here." She gestured to the pavilion, where their false laughter filtered in. "His obsession with you is weird, I admit, but I don't think he means you any harm."

Sure. Theron was a murderer, not exactly harmless.

As I approached the viewing box, I felt Theron's gaze snap to me. His eyes were dark and possessive, and a thrill ran through me at the remembered press of his hands against my bare skin, his territorial growl as he plunged his fingers inside me. No. I pushed the confusing feelings away. It was just his stupid piercing fucking with me again. None of it was real. A hidden voice in the back of my mind whispered that his magic didn't affect my emotions, just my body, and I shoved the thought away. Not. Real.

As I watched, Tannethe approached Theron, her curves pressing close to him. Her black hair cascaded down her back like a waterfall, and her dress was low cut, showing off her ample cleavage. A pang of jealousy went through me as I saw her touch his chest. Not real, I repeated. None of this was real. Just a play I was acting in to complete my mission.

Lost in my thoughts, I barely registered Raenisa's voice as she approached me where I'd stopped. "Tannethe is shameless," she said, nodding in her direction. "But she's not a threat to you. Theron's not interested in her."

Surprised by her words, I frowned at her. "I don't care if he is. I'm just a concubine, remember?"

"Of course," she laughed, agreeing with me and I scowled, walking past her up to Theron who turned to me, drawing me away from Tannethe, who glared at his back.

He must have sensed my mood because he leaned in, his breath tickling my ear, sending a shiver through me. "Jealous, Kael?" he teased, a smirk playing in the corner of his mouth.

I bristled at his words. "No," I snapped, even though I knew I was lying to myself.

Theron chuckled. "Don't worry, *Sia*. You're the only one I'm interested in," he murmured, his lips brushing lightly against my cheek as my stomach flipped.

I glared at him, and he laughed again, turning to talk to Raenisa. "Thank you for keeping an eye on her."

"No problem," the warrior said, waving it off. "But if Rhazien says anything about courting me, it's your fault. Or your concubine's, at least."

"Explain." He crossed his arms and my mouth dried as I watched his powerful muscles flex before immediately chastising myself. Raenisa told him what had happened, adding that he'd need to sacrifice Mirijana to train her.

"What about Caelia?" he asked, his brows lifting. "How's that going?"

Raenisa's expression darkened. "She's been avoiding me. I think she's trying to secure her position as Varzorn's choice. It's hard to retain power without an heir, and that's not something she can do with a wife."

"I'm sorry, Rae," he murmured, bumping her with his shoulder.

Raenisa shrugged as if it didn't matter and I recognized her attempt to hide her hurt. "It's not your fault. It's just the way things are."

The announcer called for the start of another bout and my eyes widened as I saw Xadrian appear on the sand. He wore tight leather breeches, his shirt open and revealing his muscular chest. He had an air of confidence about him as if this battle was little more than a play, and he was the star.

A deep gong rang, and a grate lifted, a guttural roar coming from within the darkness. My breath caught in my throat as the creature stepped out. It was some sort of lizard monster, easily twice the size of Xadrian, with thick scales and menacing horns on its head. It opened its massive maw, revealing hundreds of razor-sharp teeth.

"Atar's hairy balls, is that a drukkar?" Raenisa asked and Theron nodded, his attention locked on the elf below.

Xadrian held up a hand, a silvery ring glinting on his finger, and metal spears rose from the weapons rack, hovering in midair. Crackling arcane energy filled the arena, the hairs on the back of my neck lifting as he turned his magic on the creature as it sprinted toward him.

The metal deflected off its armored skin, and he leaped out of the way as the beast spun, its blackened maw snapping where he'd been a moment before. The crowd cheered, but I hardly noticed, my eyes transfixed on the battle. It swiped at him, and I held my breath as I watched him dodge the attack.

He abandoned the spears, moving gracefully as he dodged blows from the massive beast. He used his earth magic again, pulling rocks and boulders from the sand to hurl at the creature.

His magic danced at the edge of my senses, as if it was calling to me, taunting me. I wanted to be out there, in the arena with him, helping him defeat this monster. To be part of the action, part of his fight.

Xadrian continued to fight, dodging the creature's attacks and trying to find a weakness in its hide. He was desperate now. I clicked my tongue, my nerves getting the best of me.

Theron cursed as Xadrian stumbled, nearly falling in front of the beast. I wanted to reach out and help him, but I knew there was nothing I could do. Then, in a burst of brilliant magic, Xadrian brought up a spear from the sand before him, launching it up into the beast's soft belly. It roared in pain, collapsing forward and attendants ran out, dragging the thrashing beast back into the darkness. He rolled to his feet with a jaunty smile, as if he'd planned it all, and the crowd went wild.

Xadrian turned to the royal platform, bowing to the emperor before his eyes found mine.

"Salfár magic," Raenisa sniffed. "That doesn't seem sporting."

Theron lifted a shoulder. "A warrior uses all the tools at his disposal." He followed Xadrian's gaze, finding it locked on me, and scowled. "Come on. There won't be any more bouts until they fix all those holes."

He took my arm in his, drawing me away to break my attention from the man in the Colosseum.

I couldn't help but compare them.

Theron with his hungry eyes and hidden hurts, his sharp wit, and the parts of himself he was constantly hiding from the world...

And then there was Xadrian, with his air of mystery and seductive charm. He was everything Theron wasn't: open, confident, and unapologetically himself. I was drawn to him, even though he was just as bad as the rest of them.

I shook my head. These thoughts wouldn't help me on my mission. The real question was, why had his magic affected me like that? As if it was a language that I'd once spoken, half-forgotten in a new land. I needed information, and I thought I knew who to ask.

Chapter 19

Theron

"I have nothing to wear," Kael complained, frowning at her full wardrobe.

"Put on one of those," I waved at the rack of colorful dresses as I shot her an amused grin. "It's just a dinner party," I said, hiding my worry about tonight.

I'd received an invitation from Varzorn himself to attend him during a party, one to which they invited only the high houses. I knew better than to hope, but it would be the perfect opportunity for him to give me my new orders in the Niothe. And finally kick Theodas back into the ranks where he belonged.

"I don't have anything to wear," she said, her voice tight. "Can you call for Kadir?"

I frowned, and she gave me a small smile as if trying to win me over even though I knew she despised me. Though maybe I was winning her over more than I'd thought. She's been acting strange, but less combative. Perhaps things between us were changing? Regardless, it felt good to take care of her and if she wanted more clothes, then I'd give them to her.

"Of course." She smiled at me, and my heart thumped painfully. It was the first time I'd seen a genuine smile on her face, and she was *breathtaking*. Her green eyes shone like emeralds, softening the hard lines of her features into a beauty that had to rival the goddesses that once walked the earth. She had to be a daughter of Thanja because I'd seen nothing more beautiful than her at this moment. Not even the cascading waterfalls in the north or the sun setting over the seas held the same majesty. Her smile faltered at the look on my face, and I wondered what she saw in my expression.

I cleared my throat. "I'll send for the tailor." Striding away, I found the attendant in the hall and sent a message for Kadir to come at once.

Kael eyed me when I returned to the living room. I stalked forward, intent on claiming her. A knock at the door interrupted me and I swore. Damn Kadir for his punctuality.

"Come in," I called and Zora busted in with her bright smile and bubbly nature on full display as she squealed, while Oz looked serious and studious as always.

"Theron!" Zora exclaimed, throwing her arms around me. "It's been too long!"

"It's good to see you, Zora," I said, hugging her back. "And you too, Oz."

Oz nodded at me, his eyes already scanning the room for something to read before he walked over to my bookshelf and pulled one off the shelf.

"Less than ten seconds before you grabbed a book," Zora called to her twin as she flopped onto the couch, patting the space beside her for Kael to sit down. "That has to be a record, even for you, Oz."

Kael looked between us, her expression bewildered when Zora turned to her. "We've been here for days and go nowhere but the library. What's the point of coming?"

"Um." Kael shot me an alarmed look that made me laugh.

"To visit me?" I asked, sitting down on Kael's other side and stretching my arm over the back of the couch and behind her shoulders.

"And report to my mother what happens here," Oz said without looking up from his book, one of my histories of Adraedor. "She still doesn't want to risk coming to court after what happened to your father."

My expression darkened. I didn't need a reminder of that. It was etched into my mind like the carvings that Zora created, never to be smoothed away. I avoided Kael's questioning glance, instead toying with one of her curls and changing the subject. "How's the research going?"

"It's going well," he said, his tone clipped. "I'm making progress."

Kael leaned forward, curious. "What have you learned?"

"I've found some new texts regarding the rise of the Carxidor line." Oz said eagerly, "It happened at the end of the Godsfall, and isn't well known, which is strange."

"The Carxidors?" Kael asks, glancing at me and I scowled. I didn't like being reminded of my heritage. I'd rather only be an Axidor, with no connection to the throne.

Theron nodded. "Tiordan Carxidor is known as the 'Lightcursed' and was the creator of the Empire as we know it."

Zora shuddered. "Sounds like a charming fellow."

Oz continued. "Tiordan was the general under King Eiran Daelor. Eiran was a Sálfar who was a favorite of Atar and after what Kearis did—"

Kael interrupted, her expression rapt. "What did he do?"

"Well," Oz leaned back and closed his book, getting comfortable. He was in his element. Talking about his current project was a sure way to get him to stop reading. "There are conflicting accounts. One said the shattered union between Vetia and Sithos created the rift. Another contended that it was Atar's natural pride that caused it."

"That I believe," Kael mumbled under her breath and Zora gave her a confused smile. Gods, what was she doing here? My cousin was too sheltered for Adraedor. Living in the country was a gift and a curse. They avoided most of Varzorn's ire, but being here amongst the court only put targets on their backs.

"But apparently," he continued. "It was something else. Kearis wanted to follow Ydonja to the stars, but every time he tried, the atmosphere would burn his wings and he'd be forced back to the ground. He asked Atar for help. To craft him armor that would allow to him cross the barrier, but Atar refused." He paused, taking off his glasses and cleaning them with his shirt. "It's unsure why. Whether it was fear for Kearis' safety, respect for Ydonja, or plain hubris believing as the firstborn that he could choose for him. But Atar refused, and the feud began, with the Kyrie and the Elves going to war."

"In Adraedor?" Kael asked, and he nodded.

"Though it wasn't called Adraedor yet. Tiordan's son renamed it for his wife Adra."

"Fascinating," Zora said, shooting me a mischievous grin that Oz missed as his head bobbed with enthusiasm.

"Isn't it?" He said earnestly. "Eiran convinced Atar to give him a weapon that would allow them to kill Kearis and end the war," Oz explained. "They named the sword 'Endbringer,' after Atar fashioned it from his own bones to make it strong enough to defeat the other gods. The chains used to bind the gods were made from metal strengthened by his blood."

Guilt filled me again for losing one of my family's swords. It was an honor to carry a weapon like that. One that the bastard didn't deserve. Striker would pay for it if it was the last thing I did in this Atar-forsaken desert.

"According to these texts, Eiran told the humans that Atar would make them Elves if they helped take down his enemies. He used them as his fodder to attack and overwhelm the other god's peoples as they tried to defend their gods. They killed Kearis first for his slight against Atar, followed by Cetena, then Sithos and Rhaedos."

"But the humans realized they didn't want to rely on a promise from Atar to change them," Oz continued. "Instead, they saw how they might take power by creating an equal playing field since with each god they slaughtered, that god's people lost their magic and immortality. The humans stole Endbringer and murdered Vetia, Atar's daughter."

I whistled low in disbelief. "Imagine humans killing a goddess of fire by themselves. Incredible."

"Why?" Kael glared at me. "Because Elves are so superior?"

"Yes?" My brows drew up. She couldn't be serious. Humans didn't have the same strength or magic. It was an unimaginable feat and one I'd like to study. The tactics they'd used had to be incredible...

Oz glanced between us and ignored the tension in favor of his story. "Eiran took revenge on the humans, killing them, and thought the situation was finished. But with Endbringer unable to be destroyed, the risk of someone stealing it and murdering

Atar was too great. The Elves would lose their immortality. That's when Tiordan Carxidor came in."

Kael leaned back, not noticing as I toyed with her hair once more. "And then what happened?"

"The histories get muddled," Oz admits. "Tiordan killed Eiran and ordered the deaths of all the Sálfar, but it's unclear why. Then Atar disappeared, and the Svartál slayed the last goddess, Thanja."

Zora whistles. "Sounds like a real mess."

"It was," Oz agreed. "And it's still affecting us to this day. Tiordan is called the 'Lightcursed' because, after his attack on the Sálfar, we lost the ability to use the celestial metals."

I nodded. This I knew. It was one reason the Carxidor line was so unpopular. Well, that and our penchant to torture and destroy anyone standing in the way of our ambition.

Kael went still. "What about Xadrian? Was that the magic he used in his bout?" Her voice was nonchalant, but I couldn't help the surge of jealousy that rose in me. Xadrian? They were on a first-name basis? She could act as unaffected as she wanted, but I could see through it. The need to dominate her, to fuck her until she broke apart with pleasure so intense that she never looked at another man shook me and my hand tightened in her hair.

Oz nodded, oblivious to my reaction. "Yes, Xadrian can use Earthborn metals, as well as some Celestial metals from before the curse. His family has primarily Svartál ancestors, but his Sálfar heritage showed up stronger in him than his siblings."

"We have Sálfar ancestors as well," Zora put in. "Eiran's son Callyx was our Great-Great Grandfather."

"You're missing a great." Oz pointed out, and she stuck her tongue out at him.

Kael stared at me. "So you're related to both dynasties?"

I shrugged, uncomfortable. "Rhazien is too."

"Which adds to the complication of choosing an heir," Zora added, pouring herself a glass of wine, the liquid so dark it was almost black.

"So what's the difference between Earthborn and Celestial metals?" Kael asked.

Oz smiled, no doubt enjoying having an attentive audience. "Earthborn metals and alloys, like gold, silver, and electrum, affect the body, adding speed and strength or stamina and healing. Celestial metals allow Elves to manipulate stone and metal outside of their bodies, moving it or turning any object into rock. It's how Xadrian could move the boulders in his bout."

Kael opened her mouth, ready to ask another question when a knock came at the door.

"Lord Marshal, you called for me?" Kadir stepped inside, carrying clothing samples for Kael to try on for the evening. She excused herself from the conversation and went into the bedroom with the Remnant to get a new outfit.

I watched as she walked away, admiring her lithe frame and alluring curves, wanting nothing more than to feel that body pressed against me again. I couldn't stop thinking of her passion as she came, cursing me as she writhed… But I shook my head, forcing myself to focus on my cousins once more. I'd have her to myself soon, and I was determined to tempt her to my bed once and for all.

As soon as Kael entered the bedroom, Oz whipped around, his usually mild expression pinched with anger and confusion.

"What the hell do you think you're doing claiming a concubine?" He demanded. "Your father would be ashamed."

"It's not like that," I growled, heat rising up my neck as I tried to defend myself. "I've done nothing wrong. I haven't slept with her or used any magic on her, I swear."

"She doesn't seem enchanted," Zora said, glancing between us nervously.

"I claimed her so no one else could. To keep her safe." It wasn't a lie, but it wasn't the whole truth, either.

Oz eyed me skeptically before shaking his head. "Well, that's something, at least," he grumbled, crossing his arms over his chest in disapproval. "But if you plan on keeping her close, it's going to cause problems for you."

"I know," I admitted.

Zora sighed, her mouth falling open in disbelief. "You're going to end up breaking her heart, Theron. You can't just claim her and then toss her aside like she's nothing."

"I won't," I promised, guilt weighing heavily on my stomach.

"But what about when you have to marry?" Oz asked, his voice low and serious. "Then what happens? Or when she grows old?"

The thought of her growing old, changing while I remained the same, filled me with fear.

I bit my lip and looked away, not wanting my cousins to see the pain in my eyes. "I don't know," I murmured finally. "But I'll do whatever is right."

Oz softened, his voice gentle. "Are you going to steal her chance to have a full life? To have children? A family of her own?"

The image of her carrying another man's child made my vision flash red. My hands curled into fists as jealousy and possessiveness consumed me; Kael was *mine*. The idea of sharing her with anyone else caused my temper to flare. If she wanted children, I'd be the one to give them to her.

"Where will she have this mythical, perfect life?" I demanded, my voice sharp. "Living in Adraedor isn't like life on the estate. It's war. Each day fighting for survival, living on scraps. Would you rather her go back to the mines? So she can watch some imagined husband die in a collapse? So her child can live in squalor? Just for the illusion of freedom?" Zora's mouth fell open, her eyes welling with tears, and I stopped, shame filling me as I hung my head. "I'm sorry. It's just—" I floundered, at a loss.

Oz stood, kneeling in front of me, his brows drawn. "I should be the one apologizing." He glanced at his sister, pain in his expression. "I sometimes forget what you went through after Uncle Larion was murdered. I trust you. If you say you'll do the right thing, I believe you."

"We love you, Theron," Zora said, scooting closer to pull us both into an embrace. "I'm sorry we can't be here for you more."

After my cousins left, my mind was consumed with thoughts of Kael. I couldn't wait to have her alone again, to feel her body writhing beneath me as I took her, claimed her, made her mine. But as much as I wanted her, there was a nagging feeling in the back of my mind. Was I doing the right thing in claiming her as my own? Would I be able to give her the life that she deserved, or would I be dooming her to a loveless existence by my side?

Chapter 20

Kael

I stepped into the bedroom, greeted by the sight of Kadir. His iridescent scales set his olive skin aglow on his cheeks, and his pink hair was styled to perfection. He gave me a slow once-over as he raised an eyebrow at my outfit.

"Why do you say you have nothing to wear when I made you a full wardrobe?" He asked in that strange accent of his.

I shot him the rebel hand sign, but part of me wondered if he was really in the rebellion. He'd been avoiding me, and that put me on edge.

But I had bigger things to worry about right now. "I need your help," I said, leveling with him and waiting to see how he responded.

Kadir's eyes widened, but he recovered quickly. "And what makes you think I can help you?"

"I know you have connections," I replied, crossing my arms. "Tailors hear things. Words are all I offer, though."

Fuck. He was one of the spies we had that traded information, nothing more. I'd thought with the armored outfits and hair needles that he'd be willing to help me more.

"Please help me."

He stared at me a moment, taking measures breaths as he looked over his shoulder at the door before moving closer, his voice hushed. "Fine. Let's talk. But you can't implicate me. Teodosija needs me here to listen in."

I nod, relieved that he's prepared to help. "I'm here to kill the Beast."

Kadir's face drained of color and he stepped back, his eyes wide. "You're mad," he whispered urgently. "That's suicide."

I gritted my teeth and squared my shoulders. "It has to be done. There's no other way to stop his reign of terror."

He shook his head, exasperated. "And you think one person can do it? You haven't seen what he can do. I—I can't be part of this."

"Wait," I said, grabbing his hand before he could grab his clothes and leave. "My codename in the rebellion is Striker. You know that name, right?"

Kadir's eyes widened as he stared at me, understanding dawning on his face.

"Striker could pull something like this off, right?" I pressed, using my reputation to my advantage. I knew it was exaggerated, part of Teodosija's plan to give the other slaves hope, but if it gave him the confidence to help me, then I'd use everything I had. He nodded in agreement, but he still looked wary.

"What's your plan?" He asked, and I had to hide my sigh of relief.

"I'd planned on joining his harem and killing him, but that didn't work out so well."

He laughed, running a hand down his face. "I'd say not. The Marshal won't let you out of his sight."

"Exactly." I blew out a breath, putting my hands on my hips. "I just need a few minutes when the Beast is by himself."

Kadir shook his head. "He's seldom alone. That pack of concubines trail him all the time."

"But not when the emperor is near..." I said, remembering Zija's accusations from earlier.

"You can't possibly be contemplating killing him when he's with the emperor?" He asked, his eyes flying open. "You are as insane as they say."

I sighed in exasperation. "I'm not crazy."

"You are. All of this is madness. I can't help with this."

"Wait." I held up my hands. "What about if you just tell me if you hear about any opportunities? I need more eyes and ears around here. I feel like I'm just being taken from event to event, and I can't plan anything.

He nodded cautiously, still eyeing me as if I might snap at any moment. "That I can do. I'll keep bringing you new clothes to share information."

"My brother, Gavril, is in the city waiting for me. Can you pass him a message, telling him I'm alright and that I need more time?"

"Of course."

"And can you put in a place for my knife in the outfits? I want to be armed and ready for any opportunities."

He snorted. "That's going to be a challenge given what you're wearing. But I'll try." He pulled out a skimpy outfit that was barely more than strings of pearls, waggling his eyebrows suggestively. "You'll need this for the party tonight," he said with a knowing grin.

My cheeks flushed with anger and embarrassment. "I'm not putting that on," I hissed.

He shrugged, a devilish glint in his eyes. "Suit yourself. But it might come in handy if things get... heated."

I clenched my jaw, even though I knew he was right. I'd do whatever it takes to complete my mission. And if that meant wearing a revealing outfit to get close to Rhazien, then so be it.

I snatched the outfit out of Kadir's hands and stomped to the corner to put it on, glaring at him all the while.

I had to admit, the ensemble Kadir had chosen for me was… something. It wasn't truly a dress. More like an elaborate necklace of ivory pearls that cascaded down my body in clever loops that barely covered my breasts and mons. He'd put me in heels, painting my eyes and lips in soft colors. My hair was tied in a complex knot on the top of my head, leaving my entire back exposed.

When Theron saw me, his eyes flooded black as the desert night. He growled as he looked me up and down, seemingly unable to comprehend what I was wearing. I hated how my body reacted to his gaze—heat blossomed low in my stomach and my heart rate picked up. But I couldn't let him know that; instead, I crossed my arms over my chest. "What? Is something wrong with my dress?"

He blinked a few times before shaking his head. "No...I just don't know if we'll make it there with you looking like this," he rumbled, his voice deeper than normal.

A shiver ran through me, my nipples hardening, and I tried to push the feeling away. The longer I was with him, the stronger his magic seemed to be. I couldn't help admiring him; he wore a black silk shirt, open at the collar, and fitted black pants that hugged his muscular frame in all the right ways. His long hair was loose on his shoulders, and his bronze eyes glinted in the flickering light of the braziers. I breathed in his scent, my lids half-closing before I caught myself.

"Let's go," I said, leading the way to the door. The pearls swung as I walked, and I looked over my shoulder to see Theron's gaze locked on my ass. He caught my gaze and grinned, unrepentant and unbothered at being discovered.

"Come on, *Sia*." He held out his arm for me and I took it, my fingertips resting on his firm forearm as he led me through the castle.

I sucked in a breath as we entered the outdoor patio party. The entire scene was like something out of a dream—or a nightmare. Low furniture and billowing silk tents created an intimate, almost secretive atmosphere, and the fire dancers twirled and leaped around us to the beat of the sensual music. The waiters, both male and female, wore little more than scraps of cloth draped artfully over their bodies, and their flirtatious smiles only added to the charged energy of the event.

Theron sighed. "I'd hoped it wasn't one of these kinds of parties." He looked around as if looking for another exit when Varzorn called for him.

"Theron," he gestured for him to approach, a predatory glint in his eye. He stiffened beside me and I thought back to what Raenisa had said about Theron not fitting in. He guided me towards the emperor, stopping out of easy stabbing range.

"Uncle," Theron said, inclining his head. I didn't copy him, not that Varzorn noticed. His nephew was the only one who held his attention. "Thank you for the invitation."

Varzorn smiled, but it did not reach his eyes as he waved dismissively. "You know I always have a place at my table for you, nephew," he said in a voice that was both false and calculating.

"It's been years since we've shared a table, uncle. Five, actually." Theron's tone was nonchalant, but I could feel the tension radiating from his skin.

"Perhaps it's time for you to return home," he pondered aloud with a sly smile, not looking away from Theron as he spoke. "It seems like you've been away far too long."

"My duties don't allow for much time in the hollow mountains, I'm afraid."

"Indeed." He fingered the stem of his wine glass, like a spider clutching the cup. "But duty is worthless without loyalty, is it not?"

Theron nodded, his jaw tight as he clenched his teeth together. There was a pause, and then Varzorn continued slowly, emphasizing each word. "Remember what type of punishment awaits those who forget their place?"

My heart raced as I looked up to meet Theron's stare; his full mouth firmed into a line, rage heating in his eyes.

"I understand." His voice was firm but strangely devoid of the anger burning in his gaze. He inclined his head again, drawing me away without another word, his hand trembling in mine. He grabbed a drink from a passing tray, downing it in one gulp.

"Theron," I breathed, my brow furrowing in concern. "What was that all about?"

He sighed and released my hand, turning to face me with his hands on my hips, absentmindedly rubbing the pearls against my skin. I should step out of his arms, I knew I should, but

I couldn't make myself move away from him. Not when he looked like this. He glanced out towards the horizon, past the city walls as he spoke.

"My father... he fled with me from my mother." His throat worked as he tried to swallow back his emotions. "He took me to live with his sister on her husband's estate. I grew up with Zora and Oz. They were practically my siblings. We were inseparable." A wistful smile lifted the corner of his mouth.

I waited for him to go on, not wanting to push him, but desperate to hear what happened next. "We had a good life there until Varzorn sent Rhazien after us." He paused, his eyes full of fear and pain as he looked at me. "My father died trying to hold him off so I could run. His own son killed him... I still can hear the way Rhazien laughed as he bled out." His eyes were distant as he shook his head. "My brother captured me and brought me back here to Varzorn and my mother." Theron took a deep breath before continuing, his voice heavy with emotion. "Then things got exponentially worse. Rhazien was cruel and violent in ways I can't even describe. "

He exhaled and stared out into the night sky before finally turning his gaze back to mine. I drew nearer, laying my hand on his arm gently as if it could offer any comfort. He turned towards me, his eyes haunted as he went on.

"I never wanted you to be a part of this. I wanted to keep you safe. To have one thing for myself." His voice was low and strained. He stepped closer, his breath warm against my skin as he swept aside an errant strand of hair from my face. My breath caught as I tried to parse through the conflicting emotions running through me. Theron leaned down and brushed his lips over mine, sending waves of confusing sensations coursing through me. Hate warred with desire as his tongue met mine and I shuddered as I tasted him, his leather and citrus scent filling my nose.

My breath went shallow as he kissed me deeper, and a moan escaped me. He pulled back, the slash of his smile bright in the darkness.

"Gods, *Sia.* You drive me insane," he said, his voice husky.

I tried to respond, but the words wouldn't come out. Before he could continue, the music changed and a group of dancers sashayed into the space. The Empress emerged from behind them, her eyes immediately finding us in the corner. She moved sensually—her gaze locked on Theron as if she were trying to tempt him to her. But all his attention was on me. Her movements—the way her hair shimmered like liquid fire and her hips twitched—mesmerized me and barely heard Theron whisper something in my ear as he clasped me to him.

He pulled me into an empty tent off to the side and onto his lap, his erection pressing against my backside. His hands roamed over my body and desire pooled between my legs as he kissed my neck softly. Other dancers stepped onto the floor and soon couples were spinning and stripping as they moved together. Moans came from other tents and I realized why Kadir had laughed. He'd known what kind of party this would be.

My eyes drifted toward where Xadrian danced, grinding with a woman I didn't recognize. Her thigh hitched over his hip as he gripped her against him. Theron's hand stilled against my waist, a snarl escaping him when he saw who'd caught my attention. He grabbed my hips and flipped me around to face him.

"You're mine," he growled. "I'll kill him if he ever touches you." His lips crashed against mine, his possessive anger radiating from him as his hands tugged at the lengths of pearls, pushing them aside and revealing my body.

"I've wanted to taste these from the moment I saw you." He teased my breasts with his mouth, circling my nipple with his tongue before flicking my piercing. My heavy breasts ached in a way I'd never experienced, and I moaned. This wasn't me. This was some other Kael with glowing skin and curves for days. It didn't matter what *she* did. I cried out in surprise, pleasure, and anticipation winding me higher. I didn't care anymore that it was his magic doing this to me. All I could think about was having *more*. More of him. More of this overwhelming feeling cascading over me.

He freed his cock, his massive length springing up between us. My breath shuddered, unsure if I could take him into my body, but desperate to try. He was longer and thicker than any male I'd ever seen before, and that included the Zerkir Remnants.

He must have sensed my hesitation because he kissed me again, slowly, not like the frantic embrace of before. "Just slide back and forth, *Sia*," he coaxed, his eyes heavy-lidded as he gazed down at me. I rose on my knees before sinking onto him, rubbing my core along his length without him entering me.

My body responded, arching into him as my wetness coated his heavy cock.

"Gods, feel how wet you are for me," he breathed into my ear. One of his hands squeezed my backside, holding me tight against his erection as I rode him. "Tell me you don't want this."

"I don't want this," I moaned, gasping as he ground his length against my clit. "I hate you. I hate this."

His smile was wicked as he slid his hands around my hip, dragging me up and down him. "Liar," he growled against my neck. His thrusts became more insistent, pushing me higher and higher. I pressed my forehead against his, the intensity of the pleasure overwhelming me. I broke, waves of bliss radiating outward as I choked on a scream. His thick cock spasmed and his hot seed painted my stomach as he groaned, his body shaking with mine. I collapsed on top of him, panting as we both tried to catch our breath.

"Tell me I'm not alone in this," he whispered, brushing the hair from my face. I didn't respond as I lay there in his arms, trying to ignore the shame threatening to suffocate me.

Chapter 21

Theron

I watched Kael as she slept, marveling at how peaceful she looked. I couldn't believe that this was the same woman who had been glaring at me just hours before, all fire and defiance as she rode me. But even in her sleep, there was something fierce about her, like she was ready to fight at a moment's notice. What had made her this way? I wanted to know everything about her. I rubbed my chest absentmindedly, looking over my shoulder when I heard someone enter my suite.

I slipped out of the bedroom and found my Harvestmen waiting. Raenisa lounged on the sofa, appearing hungover once more; Zerek leaned against the wall and glared across the room where Herrath was standing at attention, his black hair groomed, as always.

"What's going on?" I asked, a growl riding my voice.

Raenisa was the first to speak, her sharp tongue as filthy as ever. "Your dumbfuck brother just sent half the fucking guard into the Red Wilds to find Striker."

My fists clenched at the mention of Rhazien. "Why would he do that?"

Why was Rhazien doing this now? My mind wandered back to my conversation with the emperor the night before. Was this about my return to the Niothe, or was it something more? I couldn't shake off the feeling that there were plans within plans that I had missed.

Raenisa shrugged. "He wants to steal some glory?"

"Or my sword." The thought of Rhazien taking my blade, one of the few things I had to remember my father, made me clench my fists.

"We'll have to go, too. Otherwise, you can kiss that sword goodbye." Raenisa said, tossing a grape in the air and catching it in her mouth.

"I'll go," Herrath declared, startling us all.

I raised an eyebrow at him, wondering what game he was playing.

"What are you up to, Herrath?" I asked.

He shrugged. "Maybe I'm not the paragon of a perfect son like you all believe."

I shared a look with him, remembering our previous conversation about his family's financial troubles and how he had to obey Raura to keep the money flowing. Had his parents arranged a marriage for him? Perhaps I could trust Herrath more than I thought.

Zerek groaned, pushing off the wall with a stretch. "I'll go too. Anything to avoid listening to Xavier brag about his courtship of—" He cut himself off, but the unsaid name echoed around the room.

Raenisa looked away, her eyes wet. Caelia had chosen to fight for the crown instead of their relationship, and Raenisa was hurting.

"Why don't you go with them, Rae?" She didn't need to be here with Rhazien sniffing after her and Caelia ignoring her. Even the treacherous desert would be safer for her heart.

She shook her head. "It's not safe to leave you here alone."

"I'll be fine. We should depart in the next few days. Striker is our priority."

She stared at me for a long moment before nodding, a sigh of relief escaping her.

"Good hunting. But be careful," I warned them all.

Our group fell silent as my mother entered. Her suffocating presence seemed to suck air from the room and caused my heart to hammer in my chest.

"Out. I need to speak with my son." Nyana said, his cold voice ringing with authority.

Raenisa, Herrath, and Zerek excused themselves, leaving me alone with her.

Her eyes bored into mine, the weight of her expectations crushing me. "What did Varzorn tell you last night?" she demanded, a flush rising to her pale cheeks.

I hesitated, trying to come up with a suitable answer. But my mother was not one to be kept waiting. "He said I would be returning home."

My mother's eyes narrowed, and she stepped closer to me, her expression darkening. "Home? Not the Niothe?"

I swallowed hard, a knot forming in my stomach. "Yes, home."

"Foolish boy." She glowered at me. "You're trying to usurp your brother again, aren't you? You want to take his place as heir."

I clenched my fists; the anger rising within me. "That's not true," I spat.

My mother stalked forward, her eyes blazing with fury. "You will fall in line, Theron. Or I'll make sure you never disobey me again."

My fear and anger warred inside me, and I struggled to keep my voice steady. "I won't be caged again," I said, my voice shaking. "I'll do what I must, but I won't let you break me."

Nyana's expression twisted into a wintry smile. "We'll see," she said, before turning and stalking out of the suite, leaving me to wonder what my mother's next move would be.

A scrape drew my attention, and I saw Kael watching from a crack in the door. She quickly averted her gaze, but not before I glimpsed pity in her green eyes. Embarrassment and anger flooded me as I realized she must have overheard our conversation. I stalked forward, pushing the door open as she backed up as I crowded her.

"What were you doing?" I growled.

She lifted her chin, her familiar glare in place once more. "Eavesdropping."

Stubborn woman. The only time she ever submitted to me was when I pleasured her.

I stepped closer, trapping her between my arms. Her eyes widened, and I relished the heat radiating from her body.

"If you wanted me to pleasure you, Kael, you should have just asked," I said as I leaned down, my voice low and seductive.

"Never."

"You want this as much as I do," I murmured, my lips brushing the shell of her ear. "You want to feel what it's like to have my cock buried in that tight cunt of yours."

"Bullshit. You know nothing about me," she said, trying to push past me.

I grabbed her arm and pulled her back, my arms encircling her waist.

"I know you're attracted to me," I breathed as I leaned in close, my lips hovering over hers. "But you're too scared to admit it."

She trembled in my arms and looked away, unable to meet my gaze any longer. I had found the one thing that could break through Kael's tough exterior—fear of desire itself.

Her breathing quickened, and I could see the flush of passion on her cheeks. Despite how much she detested me, her attraction was undeniable.

She licked her lips nervously before shaking her head in denial. "No."

I smiled smugly and reached out to brush a strand of hair away from her face. She gasped at the sudden contact and I stepped even closer, crowding her as I nuzzled her neck with my nose.

"You can deny it all you want," I murmured against her skin. "But your body knows the truth."

My hands moved lower down her sides as I traced the curves of her hips. Kael moaned, her body arching towards me, betraying the words coming out of her mouth.

"You're wrong," she breathed. "I hate you."

"I know," I whispered back as my hands traveled further down. Wetness slicked her sex, and I knew I was right. "I hate me, too."

Her eyes fluttered shut as I brushed against her clit, sending shivers running through her. She let out a low moan, and I had her where I wanted her as she pushed against my palm.

I cupped her ass, pulling her even closer to me and against my swiftly hardening cock. She moaned before biting down on her lower lip, trying to stifle the sound. I chuckled darkly at her futile attempt and leaned in to capture her lips with mine. At first, she resisted, holding onto my collar as if to push me away, before she melted into my embrace, her hands fisting in my shirt as she kissed me back with desperate hunger.

I roamed over her body, memorizing every curve and dip as she pressed herself against me. Heat emanated from her core, and I knew I had awakened a fire within her that she couldn't deny any longer.

I lifted her and carried her to the bed, laying her down before crawling on top of her. Her eyes were glazed with desire as she looked up at me, her chest heaving with each ragged breath. I removed her sheer night shift, baring her exquisite curves.

"Gods, you're so beautiful." I groaned, running my hands over her smooth skin, as she gazed up at me through lust-fogged eyes.

The sight of her gorgeous body made my cock impossibly harder, a bead of precum welling from my slit. I had to taste her.

I leaned down, pressing light kisses along the soft skin of her stomach until I reached the top of her panties. She shuddered and moaned as I lightly brushed against the fabric, teasing her with what was about to come. Taking the hint, she pulled them off herself, welcoming me.

"Good girl," I murmured, and she growled, yanking my hair. I chuckled and dipped my head, licking her clit with a long stroke. She cried out, her thighs tightening around my ears.

My tongue explored every inch of her as I pleasured her with my mouth. She tasted sweet and salty all at once, and I slipped deeper into a blissful trance as each moan grew louder than the last. I dipped a finger into her and she shouted with pleasure, rolling her hips.

"Fuck, you're so tight," I groaned, dragging my teeth over her hip. I couldn't wait to sink into her.

The smell of sex filled the air as Kael's body quaked beneath mine in unbridled pleasure. I focused on the piercing I hadn't activated, tugging it with my teeth, and she cried out, her back arching before collapsing onto the bed, her breathing heavy and labored. I crawled up next to her, admiring the way her chest rose and fell with each breath.

"I want to taste you," she said, her eyes still heavy-lidded as she reached for the buttons on my breeches. I helped her remove them, tossing them aside as she took hold of my cock, stroking it lightly. Her hand hesitated over my piercing before she ran her thumb over the head, spreading the seed seeping out of me over it. She began slowly as if she didn't know what to do.

"That's it," I moaned, my erection growing harder under her touch. "Fuck, that feels good."

Kael took my cock into her mouth, swirling her tongue around the head before taking me deep into her throat. I groaned, my eyes rolling back in my head as she bobbed her head up and down, taking me deeper and deeper. What she lacked in skill, she made up with sheer enthusiasm. Gods, I wasn't going to last.

"I'm gonna come," I warned, trying to hold back but unable to resist the incredible pleasure of her mouth. With a loud shout, I came, my cock jerking against her tongue. Kael swallowed every drop of my hot seed, licking her lips and looking up at me with a satisfied smile.

"Mmm, it tastes good," she said, wiping her chin with the back of her hand. I chuckled, pulling her into a kiss, tasting myself on her tongue.

"That was amazing," I murmured, and she snuggled closer. I smiled, pressing my lips to her hair. Contentment spread through me like a warm blanket as I held her tight, the steady beat of her heart against my chest comforting.

But soon the afterglow faded and reality set in. Kael stiffened beside me, and I knew she regretted what we just did. She hated me, even though she wanted me. Just more of the same in my life. I sighed and got out of bed, leaving her alone with her thoughts.

Chapter 22

Kael

I reluctantly accompanied Theron to the dinner party in the castle, my mind reeling from what had happened in the bedroom. Why did I feel such an attraction to a man whom I loathed? My body still tingled with pleasure, my core clenching on emptiness, wanting nothing more than for him to fill it. How much longer could I continue this charade before I gave in to my true feelings? I had to complete my mission and get out of here before this became any worse.

Theron put his arm around me as we entered the grand banquet hall and he handed over our invitation to a servant. He leaned closer and whispered in my ear, "I know this is hard for you, but I need you to stay by my side tonight." His proximity unnerved me, but it also comforted me somehow. I knew he wouldn't let anything happen to me.

The dinner guests were already seated in their assigned places around long tables covered in luxurious tablecloths adorned with gold trimmings. Some nobles gave me curious glances as we took our seats next to each other near the head of the table.

Caelia walked up to us, her short hair no longer mussed. She was dressed perfectly in her emerald tails, and she looked around the space as if searching for someone before looking at Theron.

"Where's Raenisa?"

His voice was icy. "She's on a mission in the desert until the court departs." Caelia's face fell at his response. "Maybe you can find something else to occupy your time, like flirting with Xavier." He spat the words with contempt, his anger towards Caelia for playing with Raenisa's feelings clear.

Caelia's eyes flashed with indignation. "I'm not here to flirt with anyone," she said, her voice rising. "I have a rightful claim to the throne as heir, and I need to prepare myself for when I assume my role."

She paused for a moment and then looked up at us defiantly. "No one can tell me who to love, Theron." Her words were strong and sure, but there was an underlying vulnerability in her eyes that caused a flicker of sympathy for her to run through me.

"It's not love to keep someone on the side so you can follow your dream with no thought of hers. "

Theron met Caelia's gaze without wavering, which only seemed to make her more determined. "How dare you?"

She stood tall despite how outmatched she was in the situation. She had to see how in the wrong she was, right? Who could profess to love someone while they kept them a secret?

Xadrian sauntered in with his usual sly grace, sensing the tension in the air. "Ah, what's this? A battle of wills?" He declared with a smirk. "Let me throw my hat into the ring."

He reached out and placed a hand on Caelia's shoulder while giving Theron a knowing look. "You can't be too hard on my sister, Theron," Xadrian said in a jovial tone. "She's just trying to find her place in the world, like all of us."

Theron didn't take the bait and instead gave Xadrian a stern glare. "Then she can do it without stringing Raenisa along."

"My sister's relationships are her own business that I'd never dream of interfering in. Just like no one would try to separate you from your charming concubine, right?"

He smiled, but the threat was there, and Theron growled. My eyes locked on Xadrian's necklace, the silvery metal glinting in the candlelight calling me like a Sirin. I tore my gaze away from the jewelry and focused on the conversation. The tension was thick; anger emanating from Theron like a storm cloud.

"Be careful with your threats, Xadrian," Theron said in a low voice. "Or you'll get more than you bargained for."

Xadrian laughed, his eyes glinting with amusement. "I don't want to fight you, Theron. I'm here to enjoy the... festivities. The show at the emperor's party last night was particularly... pleasurable. Wouldn't you agree?" His gaze lingered on me and Theron's grip on my waist tightened.

"I think it's time for you to move along," he snapped.

Caelia narrowed her eyes. "I'm not going anywhere until you tell me where Raenisa is."

"Why? Did you stop courting Xavier?"

When she refused to answer, he stood, dragging me up with him. "Didn't think so."

A wave of relief filled me as we left the tension behind and headed towards the food spread out in the banquet hall. But before we could reach the table, Theodas Vennorin and his brothers waylaid us. Theodas sneered at Theron, his brother with the silver eye beside him smirking.

"Theron and his whore. What a surprise."

"What do you want?" Theron demanded, his voice taking on a dangerous edge.

Theodas stepped forward and crossed his arms. "We just wanted to talk," he said in a flat tone. His brothers moved closer to surround us.

"About what?"

"There's a rumor going around that you're trying to steal my position," Theodas said, advancing another step toward us. "That would be unwise."

Trevyr's smile was bitter. "Vennorins don't take it lightly when someone takes what's ours. We repay it in kind." His eyes darted to me, making his intentions clear.

Theron stepped between us, blocking their view of me with his body. "Kael, why don't you go ahead and find a table? I'll be there in a second."

I held his stare for a long moment, a sense of unease creeping over me. What was Theron up to? I didn't want to leave him by himself, surrounded by enemies. I spun, looking for Raenisa and the other Harvestmen before I remembered they weren't here. When did I start thinking of Raenisa as an ally rather than an enemy? And why should I care about what happens to Theron? I hated him. They'd be doing me a favor, right?

I turned, walking away towards the food, but that wasn't my true destination. It was time to find Rhazien and end this charade once and for all.

As I stepped onto the patio, I felt the weight of someone's gaze on my back. I looked behind me and discovered Tannethe staring at me, her sharp eyes drilling holes into my skull. She had been waiting for me to separate from Theron, and she had me cornered.

"You're a sneaky one, aren't you?" Tannethe said, her voice dripping with contempt. "I've been watching you. It's bad enough that you've wrapped Theron around your finger, but now you're after Xadrian." She tsked. "Someone has a thing for second sons."

Anger boiled inside me, but I kept my temper in check. "I'm not trying to steal anyone from you," I said, glowering at her. "Maybe if you weren't so insufferable, you wouldn't be so desperate for attention."

Tannethe's face turned red with rage and she stepped closer to me, her hand balled into a fist. "You think you're so special? You're nothing more than a common whore!"

I laughed in her face. "You're calling *me* a whore? Seriously? After you've been out here acting like a bitch in heat?"

Tannethe's eyes widened with surprise and then narrowed in rage. "How dare you!" she snarled, lunging at me again. I dodged out of the way, but her fingernails scraped the side of my face, leaving a long, stinging scratch on my cheek.

I touched my cheek, seeing blood on my fingers. She used my moment of distraction to lunge at me. My instincts took over, and I attacked, my strikes landing hard on her jaw and ribs. She stumbled back in shock, her hand flying to her mouth before I was on her again, striking her with my fists. Tannethe fought back, so she had some training, but it couldn't stand up to years of scraping for survival. She wasn't the only cause of my rage, but she'd become my target.

"Stop! You fucking bitch!"

Something glinted in the light as Tannethe tried to ward me off, holding her hands in front of her face as I pummeled her. A ring on her finger. It wasn't just any ring—it was a poison ring, used by assassins to slip their victims a lethal dose. I had to get it away from her before it was too late.

I yanked her hand towards me and grasped the ring, pulling it off her finger as hard as I could. Someone grabbed hold of my arms and dragged me back, preventing me from doing any more damage. Tannethe scrambled to her feet, her eyes blazing with fury and hatred for daring to defeat her.

She slapped me across my wounded cheek, the sound ringing over the night, and I sneered at her, spitting in her face.

"Is that all you got?"

Theron was there, ripping me away from Theodas's grasping hands and pushing Tannethe back, shielding me from harm. She advanced again, her eyes already swelling shut, her mouth and chin coated in blood from her broken nose. The heat of battle faded as I looked around to see a gathering crowd, their eyes narrowed in suspicion on me. Fuck. My instincts had taken over. I hadn't thought about the repercussions of besting an elf in combat.

"Don't," he growled, his eyes flooded in dangerous black. "Touch her again, and I'll kill you."

Tannethe stepped back and glared at him before turning and walking away without another word. I watched her go, my fingers still secure around the poison ring. My lips stung, and my cheek burned with pain, but I didn't care. I relished the sharp taste of iron in the air. If I was going to die, at least I'd take a piece of that bitch with me.

Theodas stepped in then, his expression dangerous. "You're going to pay for this," he said, his voice low and threatening. "I expected more from you." He snapped at Tannethe as he joined her, throwing a dark look my way.

"Brilliant, Theron." Xadrian chuckled next to me as the Vennorin brothers disappeared after their sister. "A concubine and a bodyguard," he announced to the gathering crowd as he looked me over. "No wonder you bring her everywhere."

What? Why was he trying to cover for me? I eyed him warily, even as gratitude filled me. Perhaps I'd still get out of this alive.

Theron glared at him, and Xadrian tilted his head toward the high table, where the emperor watched intently. His eyes flooded black as he nodded once to Xadrian.

Theron's mother observed us, a calculating expression on her face, her eyes never leaving me. I had revealed myself—no longer just a concubine, but a threat. Someone who could protect and defend herself if needed. Whispers and hushed discussions hung in the air as if they floated in the mist. Theron's mother spoke rapidly to Rhazien, who eyed me like a hungry lobaros. There were too many people, too much color and noise, flickering lights and fire, faces and eyes watching me, every single eye on me. I felt more exposed than even when I was on stage at the Colosseum.

Theron took my arm and led me away through the banquet hall, his grip tight as if he were afraid I'd disappear if he let go of me. I was a puppet, a slave to their bidding once again. I yanked my arm out of his grasp and he snarled at me, his eyes still two pools of night.

In one swift move, he scooped me up over his shoulder and carried me back to our suite without a word. I struggled against him as he stalked down the corridors, my heart racing with fear at what might happen next, and he smacked my ass with a ringing slap that echoed in the stone halls.

"Put me down, you sharp-eared bastard!" I shouted as we entered his suite and he slammed the door behind him, setting me down on the floor.

"Who are you?" he demanded, his voice dark and dangerous as he stalked toward me.

Chapter 23

Kael

"Who are you?" He demanded. "What are you doing here? What do you want from me?" His voice rang out in the empty suite, echoing off the walls and onto the marble floor.

I stayed silent, frozen in place like an animal caught in a trap. I didn't trust myself to speak—words had betrayed me once before, and I was afraid of what might come out if I opened my mouth now. Anger flashed over Theron's face and he stepped closer, his breathing heavy with rage.

"Answer me," he commanded.

I swallowed hard and looked away, unable to meet his gaze.

"You're not going to speak?" His voice was low and dangerous. He took another step forward, reaching out and grasping my wrists. "Then let's see how well you can fight."

My heart raced as he pulled me closer, our bodies pressing together until I could feel the heat coming off of him in waves. I tried to back away, but there was nowhere to go—he had me pinned against the wall with no escape. He grabbed my wrists in one hand, squeezing hard enough that my bones ground against each other, and used his other hand to grab my chin, forcing me to look into his face.

"I'm going to fuck you," he growled, his eyes were two black voids as he glared at me. "Unless you stop me."

My eyes widened as he grabbed my dress, ripping it down the front and exposing my breasts. I threw myself forward, breaking his hold on my wrists and bashing my head into his chin. He swore, and I dropped the ring, freeing my hands to attack. He lunged at me, and I spun, driving an elbow into his ribs. I tried to slam my knee into his balls, but he blocked me. Pushing off the wall, I landed a kick to his knee, forcing him to the ground. I spun, aiming another kick at his face, and he caught my leg and yanked me off balance. I fell, and he scrambled on top of me, pinning me by the shoulders before he gripped my wrists, forcing my arms to the floor. His hold on me was painful as he leaned forward, a triumphant grin on his face.

"I knew it. Who trained you? Was it the rebels? Was it Striker?"

"Fuck you." I spat.

"You'd enjoy that, wouldn't you? Mixing a little business with pleasure, aren't you, *Sia*?" He growled, running his tongue over my bleeding cheek. His breath was hot on my face as he met my gaze, and for a moment I thought I saw something else in his eyes—something other than anger. But it was gone in a second and his laugh was cold before he spoke. "*Sia.* What a fucking joke. You're not some gentle flower. You're a *Sihaya*, the false little creature that lays in wait and attacks unsuspecting hands with sharp teeth."

I glared at him, knowing the creepy insect he was referring to; the one that mimicked the Areca flower and was particularly gruesome.

"I didn't ask to be plucked," I shot back, lifting my hips and attempting to throw him off of me. His erection ground against me and wetness flooded my core, only making me angrier. "I hate you."

"You think I don't know that?" He held my stare, his black eyes as endless as a starless night. "Do you think I don't recognize that expression on your face? I see it every time I look in the mirror."

He jerked his head, tearing his gaze away and closing his eyes as his breath shuddered out of him. His expression softened and I could have sworn I saw a hint of vulnerability in those dark depths before he spoke again. It was almost as if he were disappointed in himself. The moment only lasted a second before he looked at me with a dangerous glint in his eye.

"Why are you here, *Sihaya*?"

I took a deep breath, knowing that I had to come up with something believable enough or he'd kill me.

"I was taken from the mines—" I started and he shook his head.

"Bullshit."

"No, it isn't! Do you want me to tell you how we drill adits or how the dry shaker boxes work? How about fire-setting? Cause I know all of it. I've worked in those mines for over a decade."

His chest rose and fell as he took in a deep breath before turning his gaze back to me.

"They pulled me from the mines and brought me to a new life," I whispered, knowing it wasn't exactly a lie. "I only know how to fight because my father taught me. It's how I protect myself there."

He hesitated for a moment, his grip on me loosening ever so slightly before he spoke. "Is that true?" His voice was soft now—as if he desperately wanted to believe every word coming out of my mouth.

Before he could say anything else, I leaned in and kissed him hard, our tongues tangling and teeth clashing.

Heat rushed through me as I yanked my hands free of his hold and I pulled at his clothing, tearing it from his body. His skin was like velvet beneath my fingers as I explored him, caressing the hard ridges of his stomach and tracing the outline of his pectorals. He tasted like spice and fire and I wanted more, my mouth searching for his hungrily.

"*Sihaya*." He groaned, wrapping an arm around my waist as he deepened the kiss as if trying to devour me. His hands were everywhere, exploring every inch of my flesh until I was a trembling mess beneath him. Our breathing was heavy and ragged in the silence, punctuated by soft moans and whispered curses as we each fought for dominance.

The heat between us was like a wildfire and all I wanted at that moment was to feel his body against mine. His hands moved lower, running along my hips and gripping them tightly as he yanked my hips to his, pressing his heavy erection against my stomach, his precum smearing against my skin.

His lips strayed from mine, trailing along my jaw and down to the sensitive column of my throat. I gasped as he started suckling my nipples, laving them with his tongue and teasing the piercings with his teeth until I was writhing beneath him.

"Gods, yes." I hummed in pleasure, burying my hands in his thick hair and holding him to my breast.

His fingers toyed with the edges of my panties and then tugged them off as he kissed a path lower. His hands continued to move lower, trailing down my body until he reached between my legs.

I moaned loudly, arching my back as his mouth traveled further south.

He stopped, and I growled, glaring at him. "Beg me for it," he demanded.

"Fuck you," I hissed, and he grinned. His fingers moved expertly, teasing my clit before slipping inside of me. I gasped, a jolt of pleasure surging through me as he began to thrust them in and out of me.

"I will," he said, flicking one of my nipple piercings with his tongue. "If you ask nicely."

He stopped, his fingers stilling inside me as I scowled at him. "Theron..."

He grinned at me. "Just one paltry word, *Sihaya*."

I growled, trying to grind against his hand, too lost in lust to care, but he withdrew his fingers, leaving me empty. Bereft.

I swallowed hard, staring into his dark eyes. Strange how seeing them blackened didn't frighten me anymore.

"Please." I gritted out, and he smirked.

"Good girl." I didn't have time to respond before a shout left me as he sucked my clit into his mouth.

"Oh gods, oh fuck. Theron!"

His hands gripped my thighs as he went down on me, licking and sucking until I thought I'd go mad with pleasure. Every stroke of his tongue brought me higher and higher until I was adrift in an ocean of pleasure that threatened to drown me.

It was too much—too much pleasure, too much intensity—and I shouted his name as bliss raced through me like wildfire. He kept going, pushing me further over the edge until I screamed, my body convulsing in waves of ecstasy. Theron finally released me, and I panted, my legs quivering as aftershocks of my climax rippled through me.

But he wasn't finished with me yet.

Theron moved up to kiss me, my musk on his lips as his tongue explored my mouth and his hands wandered over my body, igniting new flames of desire within me. I touched him everywhere, clutching at his hair, his broad shoulders, his muscular arms, as I tried to get as close to him as possible. I wanted to crawl inside of him and live there.

He pushed me back onto the ground and positioned himself between my legs, running the head of his cock through my folds before slowly entering me. I whimpered as he filled me, his hard length stretching me until I didn't know if I could take anymore.

"You are mine, Kael," he said, trapping me with his gaze. I sucked in a breath, unable to respond, choking on pleasure as my body adjusted to his size.

Theron started moving, slowly at first, building up a rhythm that matched the beating of our hearts. Every thrust sent me higher, my moans growing louder and more desperate with each passing moment. I clawed at his back, leaving red marks as my nails dug in, lost in a haze of carnal pleasure as he thrust and retreated.

His hands roamed over my body, pinching and teasing my nipples as he continued to drive into me, deeper and harder. My climax loomed closer, and I tilted my hips, guiding him in even deeper.

"Theron," I gasped out, my voice barely above a whisper. "Please, harder."

"*Sihaya*," he groaned, slamming into me with a force that made my head spin. I cried out as pleasure raced through me, every part of me alive and on fire. It was like nothing I'd ever felt before, a wild, untamed passion that threatened to consume me completely.

I wrapped my legs around his waist, pulling him deeper into me as I matched his movements with my own.

"You feel so good," he groaned, his breath hot against my ear. "So fucking tight and wet for me."

I moaned in response, unable to form words as pleasure consumed me. Burying my face into his neck, I urged him on as he pounded into me with abandon. I was lost in a whirlwind of sensations; my skin was on fire with desire as Theron drove me closer to the brink. Tension built inside of me, coiling tighter and tighter until it threatened to snap.

And then, with one last thrust, Theron pushed me over the edge. I cried out his name as my body convulsed around him, wave after wave of pleasure washing over me. I clung to him, trembling with the force of my orgasm as he drove himself deeper inside me, grinding against my clit. Theron followed soon after, a deep groan escaping his lips as he emptied himself into me.

We stayed like that, our breathing harsh and ragged as we held each other. And then, slowly, reality crept back in. Theron pulled away, gently disengaging from me as he rolled to the side.

He gazed at me for a few moments, his stare unwavering and unreadable. He leaned in, pressing a soft kiss against my lips that I didn't refuse.

"You're mine," he whispered, his voice hoarse. "I don't care what you did before this or where you came from. From now on, you belong to me."

I shivered, unable to speak, as his words settled deep inside me. At that moment, I knew he was right. I had willingly given myself to him, to the enemy. How could I ever face Teodosija or my family again?

Chapter 24

Kael

I stirred in the morning light streaming in from the open door, my vision adjusting to the brightness. I expected to see Theron sleeping beside me, but the bed was empty. Panic rose in my chest, my mind racing with thoughts of what he could be doing. Was he gathering the guards now to take me to the dungeons? Or was he telling the emperor and setting himself back up in his position as Lord Marshal? I sat up and rubbed my eyes, trying to push away my fears. A shadow moved in front of the doorway and I tensed, ready to attack.

"Good morning, Kael," Mirijana greeted me with a smile as she breezed into the room. "Did you sleep well?"

I nodded, attempting to calm my nerves. "Yes, thank you."

"We have a surprise for you," Mirijana said, motioning towards the main living space. "We've prepared breakfast."

We? Was Theron out there?

My traitorous heart leapt, and I bit my lip hard to remind myself he was the enemy. I hurried out of the bedroom and was met with the sight of Mirijana and Aella bustling about the suite, their laughter, and conversation filling the air. Aella was in better spirits than I'd ever seen her, a glimmer of hope sparking in her eyes once more. It was a relief to see her so much happier, despite my disappointment.

"The Lord Marshal will be out for a bit and we're to entertain you," Mirijana said, gesturing for me to sit down. Aella asked about working in the kitchen today and I let out a breath, grateful for the distraction. I sat down to eat, no longer surprised by the bounty they spread before me each day. But my thoughts kept drifting back to Theron. What was he doing? Had he discovered my secrets? I couldn't help but feel a sense of unease. Was he as shaken by last night as I was?

"Kael?" I looked up from my bowl of fruit, and both Aella and Raenisa stared at me. Aella must have tried to get my attention more than once.

"Sorry, I'm still waking up," I mumbled sheepishly, and a tentative smile grew on her face as she shared a glance with Mirijana.

"I bet," she chuckled, and Mirijana shot her a conspiratorial grin.

"Here's your ring," Mirijana said, holding it out to me.

I took it, a flush creeping up my neck. They must have found our clothes tangled together on the floor and figured out what had happened. "Thanks," I muttered, slipping the ring back on my finger, grateful that she didn't recognize it for what it was.

Mirijana's eyes flicked to the door as if checking that Theron hadn't returned before she broached a new subject, feigning nonchalance. "Do you know where Herrath is? Did he go with the others?"

I hesitated for a moment before answering. "Yeah, he did."

Mirijana's face was unreadable as she nodded. But I couldn't shake the feeling that something was off.

"Well, with all of them out of the castle, that just means Aella can stay here for all of my tasks." She smiled at the other girl, who hid a pleased grin.

I hid my grimace by taking a bite. The last thing I needed was another set of eyes watching my every move, making it even more difficult for me to carry out my mission.

Thankfully, Kadir strode into the room, interrupting our conversation. "Sorry to interrupt, but I need to fit her for these clothes," he said, holding up a bundle of fabric.

I raised an eyebrow, suspicious of the sudden intrusion. But before Mirijana could object, he grabbed my arm and pulled me toward the bedroom.

As soon as we were alone, Kadir turned to me, his eyes flashing.

"What were you thinking, Kael?" Kadir hissed as he began fitting me with the new clothes, glancing at the closed door as if worried the servants would burst in at any moment. "Fighting a noble? From a high house, no less? You drew too much attention to yourself. Nyana is checking all the servants' backgrounds. They're trying to find the spies."

"I had to do it," I replied, my voice tight with anger. "I couldn't just stand there and let her attack me."

"It's too dangerous to stay," Kadir said, frustration clear in his expression. "We need to return to the base. Now."

"No," I blurted. "I can't leave yet. If I do, then everything will have been for nothing. I have to complete the mission, and make all of this worth it."

If I didn't kill Rhazien, then all I'd accomplished was fucking Theron. I didn't think I could live with that.

"You're taking too many risks, Kael," Kadir said. "Rhazien suspects something. If we stay, we'll be caught and executed."

"It doesn't matter if they suspect me." I crossed my arms. "Theron will protect me."

I hated relying on him, but I had no other choice. The more time I spent with him, the more I realized he was a prisoner here, too. I might hate him, but he wasn't the enemy I once thought he was.

Kadir sighed, but he didn't argue. "Fine. But you need to be careful. You won't have backup after I run."

"When are you leaving?" I asked, worry flitting through me despite my big talk.

"As soon as I walk out that door." He paused before continuing, his voice low. "Rhazien has been having nightly meetings with his mother. You could corner him on his way back from one of them. He takes the south servant stairwell."

My heart quickened in my chest at the thought of finally finishing the mission and removing this collar once and for all.

"Tell Teodosija that I won't leave until the job is done," I said firmly. "And tell my brother that I'll meet them in Sailtown when everything is over. The Red Wilds aren't safe. Go through the Bone gap."

"You're crazy," Kadir muttered, shaking his head in disbelief. Theron had already searched Sailtown and came up short. He wouldn't do it again, but Kadir didn't know that.

"I'll be fine. See you soon."

Kadir looked at me skeptically, but he nodded in agreement. "Good luck, Striker."

He left, pausing at the door. "You'll need to hang those or they'll wrinkle." He gestured to the pile of dresses left on the mussed bed. I hadn't even paid attention to the outfit he'd dressed me in. It was black and made of a gauzy material that flowed around me almost lighter than air, with a plunging neckline. But it was the ornate silver lilies embroidered into the skirt that caught my attention. Each one featured a tiny skull, its mouth open in a morbid grin.

"I will," I whispered, my throat tight with emotion. Kadir had risked so much to help me and now I was alone.

"I'll hang those up for you, my lady." Mirijana bustled in all smiles as she looked around, oblivious to the tension. "Aella set up the heated pool for you on the patio. We thought you may need a soak." She didn't hint about my night with Theron again, but it was there, left unsaid. Taking off my parting gift from Kadir, I hung it up before pulling on my robe and heading out onto the patio. The night sky was a deep navy blue, sprinkled with specks of stars like sugar on a cake.

The desert city was spread out below us; its labyrinth of narrow winding streets filled with shops, water forums, and markets illuminated by lanterns glowing golden against the darkness. Above them all loomed the mountains like an impenetrable fortress, standing tall against any would-be attackers. To think that once this was a place of peace; now all I saw was desperation, whether it be under a veneer of gold or sand.

The air was heavy but still comfortably warm; a gentle breeze carried scents of exotic spices, burning incense, and perfumed oils from far away.

The pool was waiting for me, a steaming cauldron of hot water with welcoming bubbles that made my skin tingle. I stepped into the pool, hissing as the heat began soothing all my most intimate aches. It had been years since I'd had a sexual partner, and none of them came close to Theron's size. The water was delicious, sinking deep into all of my aching muscles. I lay back, letting myself float on the surface while watching the stars twinkle in the night sky.

Thoughts of Theron crept into my head unbidden, his broad shoulders and dark eyes that seemed to see beyond what I allowed people; but then I remembered how he had ordered the razing of Caurium, uncaring as he watched us suffer from above, his face unmoving as if he'd been carved from stone. He wasn't a good man; he was my enemy and the only reason I felt this way was because of his magic. Who knew what intentions he put into the metal? He could increase it every time his eyes flooded black, and I'd never know. None of it was real. I had to focus on completing the mission. It was the only thing that mattered. I shook my head in frustration; it was all just too much for one night.

I closed my eyes and let out a sigh as I sank further down into the hot water until I was completely submerged.

I felt a gaze on me, heavy and intense. My eyes flew open to see Theron standing at the edge of the patio, watching me float in the water with an intensity that made my heart thump painfully fast. He began unbuttoning his shirt, looking like something out of a dream as he bared his muscular chest. His dark hair hung loose around his chiseled face, and he held my gaze as if daring me to look away first.

"Are you sore, *Sihaya?*" He purred, and I glared at him.
"What does that matter?"

His dark eyes locked with mine and his expression said it all; he wanted me. He took his time stripping off his clothes before stepping into the pool, joining me in the warm embrace of the water.

"So I can decide if I'm going to fuck you with my cock or my mouth." His erection bobbed in front of me and I swallowed hard, a mix of desire and rage rising within me. Theron had caused so much pain and destruction, yet I couldn't deny the pull I felt toward him. It was his magic, I told myself, but deep down something whispered in me it was more than that. His muscular frame pressed against mine, his lips finding my neck as his hands roamed my curves. I moaned despite myself, my body betraying me with each touch.

"I'm fine," I murmured. "It doesn't hurt."

Theron pulled back, locking eyes with me again. "Tell me you don't want this, Sihaya," he challenged, his voice low and dangerous.

I wanted to resist him, to push him away and remind myself of everything he had done, but I couldn't. Instead, I leaned forward, capturing his lips in a fierce kiss. Our tongues met, intertwining in a whirlwind of need and desire.

Theron's hands moved lower, cupping my ass as he lifted me, pressing me against the side of the pool. His fingers roamed over my body, tracing the curves of my breasts before sliding lower to squeeze my backside. I moaned against his lips, grinding my hips against his as our bodies melded together in perfect harmony.

He pulled away, his eyes burning bright with desire as he gazed down at me. "I want you, Kael. All of you," he murmured, pressing his forehead against mine.

My eyes fluttered shut, a surge of longing sweeping through me as I nodded in agreement. Theron moved closer, his lips capturing mine in a passionate kiss as his cock pressed against my entrance. I opened for him, my body welcoming him as he filled me up with each thrust. His mouth found my neck, sending sparks of pleasure through my veins as I clung to him, our bodies merging in the water's warmth. It sloshed around us as we moved together in a frenzy of desire, each touch igniting a fire inside of me. Theron's thrusts were powerful and deep, each one sending ripples of bliss through my body. Our bodies moved in perfect unison, each touch and caress a symphony of passion. I wrapped my legs around his waist, pulling him even closer, wanting him to fill me completely. He groaned against my neck, his grip on my hips tightening as he increased his pace.

I dug my nails into his back, urging him on, my body screaming for release. It hit me, a tidal wave of ecstasy that consumed me whole and I cried out his name, my legs shaking with the intensity of my orgasm. Theron followed suit, his cock jerking as he spilled himself inside of me with a shout.

We clung to each other, panting heavily, our bodies entwined in the warm water. For a moment, we stayed there, lost in each other's embrace, enjoying the quiet stillness of the night. I looked up and my breath caught in my throat as I saw a figure standing on the balcony of the palace, watching us silently. It was the empress. Her face twisted in anger and hatred, her eyes blazing with rage as she stared down at me. The surrounding air seemed to thicken, and a chill ran through me as our gaze met.

Theron didn't seem to notice her presence, but I did. And for some reason, the sight of her made me fiercely possessive of him; wanting to prove that he belonged to me and no one else. So I stayed where I was, wrapping my arms around Theron's neck and pressing myself against him possessively as I ground against him, encouraging his softening cock to harden once more.

"Again, *Sihaya*?" He grinned, stirring his hips and making me gasp.

"Yes," I moaned, looking up and meeting her gaze as he began to slowly thrust into me once more. She sneered, drawing away into the darkness and I let myself go, lost in the pleasure of Theron's body once more.

Chapter 25

Theron

I lay in bed with Kael, the morning light creeping in through the cracked bedroom door. I gazed at her sleeping form, content and happier than I could remember being in years. She'd been incredible the night before, so passionate and demanding. I was finally getting to know the real her, beyond the hostile facade she presented to the world. I ran my fingers through her silvery hair and down her back, circling the dimples at the base of her spine.

A knock sounded, interrupting our peaceful moment. Irritation pricked me, and I rolled out of bed, pulling on a pair of loose sleeping pants. I opened the door to find the empress standing before me. I glared at her, ready to shut the door in her face, but she stopped me with an upraised hand.

"Wait. It's important."

"What do you want, Raura?" I growled.

The empress entered the suite; her gaze flickering into the bedroom and over Kael's sleeping form. My protective instincts flared, and I stepped in front of the doorway, blocking her view of Kael. No one else was allowed to see her when she was soft and relaxed, only me.

"Theron, darling, I need to speak with you," Raura purred.

I rolled my eyes, not falling for her flirtatious attempts. "We have nothing to talk about, Raura. I'm not interested in your games."

Raura clicked her tongue and sauntered closer to me. She ran a manicured nail down my chest and smirked. "Come now, Theron. Don't be so uptight. We're adults here."

"I didn't know you liked adults," I spat, and her eyes flashed.

"Theron..." She reached out again, and I grasped her wrist and pushed it away from me, my expression darkening further. "Don't touch me," I hissed between gritted teeth. "Say your piece and leave. I have nothing to say to you."

Raura took a step closer to me, her body was as beautiful and sensual as I remembered. Too bad it covered a heart as black as pitch. "Theron, please, hear me out. Your mother is planning something, and I fear she may have turned on me."

I narrowed my eyes at her. "I don't want anything to do with your political games, Raura. Being the heir means nothing to me. And if you're interested in power, then you're trying to fuck the wrong brother."

Raura's eyes widened in surprise and anger. "This concerns you too."

"I don't see how."

"Who do you think Rhazien is going to target first once he ascends the throne?"

"If you think that scares me, you're mistaken. I've been dodging murder attempts from him my entire life."

"But this time, it won't just be you. He'll come for your pretty little concubine, too. You can defend yourself, but can you protect her?"

I clenched my fists in anger, a chill running down my spine as I realized Raura was right. If Rhazien took power, then Kael would be in danger. And I couldn't be sure that I could keep her safe.

I held my tongue, unwilling to be drawn into her machinations. But Raura wasn't easily deterred. She stepped closer and laid a hand on my forearm, her stiff fingers like icicles against my skin. I jerked away from her and shook my head.

I stepped back, breaking Raura's hold on me. She looked startled and tried to take my hand in hers, but I stopped her, keeping my distance.

"Thank you for the warning, Raura," I said icily. "But don't forget, I'm not one of your pawns. Never again."

Kael stood in the doorway, her attention focused on where I held Raura's wrist. Anger flashed across her face as she stormed over to my side. She grabbed my arm, pulling me away from the empress as she glared daggers at her.

"What are you doing here?" she demanded, her eyes flashing dangerously.

Raura's lips twisted into an ugly smirk. "Just having a conversation with an old friend."

Kael scoffed and pulled me closer to her side. "It's time for you to leave," she snapped, her grip on my arm never wavering.

Raura's eyes hardened as she took her in.

"I'm done here," she said coolly, turning away from us. "Don't forget my offer, Theron. My door is always open for you." She gave me a smirk before walking off without another word.

Kael glared after the Empress. "What did she want?"

"It doesn't matter," I replied, pulling Kael closer to me. A flicker of guilt flashed in her eyes, and I pulled back, forcing her to meet my gaze once more. "What's wrong?"

She hesitated for a moment before admitting. "Raura saw us in the hot tub last night." She watched my face, biting her full lower lip as she waited for my reaction.

"What?" My eyes widened before my brows furrowed together, my stomach queasy. That disgusting woman soiled everything she touched. The idea of her seeing Kael while she came undone... A growl escaped me. "Why didn't you say anything?"

She shrugged, unable to meet my stare. "I don't know."

I thought of the night before, the way she'd clawed my back, as if desperate for me as she coaxed my cock into her once more. "Was all that just a show for her?"

She shook her head. "No. She left right away. I don't know why I did it. I wanted her to see that you're—" She cut herself off. "It doesn't matter. What did she want to talk about?"

"An alliance."

"And you said...?"

I snarled. Just the thought of letting Raura have power over me again sent a visceral rage through my veins. "I'd never ally myself with her. She's worse than Varzorn. I'd kill her if I could."

Her eyes flew open, shocked by my vehemence. "Why do you hate her so much?" Kael asked, her voice softening as her brows drew down.

I hesitated, undecided if I wanted to reveal the true depths of Raura's depravity, uncertain of Kael's reaction. Maybe she would understand? I'd told no one before, and I didn't know if I was ready to relive the memories of my past.

"I told you that Rhazien killed my father," I said, my voice low and pained. "And that he brought me back to court with him. But I didn't tell you what happened after."

Kael's hand tightened on my arm, her eyes locked on mine.

"I was kept in a cage, like an animal," I continued, my stomach quaking with the memories before I took a deep breath. "Rhazien would come in and beat me, pretending it was for interrogation or teaching me a lesson. But it was just because he was a sadist and I had become his toy."

Kael gasped, horror and anger warring on her face.

"I lived in fear for years," I explained, my voice barely above a whisper. "Hearing his voice was enough to make me shake in terror. My mother would ignore me for months on end, trying to force me to obey her every whim just for a shred of affection. I was alone, missing my cousins, mourning my father..." I shook my head, my eyes distant and seeing the palace under the mountain that had been my prison. "Then Raura found me and pretended to be my savior. Doting on me and showering me with praise. She seduced me and made me think she loved me. But really, she was trying to use me to get pregnant because she hadn't conceived for the emperor."

Kael's eyes were filled with tears, her hand shaking on my arm.

"I was only thirteen. Too young to truly understand."

"Theron, I'm so sorry." She said, her expression tortured. "She's sick. Anyone who touches a child doesn't deserve to live."

I nodded, an unexpected release spreading through me as I met her gaze and saw nothing but understanding. I hadn't understood how much I'd been holding in until I spoke the words aloud.

"After I grew older and realized what her intentions were." My voice hardened as I continued. "I vowed to never let her touch me again. To never let my heart be controlled by anyone else. Ever."

Kael nodded, her expression unreadable. She cupped my face in her hands and looked at me with so much understanding that I knew she'd experienced something similar. She held me close, stroking my hair and murmuring soothing words I couldn't make out.

Warmth spread through me that had been missing for so long and I realized hope wasn't lost after all. Maybe there was still a chance for happiness in this world, if only I could look deep enough within myself to find it. Kael's touch was like a balm on my soul. Healing wounds I thought would never close. I leaned into her, my eyes closing in gratitude. It was the first time I felt protected.

As she pulled away from me, her eyes met mine, and I knew at that moment that I wanted her with me always. Not for a physical release, but for the connection we shared. I'd known from the moment I'd seen her she was meant to be mine, but now I understood why.

"Kael," I whispered, reaching for her, but she stepped back, shaking her head.

"Not now, Theron," she said, her voice low and hesitant. "I can't. Not yet." I'd never seen her look so vulnerable.

I nodded, understanding, but that didn't stop the ache in my chest. I wanted to lose myself in her, forget about the pain and the past. But that wasn't fair to her. Not after what we had shared.

"I'm sorry," I said, stepping back. "I didn't mean to push you," I said, embarrassment reddening my neck. "Just... I don't know what came over me."

Kael stepped closer to me, the heat of her body pressing against mine. "I understand," she whispered as she drew me into her arms, holding me. I sighed, feeling as if something I'd been missing had finally settled into place. Maybe I was yearning for somebody who comprehended the suffering I had endured. Someone who understood what it was like to be used. I didn't know what it was, only that Kael had become the answer to my every question.

She tilted my head up and pressed a tender kiss to my lips.

"You need a bath," she said, wrinkling her nose. "You stink."

A laugh escaped me, and for the first time in my life, I felt light. "No, I don't."

Her eyes twinkled merrily and my breath caught in my chest. Has any woman ever been as beautiful as she?

"Let's wash up," she murmured, her voice gentle as she stood, readying a bath. My gaze softened as I watched her gathering the supplies to bathe me, the firelight framing her face. Every other woman paled in comparison compared to the intensity of my feelings for her. I'd never felt like this before.

The warmth that filled me when we touched, the trust I had in her, and the way my heart skipped a beat when our eyes met. Was this love? If so, it was far more intense than anything I'd ever experienced before.

It didn't matter. All I knew was that I wanted to spend every moment of my life with Kael and never let go.

Chapter 26

Kael

I walked along the halls of the Martial gallery, Mirijana and Aella trailing behind me like ghosts. A faint light from the morning sun had filled the sky and I yawned, ready to sleep but unwilling to face Theron to do so. The haze of daylight cast the stone-lined halls in soft purple-gray rays. The air was still and quiet, broken only by the occasional rustling of my dress and the sound of our footsteps. I kept circling the servant stairwells, trying to catch Rhazien as he returned from plotting with his mother.

I didn't have a plan, not truly, but I was desperate to leave the palace and willing to do anything to escape the shame and confusion twisting my stomach in knots as I spun Tannethe's poison ring on my finger. My mind raced with conflicting emotions, like a sandstorm inside my head. Theron's revelations had left me reeling, and I was struggling to make sense of it all.

As we walked, I thought about how broken he'd looked in the darkness, his face half in shadow as he confessed what Raura had done to him. What they'd all inflicted on him. I couldn't help but sympathize. I'd experienced much the same, even if I didn't remember most of it. My body still did.

But I loathed him. I hated that the more I learned about him, the more I realized we shared similar histories. We'd both lost our fathers young, both were taken from our homes and abused. But the difference was that Haemir had saved me, while Theron had no one to turn to. He had been on his own, and that made me pity him.

Then, just as quickly, that pity would switch to rage. All the horrible things that we had in common were his fault. He was the reason I had no home, the reason my father had died, and I had been made a slave. It didn't matter what had happened to him; he still perpetuated his pain on others. I'd suffered because of what he did. And I knew I wasn't the only one. Theron's actions had hurt countless others. Even if I could forgive his sins against me, I refused to forgive him for what he'd done to others.

My thoughts chased each other as I walked the halls, trapped between these two opposing emotions. It was like being caught in a whirlpool, constantly being pulled in different directions. I looked over my shoulder at Mirijana and Aella, who were chatting amongst themselves, not paying attention to me. Exactly as I wanted, if only Rhazien would appear.

The conflict inside me was overwhelming, and I wanted to escape. I wished to just forget about Theron and all the feelings he brought out in me. But no matter how hard I tried, I couldn't seem to push him from my thoughts. I had to reconcile what I felt for him.

As I paced the Martial Gallery with my two companions trailing behind me, my eyes were drawn to the glittering tiara on display once more. If what Oz said was right, then Theron's ancestor had worn this crown before his grandfather killed her and ended the Godsfall...

The shadows deepened around us, blanketing the floor and casting a chill over it as if the stone was alive and aware. The smell of iron and old stone hung in the air, like blood on the wind, and I thought of the story Oz had told us. That the war had started here, in this very castle. The Elves stored power in metal and stone. It stood to reason that the palace was still infused with remnants of that battle. I stepped closer to the display, reaching out to open the glass case. It was as if the tiara was calling out to me, begging me to try it on and feel the weight of the crown upon my head.

I couldn't rid myself of the sensation that something dangerous was hidden, prepared to attack.

Mirijana and Aella were oblivious to my inner turmoil, chatting quietly amongst themselves. But I couldn't shake the idea that I was being watched. That the shadows themselves were alive and aware, coiling around me like tendrils of smoke and snakes.

My heart raced as I reached into the display case. I was afraid to touch it, worried about what I might discover about myself if I did. But something drew me closer, a magnetic pull that I couldn't resist. I forced myself to reach out and touch the crown, one finger connecting with the embossed leaves. Heat and lightning ran through me, some hidden part of me blooming and coming to life. The quiet was a heavy blanket, smothering everything in my vicinity, silencing the entire world. All that mattered was the magic beating in my blood. But I knew better. It was the metal, as I'd never experienced it before. It sang to me, a melody playing in the back of my mind that I'd never been able to decipher the words. Now though…

Shock coursed through me, and I sucked in a breath. Was I some sort of Sálfar Remnant? Were those even possible? I'd never heard of such a thing. The implications of it were staggering. I had never identified what type of Remnant I was, always assuming I was descended from a Wraith or perhaps Fae or Zerkir. But to be part Elvish... It would explain how my father knew the language, and why he taught it to me—footsteps sounded behind me and I jumped, breaking my train of thought. Magic shot from me, shattering the case and sending glass and metal flying.

My heart pounded in my chest as I scrambled away from the shattered display, trying to hide the tiara I still held. I glanced around anxiously, sure that everyone must have noticed what I had done.

I took a steadying breath and forced myself to calm down. If anyone discovered my magic, I would be killed—only Elves were supposed to possess magic. That was the point of their wars, of the Godsfall; to consolidate their power so no one could oppose them.

"Kael! Are you alright?" It was Mirijana, her eyes wide with shock as she looked at the wreckage of the display case in horror. "What happened?"

I hesitated before speaking, unsure of what to say or do next. "Um. I'm not sure." I glanced up to see the owner of the footsteps that had surprised me. Xadrian stood there watching me with an intensity that made my stomach twist into knots. "I must have bumped it."

Xadrian's black eyes studied me as he approached, his confident grace and flirtatious manner tinged with a vague threat as he leaned into my space. I tried to focus on my breathing to keep my thoughts and emotions hidden. He was a clever one, and I had to tread carefully.

"Are you alright?" He stopped inches away from me, crouching beside me and offering me a hand up.

My heartbeat quickened as I met his gaze, forcing myself to be still despite the overwhelming urge to flee. "I'm fine," I grumbled, the words burning in my throat as my face reddened. He held my stare for a moment before smirking and stepping back.

His expression shifted then, and he crossed his arms in front of him. "What brings you here? It doesn't seem like your usual sort of place, seeing as Theron is nowhere to be found."

My throat went dry at his question as I frantically searched for an answer that wouldn't make me sound suspicious or reveal too much about myself. "Just taking a walk."

"You seem nervous," he said, a small smile playing at the corners of his mouth.

"You're mistaken," I replied, my voice steady despite my inner turmoil.

"Are you sure? You look like you've seen a ghost."

My mind raced as I tried to think of a way out of the situation.

"I don't know what you're talking about," I muttered, my tone unsteady. "Excuse me, I need to get back."

Xadrian's smile turned into a smirk. "A pity. I thought we might discuss jewelry. Your taste seems to be so similar to my own."

I wanted to scream. Did he know or just suspect? One wrong move and I could be dead.

"Maybe later," I said, trying to sound convincing.

Xadrian nodded. "Good. I'll see you around, Kael."

As he walked away, I let out a breath I hadn't realized I was holding. I had to be more careful than ever now. Xadrian was onto me, and I didn't know what he was capable of. But one thing was certain: I couldn't let anyone find out about my magic. Not if I wanted to stay alive.

I glanced down and noticed I was squeezing the tiara so hard that it had sliced my hand. Mirijana stepped forward and took the tiara from me, setting it back on its display case before turning to me with concern in her eyes. "Let's get you cleaned up," she whispered, taking my arm in hers as she led me toward the suite.

Aella quickly joined us, fussing over my wound while worrying about whom to tell about the display case. Mirijana ushered me back to the suite, trying to convince me that I needed medical attention.

"I'm fine," I argued as I held a cloth to the cut. "Seriously, I've had way worse than this."

"We need to find the Marshal so he can use the healing plate." Worry still lingered in her expression as she urged me to sit down as if I'd faint from a cut on my palm. It was then that I realized why Mirijana wasn't in the rebellion. She didn't care about power or fame; Mirijana was more than happy to remain in the shadows and take care of others, even if that meant sacrificing her freedom. Her heart was too kind for bloodshed, and I couldn't help but admire her for it. Allowing yourself to have a soft heart took more strength than covering it with stone.

She reminded me of Haemir. He was the same way; a doting father to Gavril and me, his first thought always of others. It didn't matter how exhausted he'd been after working in the mines, he'd always have time for us, putting our needs above his every time. People like Haemir and Mirijana desired to help and care for others, but only if they are valued in return. For Mirijana to be content with her life, Theron must show her respect and appreciation. I scowled, angry that I was learning more about Theron than I wanted to hear.

As if my thoughts had summoned him, the door opened and Theron strode inside. His gaze focused on me as he noticed the bandage on my hand.

"*Sihaya?*" His eyes studied me intently before he moved forward to stand in front of me. He mesmerized me as he bit his lip, concentrating as he took both of my hands in his and carefully examined them.

"Kael, what happened?"

"It's nothing. Just an accident. "

He let out a small sigh before retrieving a metal plate from his pocket. His touch was gentle and intimate as he covered the wound with the plate, his eyes flooding black as he funneled magic through the metal. It warmed, feeling like he'd planted a passionate kiss in my palm and I inhaled sharply. As soon as he finished, the cut disappeared as if it had never existed in the first place, leaving only smooth skin behind.

We both remained silent for a few moments, gazing into each other's eyes while neither of us said anything and yet somehow communicated volumes. I was more confused than ever as I tried to decipher this strange pull between us. He finished applying the healing plate and stepped away, breaking our intense connection.

"Thanks," I mumbled, not taking my eyes off of him as I strived to make sense of it all.

Chapter 27

Kael

Theron and I stepped onto the royal viewing deck of the colosseum, a strange sense of déjà vu filling me. The arena was bustling with activity as people milled around and shouted over one another. It was a cacophony of energy, with everyone eager to see the outcome of the next match. People filled the stands, some cheering, others shouting out their bets, holding glinting coins in the air. Enemies surrounded me, the crowd a tide of angry faces threatening to drown me. Theron buzzed with excitement, nervous energy flowing from him in waves, and seemingly oblivious to my apprehension.

The air filled with anticipation as Varzorn stood. The gathering fell silent as the emperor stepped to the podium. He was a formidable presence; dressed in royal vestments—the gold of his crown—and the glint of his weapons, belying his status as the most powerful ruler in Maeoris. His gaze swept over us all and I shivered despite myself.

"Tradition is fickle." He announced, looking over the hushed crowd. "It says that a child of my loins should rule." I glanced at Raura and the sour expression twisting her perfect features. I stared daggers at her, wishing I could kill them all. They were all monsters hiding under beautiful facades and I wanted nothing more than to tear down their twisted kingdom, once and for all. "But bloodlines aren't what it takes to create an empire. It's strength. Ambition. Power." His gaze drifted over the gathered nobles, picking out the potential heirs with his keen eyes. *Let us see who has the fortitude to take what he wants.*

The presenter took the lead as Varzorn sat, watching with a cruel smirk. He glanced over at us and dread twisted my stomach into a knot.

"Xadrian Sarro," the announcer called, his voice booming through the arena.

The crowd roared as Xadrian walked onto the viewing deck. His hair was slicked back, accentuating his chiseled jawline. He flashed me a lopsided grin, and a tremor ran through my chest.

"Versus Theron Axidor."

Fuck.

Theron stepped forward, drawing the attention of the assemblage as they shouted his name. His face was hard, and he squared his shoulders in a challenge.

My heart leapt into my throat, and I glanced at Theron. His demeanor was stoic, but I recognized the apprehension in his eyes as he turned to me; it wasn't for himself. He stepped closer to me and placed a comforting hand on my lower back. "Stay by the railing where I can see you," he warned. "Don't leave with anyone."

I nodded, touched that he was more worried about me than himself as he went to battle a man that had slain a lizard beast twice his size.

As Theron descended into the arena to face off against Xadrian, I watched, trying to focus on my breathing. Theron wore his bone armor, a tactical move against Xadrian's metal manipulation magic. I couldn't help but worry about him, even though I knew I shouldn't care.

They circled one another, saying something that I couldn't make out, but Theron's eyes darted up to me.

"His foolish infatuation with you is going to get him killed." Nyana pointed out, drinking from a golden goblet as she joined me at the railing. "Look how he leaves himself open because he watches you."

I frowned because she was right. Theron kept glancing up at me, ignoring Xadrian as he circled him.

"I'm sure that you're standing beside me for precisely that reason," I said, turning my attention back to the battle, where Theron parried an attack of Xadrian's sand.

"Clever." Her voice dripped with venom. "I almost wish that you'd outlive the day. You'd make for superb entertainment for Rhazien." She waited for my fear, her eyes narrowing when I didn't react.

"Good luck dealing with Theron if you succeed," I warned, my eyes tracking him as he ducked one of Xadrian's spears.

Nyana laughed a cruel sound that sent shivers down my spine. "Are you trying to threaten me? You're nothing but a little girl playing at being a warrior. You're not even worth the dirt beneath my feet."

I clenched my fists, the desire to hurt her rising in me before I reined it in, focusing on Theron once more.

Theron and Xadrian moved with blinding speed, their swords clashing against each other in a deadly dance. Theron blocked the metal spears that Xadrian launched at him with ease though Xadrian's magic made him a formidable opponent. Still, Theron was the better warrior. The crowd murmured about how he was able to hold his own without the use of his magic.

The arena rumbled with the sound of metal on bone, as the two men continue to circle each other, clashing and breaking apart once more, looking for an opening. Theron's sword pommel flashed in the sunlight, his movements blindingly fast, while Xadrian's metal armor glinted as he darted out of the way.

I watched from the sidelines, my heart pounding in my chest as Theron ducked a blow that would have killed anyone else.

The fight came to a sudden end, with Theron's sword at Xadrian's throat and Xadrian's spear hovering dangerously close to Theron's back. They stared at each other, the tension between them palpable. The crowd waited with bated breath for the outcome, wondering who would emerge victorious.

I released a sigh when the announcer called the bout a draw.

Theron and Xadrian returned to the viewing platform, their bodies glistening with sweat and blood. Theron rushed over to me, his eyes filled with concern. A rush of something warm squished in my chest at his protectiveness.

"*Sihaya*, are you alright?"

"I'm fine," I said, trying to brush off his worry. "You shouldn't have worried about me during the fight. You kept leaving yourself open."

"I can't help it," he replied, his gaze intense. "I can't bear the thought of anything happening to you."

A blush crept up my neck at his words, but then my attention was diverted as the announcer called for the next bout.

"We have a newcomer to the arena today. Tannethe Vennorin." He called, his voice echoing over the cheering crowd.

She strutted onto the sand, her golden armor gleaming in the late evening sun, an enameled blue viper on her chest plate.

"Who do you challenge, Lady Vennorin?"

Tannethe smirked, enjoying the attention as all eyes locked on her. She lifted a hand, pointing to the viewing box.

My heart plummeted when I realized she was gesturing at me. I followed Theron's gaze to Rhazien, who laughed with his mother, no doubt relishing the shock and terror on my face.

"Lady Tannethe has chosen Prince Theron's concubine, the Desert Lily!" Gods, they didn't even know my name.

This is what Nyana meant. The only reason they wanted me to fight Tannethe was because I had publicly beaten her and they needed to make an example of me for standing up for myself. Killing me reinstated order in their world. Because in what world would a lowly Remnant take on the ones who'd killed gods?

"Kael isn't trained. This isn't a fair fight," Theron argued, his eyes wild as he looked around for an ally and found none.

Nyana lifted a shoulder. "You flaunt her like she is one of us. Let her prove it."

Nothing was going to get me out of this. All that would happen was that Theron would get himself killed. I swallowed down my fear and spoke. "I'll fight."

Theron's eyes widened. "Kael, you don't have to do this. It's one thing to brawl in the mines, but fighting in the arena is another."

"I don't have a choice," I replied, bracing myself for the battle ahead.

Theron's expression darkened. "I won't let them," he growled. "I'll fight for you."

I shake my head, knowing that it's not that simple. "I have to do this."

Theron looked like he wanted to argue, but then the announcer's voice cut through the air. "Let the battle begin!"

I took a deep breath, my eyes locked on Tannethe as he smirked at me, her eyes filled with malice.

I stepped forward and gave a curt nod. Nyana's face lit up in ghoulish anticipation, and my stomach churned. The emperor gestured to the stairs leading down to the sand below, a cruel smirk twisting his lips.

I began walking down the stairs, feeling as if every eye in the crowd was on me. My steps were steady, but my heart was pounding in my chest. My eyes darted around the arena, taking in the sand-covered floor, tall stone walls that towered above us, and the distant roar of the masses. Their anticipation growing with each passing moment.

I took off the heels I wore, tossing them behind me as I tore my skirt, ripping the fabric until it was short enough to swing without hindering my movements. Hoots and calls came from the stands, but I ignored them, my thoughts only on the battle ahead. Tannethe strutted around the sand, wearing metallic armor in gold and copper, and I racked my brain trying to remember what copper did. Gold added strength... Better to end this quickly before she wore me out.

I stepped onto the sand; it was hot against my feet, but I welcomed it as if it were a familiar friend. She wouldn't be as used to fighting on the sand as I was.

As I ventured into the stadium, I could feel both Xadrian and Theron's eyes on me. But it was Theron's gaze that held me rooted to the spot. It was like lightning flashing between us;

despite all odds, I knew I wasn't alone. Taking one last look at Theron before turning away from him, I squared my shoulders and marched into the center of the arena.

I swept my eyes around the arena for a weapon and saw a rack of swords and blades. I strode across the sand towards them without hesitation, picking up a short sword that was like the one I had stolen from Theron. The hilt felt good in my hand as I wrapped my fingers around it; this would do. Then, without pause, I took hold of a dagger too—at least with it in hand, I wouldn't be completely exposed if Tannethe had any tricks up her sleeve.

Holding both weapons aloft, I turned to face my opponent. She stood tall and proud—her armor gleaming, a whip coiled around her waist like an extension of her body. Her eyes were sharp and calculating—as she sized me up and down—while a smirk twisted her lips into a cruel expression that sent chills up my spine.

"Ready to die, whore?"

I had faced death before—many times—but none of it compared to the fear I felt now. They wouldn't let me leave this arena alive. But I refused to run—I was no coward. Instead, I held my weapons firmly and stepped forward.

"Let's see what you've got," I said, my voice strong.

Tension filled the air around us as we both waited for the signal to begin. Then, with a single nod from the Emperor, the battle started.

Tannethe struck first, her whip snaking toward my wrist like a viper. But I moved faster, dodging her strike and lunging forward with my sword. She blocked my attack with ease, her armor deflecting my thrust. A surge of dread ran through me as I realized I had underestimated her fighting prowess.

A flurry of parries, thrusts, and blocks followed, and soon the battle was in full swing. I dodged her strike with my own while attacking with my dagger. But her armor was too strong. I needed to find a way around it.

"Don't worry, after you're dead, I'll comfort Theron for you."

Tannethe's smirk widened, and she stepped closer, her whip cracking in the air.

That's when I saw my chance. With a fierce cry, I lunged forward and cut her whip in half with a single stroke. The crowd gasped in shock as the weapon fell to the ground in two pieces, and their fear was palpable as they realized what was coming next.

I closed the space between us and brought my sword up, plunging my dagger into the gap of her armor in her armpit.

Tannethe crumpled to the ground, and everything went silent. Or the roaring was so loud that I couldn't hear anything else. I couldn't tell anymore.

She struggled to remove her chest piece, blood pumping out of her as I watched. Blood dripped from my knife onto the sand.

"You fucking bitch," she said, her voice full of contempt and pain as she glared at me. "I'll kill you."

I glanced up to see Theodas and his brothers running toward us, their eyes wild with anger. I stepped back to let them attend to their sister, as Xadrian had when Caelia was injured. But they didn't go to her.

Theodas pulled his sword with a shout, advancing on me, his features contorted in rage.

"You'll pay for this," he sneered, an evil grin on his face.

Trevyr's silver eye rolled in anticipation as they surrounded me, ready to attack. My heart raced and my palms started to sweat—I was outnumbered and outmatched. But I had overcome fear before, and I could do it again. Fear is the mind-killer, and I would not die today.

The brothers all attacked me at once, their swords cutting through the air as they fought viciously. I whirled around them like a dancer, flipping and spinning away from their blades. Only Tykas pulled his punches; the other's strikes were aimed to kill me.

Adrenaline surged through my body as I fought for my life. I flipped and twisted on the sand, desperately trying to defend myself against their onslaught.

Theodas's blade sliced my arm, and I cried out, my skin going numb. I started moving slower, my limbs feeling heavier with each second. An icy sensation flowed through me as I realized I had been poisoned.

But I wouldn't give up. With every bit of strength left in me, I kept fighting, dodging strikes, and parrying blades.

Then Theron was there.

He charged into the fray like a wild beast, his sword smashing into theirs and sending them scattering. A surge of hope filled me as he fought ruthlessly by my side, easily overpowering Theodas and his brothers. He fought alongside me like a demon, our movements in sync, as if we'd been fighting beside one another all our lives.

I tried to stay conscious for as long as I could, but my body was failing me; I could feel the poison seeping through my veins, weakening my limbs and slowing down my movements.

Theron scooped me up in his arms, cradling me against his chest like an infant. His eyes were full of concern as he looked down at me with love and admiration. Darkness flooded my vision as I succumbed to exhaustion and drifted away into unconsciousness...

Chapter 28

Theron

As the sun set over the colosseum, I held Kael in my arms, her breathing shallow and labored. The Vennorins lay scattered around us, sand in their mouths and blood on their skin, but that was the least of my concerns. Poison coursed through her veins with every heartbeat. I could lose her.

I ran as I had never run before, my feet barely touching the ground as I crossed the sand, sprinting to the gladiator barracks. "Help! Bring a healing plate!" My desperate shouts echoed throughout the arena, the gathered crowd frozen in shock. The attendants backed away with their hands raised in surrender, their eyes wide at the sight of me, wild-eyed and crazed. I laid Kael down on a cot, fear coursing through me as I tore through the cabinets, ripping bottles off the shelves, uncaring as they crashed to the floor as I searched for something, anything, to save her.

I reached the corner of the barracks, where several healing plates lay scattered. Grabbing one, I sprinted back towards Kael as she gasped, her back arching as foam coated her lips.

"Kael, oh gods." I put the electrum plate on her chest, desperate to heal her, yet knowing that this would not work against a poison of this caliber. Her pants were becoming increasingly shallow now and panic gripped my throat until my breath whistled out of me.

"Come on… come on!" I murmured as I kept pushing more and more magic through the metal. Her cuts healed, but her lips were deep purple and swollen. Her body slumped, and I couldn't tell if she was still breathing.

"*Sihaya*, no. Please, no." A stream of curses and prayers left my lips as I called on every god, living or dead, to save her. I swore I'd do anything if only she'd live. A dark figure emerged from the shadows.

Xadrian.

He carried a vial of blue liquid, rushing toward me to kneel at her other side. "Is she still alive?"

I growled, my first instinct to plunge my sword into his chest. Then I noticed he wasn't smirking or gloating like usual. Anxiety clouded his gaze, his brows knitted together as his eyes scanned her motionless body.

"Barely," I replied without looking up. My only focus was on funneling more power into her.

He reached toward her face and I snarled before he could touch her.

He held out the vial, his eyes intense.

"This is the antidote. Let me help her, Theron."

His gaze didn't waver, and I nodded. "Do it."

Xadrian shifted closer to her, pressing on her chin, and carefully poured the liquid into her mouth, his hands dark against her pale throat as he rubbed it to encourage her to swallow.

"Come on. Come on…" He muttered, and I had to fight the urge to smack his hand away. Each moment felt like an eternity.

Then Kael sucked in a breath, her lips and cheeks pinking once more.

"*Sihaya*... Thank Atar." Relief flooded me and tears pricked my eyes. I had almost lost her. Another feeling crept through my relief, poisoning it. Fear. Fear that I might be falling for her, fear that she might be taken away from me. I'd already lost my father. I didn't think I could live through that again. She was so fragile, despite her fierceness.

I took Kael's hand in mine and kissed it gently before looking back up at Xadrian, who watched us with an unreadable expression.

"She'll need rest, but she'll recover," Xadrian said, standing and slipping the empty vial into his pocket.

"Thank you," I murmured, unsure if he heard me as he melted back into the darkness.

Back in my suite, I put Kael gently on the bed, making sure the blankets were snug around her, and put a glass of water on the nightstand before shutting the door, leaving it slightly ajar to hear her if she called for me. I leaned against the wall, taking a shuddering breath. I'd almost lost her. The door to my suite flew open; my mother and brother barged in.

"What were you thinking? Attacking the Vennorins? You made us look weak and jeopardized our alliance," Nyana hissed, her eyes blazing with fury. "All for a whore."

Rhazien sneered at me, his eyes full of contempt. "You've lain in filth for so long that you've become a cur, chasing after any bitch in heat."

I snarled at him, anger boiling within me. "At least I'm not a desperate, spineless coward like you, Rhazien."

He scowled and took a step closer. "What did you say?"

My fists tightened, and my heart thudded in my chest. I'd been afraid of Rhazien since I was a child, but not anymore." I said that you're a coward," I replied, looking him dead in the eye.

Rhazien lunged at me, and I dodged, a kick connecting to his stomach. He threw a punch that landed on my jaw and stars burst through my vision as pain shot through me. Gritting my teeth, I threw an uppercut of my own and soon we were brawling, each of us snarling as we tumbled across the floor. My fists connected with Rhazien's ribs, all the rage and fear that I'd hidden for years pouring out of me in a rush. But it made me sloppy and Rhazien managed to pin me down on the floor, sitting on top of me, panting as he gripped my hair, slamming my head against the stone, and I groaned.

"Rhazien, enough." My mother intervened, her voice dripping with veiled threats. "You need to come to heel, Theron. You're jeopardizing everything we've worked for."

I shook my head, my resolve hardening. "No. I'm done listening to you. I'm not afraid of you anymore. I'll leave the empire and give it all up if that's what it takes."

Rhazien gripped my throat, his eyes cold and menacing. "You're not going anywhere. You're going to do what we say, or else."

I snarled, no longer cowed by his threats. "Or else what, Rhazien? Do you think you can intimidate me? You have no idea what I'm capable of."

I was done being their pawn; I had found someone who cared for me and I refused to be treated like this anymore. Pulling an arm free, I slammed my armor-encrusted forearm into his temple. He fell, and I rolled from underneath him and scrambled to my feet, kicking him in the stomach again and again.

"Fuck you, Rhazien." Rhazien lay on the floor, groaning in pain as Nyana pushed me away. I panted, my fists still clenched as I glared at them both, my chest heaving. My mother looked at me with a mixture of anger and fear in her eyes.

"You're making a grave mistake, Theron. You'll regret this."

"I won't," I replied, my voice steady. "I'm done being your puppet. You can't control me anymore."

My mother shook her head, her eyes glinting with malice. "You'll come crawling back to us. You always do."

But I knew that was a lie. I had Kael now, and she was all the family I needed. "Not this time," I said, pointing to the open door. "Get out."

Rhazien scowled as he limped out the door, Nyana sending a last glare over her shoulder at me before I closed it behind them, a sense of giddy relief washing over me. I had stood up to them, and I had won.

But it didn't matter. I knew what I had to do. I had to leave this city, leave this family, and start a new life with Kael. But first, I had to make sure she was safe.

I rushed back to my suite and found her sitting up in bed, the glass of water in her hand. She looked up when I entered, her eyes softening at the sight of me.

"You're awake," I breathed out, relief coursing through me.

She gave me a hesitant smile. "Thanks to you."

I sat down next to her on the bed, taking her hand in mine. "I won't let anything happen to you again."

Kael's eyes flickered with emotion as she gazed at me. I could feel affection emanating from her, and my body reacted to it, my cock throbbing. We looked at each other for a long moment, the air thick with unspoken words.

She spoke, her voice low and husky. "Theron... There's something I need to tell you."

I smiled, my heart thumping painfully. I'd already figured out that she was a rebel—how else could she have fought so well without training—I'd known from the moment she picked up the sword. And she finally trusted me enough to tell me.

I wasn't alone in this.

"It's alright, I know. And I don't care."

Her eyes flew open. "You do?"

"I don't care that you're a rebel. None of that matters anymore. We're leaving."

Kael stared at me in confusion. "What do you mean?"

"I'm leaving this city and taking you with me. We can't stay here any longer. I'm tired of living in fear. This is our chance to start anew, to have a different life. Together."

Kael shook her head slowly, and my stomach dropped.

"I can't go with you."

"Why? There's nothing here for us. Do you want to keep scratching out an existence in the mines, spreading whispers, and hoping that one day your rebellion will win? Because it won't. There's no way they can beat back the tide of Varzorn's ambition." I held her hand, gazing into her eyes. "But you and I? We can disappear. Go to Eprios or anywhere the empire hasn't reached. I can keep you safe."

"What about your sword?" Kael asked softly, her gaze searching mine. "And Rhazien and the emperor? They're just going to let you go?"

I smiled sadly, taking her hands in mine again. "I don't care about my sword anymore. Striker can have it. If I'm lucky, he'll stick it in Rhazien's black heart." I laughed. "It's what I've always wanted to do with it."

"Theron—"

"All I want is you."

Kael shifted uneasily as she stared at me, trying to gauge if I meant what I said or not.

"What is there here for you? Please come with me." My voice was desperate now, desperate to make her understand the urgency of this situation. But she seemed rooted in place, her gaze distant as if she were looking at something far away. I swallowed, fear hollowing my stomach. "I—I love you."

Her eyes shot open in alarm, and she scuttled backward on the bed to the headboard.

"What? No."

I recoiled as if she had slapped me. Her rejection hurt more than any physical wound I'd ever endured. "What do you mean, 'No'?"

Kael shook her head, her eyes burning into mine. "You don't love me. You're just desperate to escape your family. You don't even know me."

"That's not true," I protested, a lump forming in my throat. "I know you better than anyone else. I know that you're strong and brave. That you have a soft heart hidden under that stony exterior."

Kael's expression was still contorted in fear. "That doesn't mean you love me."

"I do," I insisted, a surge of anger mingling with my heartache as she denied my feelings. "I love you, Kael. And I know you feel something for me, too."

"No. I don't." She shouted, her eyes wild. "Because none of this is real. I *hate* you." Her mouth twisted into an ugly expression, one I was too familiar with.

"You hate me?" I growled. "You didn't hate me when you were screaming my name as I fucked you."

She glared at me. "As if I had a choice. Your magic and that stupid piercing took that from me. That's all you sharp-eared bastards do is take and take and take." She was shouting by the last word. "I would *never* want you. You're a monster."

It felt like she'd punched me in the gut, her words cutting deep. I stepped back, stunned and reeling from the force of her accusation. Never had I thought that she would believe I was capable of using my magic on her. An unbearable weight descended upon my chest, squeezing the air from my lungs. How could she think so little of me?

"I *never* used magic to make you want me," I said, fighting to keep my voice steady.

She scoffed and looked away. "Right," she muttered sarcastically.

I moved closer to her, desperate to have her understand what I was trying to say. "*Sihaya*, look at me," I growled, gripping her chin and forcing her to meet my eyes.

She reluctantly met my gaze, pure hate filling those green depths. My heart constricted painfully as realization dawned on me. It had been real for me, but not for her. Shame and anger threatened to choke me.

I leaned close to her, our lips almost touching. "I *never* set any intention in that stone. Every single time I made your cunt wet, every time it squeezed my cock as you came, was all you. "

Chapter 29

Kael

"You're lying."

I glared at him, ignoring his intoxicating leather and citrus scent as his body pressed close to mine, sending a shiver through me that only made me angrier. He had to be lying. There was no other explanation for the things that I'd done. Shame roiled in my gut, and I swallowed back acid in my throat. It was one thing to believe that I was out of control. That it wasn't my fault for what we were doing. But if he was telling the truth, then *I* had wanted it. Those feelings—of being so overwhelmed by him that I felt like I'd break apart if he wasn't inside me—had all been me...

"I would never do that on my own."

He dipped his head until we were nose to nose, his eyes blazing. "Tell yourself that all you want, *Sihaya*. I know the truth."

"I hate you."

"You expect me to believe that?" he growled. "You don't have any feelings for me? That all the time we've spent together meant nothing?"

I met his gaze, my heart pounding. "I never said I felt anything for you," I said, my voice cool and even. "And you don't love me. You might be lying to yourself, but I'm not. This—" I motioned between us. "—changes nothing."

But even as the anger and frustration bubbled inside me, I couldn't deny the way my body responded to his touch. I hated how he could make me feel so alive and so weak all at once.

"You're deceiving yourself, *Sihaya*," he said, his voice low and husky. "You can say what you want, but we both know the truth."

I clenched my fists, trying to push him away, but he was like a magnet, drawing me closer and closer until the heat of his body melted my core.

"I hate you," I said again, but it was more of a whimper than a fierce declaration. My resolve was crumbling with each second that passed. He was dangerous in every sense of the word, but I couldn't resist him.

"Lord Marshal, you're—" Mirijana paused, her eyes wide as she took in the state of us. "Varzorn requested everyone's presence in the throne room, my lord." She picked at her dress nervously. "He's about to announce his heir."

"Thank you, Mirijana. We'll attend to him shortly." Theron said, his tone steady without breaking his stare with me, as if we hadn't just been arguing.

My heart thudded painfully against my chest, despite my cool exterior. The court was not one I wanted to see after what had happened in the arena. Gossip would be rife and I'd have to face their wrath, that a lowly concubine had dared fight against one of the high houses, and that their prince had joined me on the sands.

"Get dressed," Theron growled, turning his back on me. "I'm not leaving you here alone."

"Mirijana is—"

"As if that poor girl could stop you." He threw over his shoulder.

"I would never hurt Mirijana."

"You're coming with me. Put. Some. Clothes. On," he snarled at me.

I wanted to protest, but I knew it wouldn't do any good.

Stomping to the jug of water, I dunked a cloth into it, scrubbing the blood and sand from my skin. Theron slunk away from me, angrily tearing his clothes off and letting them fall to the floor. My mouth dried as I took in his gorgeous body. Anger rushed through me like fire burning in my veins. I shouldn't be this attracted to him, godsdamnit.

I opened the wardrobe and pulled out a dress of deep emerald silk, the fabric glimmering in the light as though it had been spun from stars. The bodice fitted snugly around my curves and fell to my ankles, the thin straps crossing delicately over my shoulders before the skirt billowed out around me like a magical cloud of green mist.

Theron dunked himself in the tub, rising from the water like a god, and I turned my back on him as my breath caught, focusing on dragging a brush through my hair instead. He dressed, his hair still wet as it hung over his shoulders. How quickly I'd changed. Only days ago, I would've bemoaned the waste of water, but now it was an afterthought. How easily I'd grown accustomed to a life of ease in the castle, to my stomach always being full and my mouth moist. I pinched my arm, feeling a layer under my skin that hadn't been there a week ago. Water-fat, just like all those soft lords and ladies I'd mocked before. Was I truly that different from him? Theron had spent his whole life in palaces; the desert had molded me. I should know better, but still, I was drawn into the empire's web, ensnared like the rest of them.

Theron held my arm as we made our way through the castle, as if afraid that I'd run. All the eyes of the court were on us, whispers of what happened in the colosseum following close behind. I kept my head held high as we finally reached the throne room and were ushered in.

The massive throne room was at the apex of the ziggurat with immense windows overlooking the endless desert. The walls were black stone, polished to a shine, with intricate carvings depicting battles from long ago. Golden torches lined the walls and hung from their sconces like stars, illuminating the space. At the center stood a dais and on it was an ancient wooden throne, worn but still regal in its stature. It had been carved out of a single tree that must have been hundreds of years old, its once rough bark now smooth with age. Velvet cushions lay atop it in hues of scarlet and black thread adorned each cushion in the Carxidor sigil of a vanira that glimmered gold in the light.

On either side of the throne sat carved statues, each one depicting a different god or goddess, with Atar at the forefront. The air was heavy with anticipation as Varzorn stepped onto his dais and surveyed us all.

"My people," he began, "for many years now, I have searched for a suitable heir to take my place when my time eventually comes to pass." He paused for a moment to survey us all, as if daring one of us to comment before continuing, "After much consideration, I have decided to name my nephew Rhazien as my heir. He has proven himself to be loyal and ruthless, and I am confident he will lead our empire with strength."

Theron's face was still as if carved from the stone that surrounded us, but his eyes betrayed his anger. It radiated off of him in waves. He stood there in silence, looking on without argument or protest. Despite his desire to oppose Varzorn's decision, he remained steadfastly silent and bowed his head in acknowledgment of the new heir.

The court erupted into cheers and applause at Varzorn's proclamation and people crowded around Rhazien to congratulate him on his new position. Caelia Sarro scowled, her brother whispering something in her ear as they looked on.

Rhazien stepped forward from where he had been standing at the back of the room next to his mother and bowed low before Varzorn. "Thank you, uncle," he said humbly as if the gathered nobles didn't know what he was truly like. "I am deeply honored by your decision."

Varzorn nodded before turning his gaze to Theron, who stood with clenched fists at his side. His face was unreadable, but there was something in his eyes that spoke volumes.

"But that isn't my only order of business," Varzorn said, gesturing towards Theron with a wave of his hand. "My nephew, Theron, will be reinstated as Field Marshal of the Niothe and Warden of the West, effective immediately. It's been too long since our ranks were guided by his leadership."

A collective gasp ran through the room, and Theron's jaw slackened. My heart pounded in my chest as everyone began whispering again among themselves.

Theron inclined his head, accepting the position, while his mother glared daggers at him. Varzorn looked away, speaking to another noble I didn't recognize, and Theron stirred beside me.

"Let's go," he growled, taking hold of my arm. "We need to finish our conversation. "

"Fine," I snapped, ready to leave when Xadrian stepped forward.

"Congratulations, Lord Marshal," he nodded to Theron, before turning to me. "I'm glad to see you well, my lady."

"Thank you?" I said, glancing between the two men, attempting to figure out the strange energy that seemed to pass between them.

"Xadrian provided the antidote to the poison Theodas used on you," Theron explained grudgingly.

"Oh. Thank you."

Xadrian looked at me expectantly and I stood there at a loss, unsure of what else to say. I wanted to argue with Theron more, not deal with this confusing elf.

He opened his mouth to speak, but before he could get a word out, Varzorn approached.

"Xadrian," the Emperor said, his voice deep and powerful. "No doubt congratulating your new commander?"

Standing so close to the emperor made my skin crawl. Xadrian bowed low, his voice slightly louder than usual as he answered. "Your Highness, I simply wished to congratulate Theron for his spectacular performance in the arena," he said, keeping his gaze low.

"It was quite entertaining." He grinned wickedly. "You did well, Theron, as I knew you would. But I must admit my surprise when I saw how well your concubine fought. An interesting choice to keep such a dangerous creature close." His eyes flickered toward me briefly before returning to Xadrian who took the hint and excused himself.

"Yes, Your Majesty," Theron said, drawing the Emperor's attention back to him, as if trying to avoid him looking at me for too long. "I am grateful for my reinstatement, but my concubine is the only danger I plan on keeping near. I don't trust Theodas and want the snake out of the Niothe."

Varzorn sent a sly smile toward his sister's back before he surveyed Theron once more. "I agree. As Lord Marshal, I give you leave to make that your first order of business." What game was he playing?

Varzorn glanced at Rhazien once more before turning back towards Theron and motioning for him to follow.

"Come closer," he said gruffly, beckoning Theron forward with an authoritative wave of his hand. "Rhazien will remain my heir—for now. Your mother can't know that I suspect her. Come and attend me in Athain once you've settled in and cleared the ranks in the Niothe of Theodas' spies. We have much to discuss." His voice trailed off, and he looked away, leaving Theron standing in stunned silence.

Varzorn directed his attention towards me once more. His intense gaze made me feel like a mouse on the sands, just waiting for a hawk to snag me as he studied me. "You look so very familiar. Strange." He turned back to Theron. "Don't make me regret this."

Theron dipped his head and Varzorn patted his cheek as if he was a child and a shudder ran through him. I looked up to find Nyana watching the interaction; her face a mask of barely concealed anger.

I watched as Theodas and Nyana's eyes locked onto each other, a silent conversation passing between them. I could almost feel the energy crackling in the air as they silently hatched a plan. Theodas took a step closer to Nyana, their faces inches away as he whispered something to her. She smiled and nodded, barely perceptible to anyone else but clear to me she'd agreed to whatever scheme Theodas had brewing in his mind.

"Come on," Theron said, tugging me toward the door.

"Kael, wait!" I turned to see Xadrian trying to reach me in the crowd, but it moved in the opposite direction, dragging him away. So quickly that I couldn't even be sure I saw it—Xadrian flashed the rebel hand sign to me. My breath caught in my throat. There's no way. How could he be—Theron took advantage of my distraction, pulling me away and back to our suite.

Chapter 30

Kael

I was still reeling from the events in the throne room as I entered Theron's suite. There was no way that Xadrian was part of the rebellion, was there? It had to be some kind of trick, some game within a game.

I cast my mind back, thinking of all the strange moments that I'd run into him, landing on the night that I'd freed Gavril and the others. What if he'd been outside on his way to free them as well? Theron slammed the door shut behind us, his face twisted with anger, interrupting my thoughts.

"What the hell was that?" I demanded, spoiling for a fight, still angry and embarrassed that I'd allowed myself to be tricked by him. "I thought you'd be happy. Finally getting out of this fucking desert, right?" I said, venom dripping from my words.

"You don't know what you're talking about," he growled.

I didn't back down, matching his fury with my own. "You're a liar," I spat. "You said you wanted to run away with me, but the moment you got reinstated, you came running back to the emperor with your tail between your legs."

Theron's eyes sparked with anger as he retorted, "I might as well, given how wrong I was about you."

His words cut deep, but I refused to show it, instead goading him further. "I'm not surprised. You're just like the rest of them."

"That's what you wish, isn't it, *Sihaya?*" Theron moved closer, his eyes darkening as his voice rolled over me like thunder. "It would be easier than admitting the truth. That you crave me as much as I do you." I tried to resist the pull of his words, but my body betrayed me as he leaned in closer, his breath hot against my ear. "Because you know nothing has ever felt as good as when I buried my cock in you."

I gasped, heat pooling between my legs at the memory of our last encounter. I hated myself for it, but I couldn't deny the physical attraction that I felt toward him any longer.

Theron pulled back, a smirk playing on his lips as he saw my reaction. "Fight against it all you want, but this is *real.*"

My heart raced in my chest as he took a step closer, his hand reaching out to cup my cheek. Energy crackled between us, the tension that had been building since the day he'd claimed me. I wanted to hate him, to deny him, but there was something about him that entranced me. I attempted to focus on my anger, to remember all the reasons that I hated him, but it was difficult when every inch of my body screamed with desire. I responded to him, and I hated it.

"You're wrong." I tried to shove him, but he was relentless, unmoveable, his voice low and husky as he whispered in my ear.

"I know you feel it too, *Sihaya.* Don't deny it."

I tried to push him away again, but he grabbed me roughly, pulling me closer until his erection pressed against my stomach. The heat of his body against mine made my mind go blank. I wanted him, even though I knew I shouldn't.

"Stop," I said, my voice barely a whisper.

"Why?" Theron leaned in, his lips brushing across mine softly at first, then with more urgency as I responded to his kiss. "You hate me, so this shouldn't mean anything."

I tried to turn my face away, but he was too strong. He started kissing me, his hands wandering over my body. I wanted to resist, but my body gave me away, responding to his touch as I arched into his palms.

Gathering my will, I shoved him hard until there was a space between us once more. "I can't do this."

He stared at me, his eyes black with desire as his chest heaved. "Why not? We both want each other."

I shook my head, the surge of longing making it spin. "It's not that simple. I hate you."

Theron laughed, low and bitter. "Do you, Kael? Do you really?"

I turned away, unable to meet his gaze. I knew the answer, but I didn't want to admit it. He took my silence as the acquiescence it was, moving closer to me once more. I couldn't deny him any longer.

I wanted him. I wanted him more than anything I ever had before. His hands were rough against my skin, but it only heightened my pleasure as he touched me. I moaned into his mouth, my body arching towards his as he continued to kiss me with an almost savage passion.

He cupped my face in his hands and kissed me deeply, his lips exploring mine. I melted into him, allowing myself to surrender to him. All the loathing and fury between us ignited a fervor so intense that I felt as if I'd explode.

I tugged his mouth down to mine, my tongue dominating his as if I was trying to claim him. Theron's hands were all over me, his touch igniting a fire deep inside me. I wanted him—needed him—and nothing else mattered. I pulled him closer, my hands fisting in his hair as I kissed him fiercely.

Theron was just as desperate, his hands roaming greedily over my body, exploring every inch of me. I moaned his name, my hips bucking against his as he pressed me against the wall. He broke the kiss, trailing fervent kisses down my neck, nipping and biting at my skin. I gasped, my skin shivering with pleasure. Theron lifted me, and I wrapped my legs around his waist, grinding against him.

"Gods, Kael," he growled, his breath rasping in his chest. The sound was delicious in my ears. "You are the most beautiful creature I have ever laid eyes on."

Theron groaned, his hands slipping down to grip my backside. The hardness of his arousal pressed against my thigh, and it sent a shiver down my spine. His hands moved to the hem of my dress, pulling it up over my head before tossing it aside as I wrapped my arms around his neck. He trailed kisses down my throat, dragging his teeth over my pulse and making me moan in pleasure.

"Bed. Now." I demanded, and he gripped my ass, carrying me into our bedroom. I reached for his shirt, tearing it off his body, hungrily running my hands over his chest and abs as he sat me down. He was hard and muscular, and I couldn't get enough of him. I wanted him bare, to have every inch of his skin pressing against mine.

He pulled off his pants, and his hard cock sprang free, thick and pulsing with desire. My eyes widened as I stared at it, a sudden ache filling in my core. I spread my legs for him, silently begging for him to take me.

He crawled onto the bed, his body looming over mine. He kissed me deeply, his tongue exploring my mouth as he ground his hips against mine. His cock pressed against my clit, and I moaned into his mouth.

Theron broke the kiss, trailing fiery kisses down my neck, over my breasts, and down to my stomach. He nipped at my skin, making me gasp with pleasure. Hooking his fingers in my panties, he pulled them down my legs and tossed them aside. He spread my thighs wide, his eyes fixed on my glistening folds.

"Gods, Kael," he groaned.

He buried his face between my legs, licking and sucking at my clit. I cried out, my fingers tangling in his hair as he devoured me. His tongue darted in and out of me, flicking over my sensitive piercing until I was gasping for air.

"Theron," I moaned, my toes curling in pleasure. He moved his mouth closer to my entrance, his tongue dipping inside of me deeper. I felt like I was going to explode from the sensation, and my hips bucked against his face as I came closer to release.

I growled as he moved up, kissing my neck and chest as he positioned himself at my entrance, locking eyes with me.

"You're *mine*," He rumbled as he grasped his cock, pushing it inside me inch by inch until he seated himself fully inside me, filling me completely. I gasped at the sensation, my back arching off the bed as he began to thrust. He moved in and out of me, each stroke sending waves of pleasure through my body. He sped up faster and faster, pushing me toward the edge. My hands clutched at his back, my breath coming in shallow pants. My release built inside me, my body trembling with anticipation.

Then he stopped.

"Theron? What—"

He rolled over, pulling me with him until he was on his back and I straddled him, his thick cock still buried inside of me. My core fluttered around him; he was so much deeper in this position, almost brushing my womb.

"You say that you don't want me?" He whispered, his voice intimate in the shadows. "Then prove it. Get up and leave." He thrust up into me, making me gasp as his thumb brushed my clit. "Unless that was a lie."

"Theron..." I breathed, my heartbeat pounding where we were connected as his cock throbbed.

"Ride me and take what you want." He murmured, squeezing my backside. My breath came in short pants, my nails digging into his skin. He was right. I could get up and walk away right now. But I didn't want to. Shame and desire melded into one as I rolled my hips, taking him even deeper inside me.

"Yes, *Sihaya*," he groaned.

I rode him harder, faster. The sound of our skin slapping together filled the room. Sweat beaded on my forehead and the heat in my core spread through my stomach as I moved up and down on his cock. Theron's hands were on my hips, guiding me, urging me to go faster.

My body was on fire, my skin sensitized to the slightest touch. I leaned forward, pressing my breasts into his chest as I continued to ride him. His hands went to my ass, pulling me down harder onto his thick length. I inhaled sharply at the sensation, bliss coursing through me like a current.

Theron's mouth was on mine, his tongue pushing past my lips as he kissed me hard. His hands were everywhere, kneading my breasts, pinching my nipples, gripping my ass.

I sat up, whipping my hips over him and making us both cry out.

Tension built inside me with each thrust, spiraling me higher and higher. Theron's eyes were locked onto mine, gripping my hips tightly as I rode him. Every time I slammed down on him, I came closer and closer to the edge.

My breasts bounced with each movement, and Theron took one of them into his mouth, sucking hard until I cried out in pleasure. His other hand trailed down to my clit, and he stroked it, sending me over the edge. I screamed his name as I came, my body convulsing around him.

Theron flipped me over, pushing me onto my knees. He shoved his cock deep inside me once more and I groaned, overwhelmingly full in this position. He pounded into me, his thrusts becoming more erratic as he chased his release, slamming into me so hard that his sac slapped my clit with each thrust.

He shouted out my name as he came, his seed spilling inside me in hot ropes. I collapsed forward onto the bed, gasping for breath, my body still tingling with pleasure. Theron draped himself over me before sinking beside me, wrapping his arms around me and pulling me close. His cock was still inside me, as if he couldn't bear to be separated, our release slicking my thighs and soaking the sheets.

I melted into his embrace, my heart heavy with conflicting emotions, and rested my head on his chest as we both recovered. I felt safe in his arms, despite knowing he was my enemy. I turned to look up at him, my heart aching with longing and confusion.

His eyes were soft as he gazed down at me and caressed my cheek with the back of his hand. He seemed to understand the turmoil inside me and I wanted nothing more than to stay in this moment forever. But I had a job to do, and no time left to see it done.

Chapter 31

Kael

The atmosphere in my room was heavy with the gravity of my task ahead. Dressing in the dark so as not to wake Theron was an exercise in uncertainty—I didn't know what awaited me when I left the suite. I pulled on the dress that Kadir had made me, the one with the lilies and skulls that he'd given me as a parting gift. He would be with Gavril by now. And if this went well, I'd be with them within a few hours. Never to return to this palace again.

I let my eyes wander over Theron's sleeping form, watching his chest move in time with each breath he took. My fingers brushed against the thick collar around my neck, a tangible manifestation of my inner turmoil. It didn't feel like a chain anymore, but a promise.

I fastened my stolen poison ring onto my finger, the small vial of deadly powder hidden among the intricate gold design. I had no idea what its effects would be, but I wanted it in case I failed with my knife. The emperor and his entourage had just left the castle, and I knew the Beast wouldn't be far behind. Time was running out.

Taking a deep breath, I let my eyes sweep over Theron for the last time, memorizing his face before I left our suite, ready to end this, one way or another.

I moved through the castle like a ghost, my feet making no sound as I slinked through the shadows. Every step was calculated and precise; I knew I had to be careful not to alert anyone to my presence. Laughter and conversations came from rooms I passed, servants relieved to be free of their duties serving the expansive court.

I arrived at Rhazien's suite. Taking a deep breath, I opened the door, expecting to find the Beast lounging amongst his concubines, but found an empty room. The silence was heavy and oppressive, only broken by the occasional creak from the floor above.

I caught a whiff of Areca smoke. He always seemed to smell of it; an addict, for sure. Voices came from the hall. Fear and adrenaline surged through me as I stepped inside and closed the door, my eyes darting around for any sign of him.

The room was opulent, filled with luxurious furniture and decorations. In one corner was an enormous bed draped in deep red fabric, ornately carved with an intricate design. It was fit for an emperor—a pile of silken sheets and sumptuous pillows overflowing onto the floor, all framed by four lavishly carved mahogany posts. A grand balcony opened up to reveal a breathtaking view of the desert city below.

I took in every detail as I moved around the room—but there was no sign of Rhazien or his harem anywhere. With my heart pounding in my chest and my senses on high alert, I searched for a hiding spot to ambush him when I had an idea.

Stepping closer to his hookah pipe, I took off Tannethe's poison ring and carefully unscrewed its top to reveal the small pile of deadly powder inside. I tapped out all the powdered poison into the bowl of the hookah and mixed it into the crushed flowers using the mouthpiece, careful not to get any powder on my fingers. Stirring it until it was unnoticeable, I put the ring back on my finger and stepped away from the hookah as he entered the room flanked by his harem of wicked concubines.

"Well, well, look who we have here," Rhazien said in a low voice that sent a chill down my spine. "Where is your valiant prince now?" He chuckled malevolently and motioned for his concubines to circle me, tightening the ring of their harem until I was trapped within its confines. He looked around the room as if searching for Theron before tutting. "I'd wanted to do this in front of Theron," Rhazien said with mock disappointment. "No matter."

The concubines laughed and sneered as Rhazien approached me. They wore sultry lingerie that clung to their lush bodies, with high heels that clicked on the ground as they walked. Rhazien was clad in an expensive silk coat that shimmered like liquid gold in the torchlight, his dark eyes twinkling with malicious delight as he surveyed me from head to toe. I stood tall, refusing to cower before him. My heart raced in my chest, but I refused to let him know he had any power over me. "What do you want, Rhazien?" I demanded, my voice sharp.

The harem giggled at my boldness, but Rhazien simply smiled. "To see what you're made of, little whore," he said, moving closer until he was close enough to touch. "You've been quite the distraction for me, you know. I've been waiting for this moment for some time."

I stiffened at his words, my fingers twitching against my poison ring. If he suspected anything, he gave no indication. Instead, he took another step closer, his hand reaching out to brush against my cheek. I wanted to recoil from his touch, but I forced myself to hold steady.

"You won't get away with this," I said, my voice unwavering despite the fear that was building inside of me. "Theron will come for me."

"I'm counting on it." He stepped closer to me, his eyes glinting with a dangerous kind of pleasure. Rhazien stopped mere inches from me, looking down at me with an expression of pure evil. His black eyes stared into my soul, and I felt fear coursing through my veins like icy water.

"Are you going to beg for mercy?"

"Fuck you," I spat.

Zija attacked me from behind, one hand on my throat and the other clawing at my face. I pushed her away with all my strength and she snarled like a wild animal as she drew blood with her nails.

I pulled my knife from its sheath, but before I could even think about using it, Rhazien kicked it away somewhere under the bed. With my blade out of reach, I had no choice but to fight with my bare hands. Rhazien advanced on me, raining down blows that seemed never-ending. I fought back as best as I could, ducking and dodging their attacks while trying to escape. But everywhere I looked held only more grasping limbs and stomping feet.

I began to tire, my movements becoming sluggish as I tried to dodge the constant barrage of attacks. Rhazien's concubines were vicious, their nails sharp and their kicks and strikes precise. Bruises bloomed on my skin, and blood trickled down my face. Rhazien laughed cruelly as he struck out with his fists, landing punches that sent searing pain through my body while Zija threw wild kicks.

"Look how the mighty warrior has fallen," Rhazien taunted.

I kicked my leg out, connecting with Zija's knee and sending her stumbling back. The other concubines closed in, but I was quick, sidestepping their grasp and swinging my fist toward Rhazien's face. He dodged easily, a cruel smile on his lips as he grabbed me by the collar of my dress and slammed me against a wall.

I gasped in pain, momentarily stunned, as he tightened his grip around my throat. Every inch of my body screamed with agony, and I couldn't catch my breath. One of my ribs was broken. He grasped the front of my dress, ripping the fabric from me and baring my naked body underneath. I gasped in shock and humiliation as they laughed and jeered at me. He kept tearing until I had nothing left covering me. I wiped the blood from my mouth, glaring at him with a quickly swelling eye.

"You're going to beg for me to fuck you, you little whore."

Rhazien moved closer, cupping his hand around my sex and pushing his magic into the piercing. An overwhelming wave of pleasure washed over me as if someone had flipped a switch inside my body. My skin tingled with delight, heat radiating from Rhazien's touch.

I moaned, writing against his palm shamefully. I couldn't control myself, my hips bucking of their own accord, and I knew at that moment Theron had been telling the truth. Being with him felt nothing like *this*. It was like Rhazien was ripping pleasure from me painfully, wringing me like water from a cloth. There was no buildup, or even release. Just waves of unbearable pleasure, and yet I couldn't help but enjoy it as tears clouded my vision.

"Poor Theron. His whore is so fickle." Rhazien taunted. "Let's show him who his little pet really is."

He nodded to Zija, who grabbed hold of my nipple piercing, ripping it free in a mess of blood. My body shifted, the magical intention leaving once the metal was removed, my breasts returning to their original size. I screamed, so loud my vocal cords tore as she ripped out my other piercings from my nipple and ears.

"Vetia's horns, her ears are pointed," Zija said, but I couldn't pay attention; I was lost in a haze of pain and pleasure. Tears streamed down my face, mixing with the sweat and blood on my skin as Rhazien circled me like a predator, licking my blood from his fingers and delighting in my agony before he unbuckled his belt.

Vivid memories of when I first arrived in Adraedor came rushing back to me like a tide; drowning me. The stench of the mens' breath, the feel of their stiff hands as they roamed my tiny body, and the sound of taunting male voices. They forced themselves upon me in ways I could barely comprehend. I felt wrong; like an animal was taking over my mind and body and I had no control.

The memories flooded through me in inexorable waves of terror and shame, each more tormenting than the last, mixing with the agonizing sensation of him invading me with his foulness, the vile force that stole away my innocence and left me broken in its wake. The horror of knowing there was nothing I could do to make it stop or escape from this misery inflicted upon me.

Zija's laughter echoed endlessly through my consciousness like a never-ending nightmare as he took me. Her sadistic pleasure at watching another suffer by their hands; like a twisted spectator to one of their sinister games.

My stomach churned as he grunted. Waves of forced pleasure and shame rolled over me and I vomited, uncaring that it covered me. Tears streamed down my cheeks as I curled into a ball, shuddering with fear and revulsion, unable to take the memories any longer. I screamed out in anguish, trying to expunge them from my soul, but it was too late and he was starting again.

"I told you to beg for mercy," Rhazien whispered in my ear, his foul breath in my face as he forced himself inside of me once more. I clamped my eyes shut, wanting to scream out at the agony of his touch, but I couldn't bring myself to do it. Biting my lip, I tasted the blood that pooled in my mouth while I struggled to resist the urge to throw up again.

Theron will come for me. He'll come for me... The thought became a mantra, but even that wasn't enough to pull me from drowning in the onslaught of memories. The pleasure mixing with pain seemed never-ending until, mercifully, I blacked out.

Chapter 32

Theron

I woke up to the sound of Mirijana screaming for help. My heart raced as I leapt out of bed, my body already moving before my mind could even register what was happening. I ran to the doorway and saw Mirijana standing over Kael's blood-covered and beaten body. Every inch of her was covered in blood, turning her silver hair a dark matted brown. She was barely breathing.

"Kael!"

I scooped Kael up, carrying her to the couch, feeling her broken bones shift under her skin.

"Mirijana, grab my healing plate!" I shouted, my focus solely on Kael. My hands shook as I held her, anger simmering deep inside me. Never had I witnessed such devastation wreaked on another. It made my skin crawl with wrath.

She stirred, and I cupped her cheek, but she flinched away from my gentle touch. Rage filled me as I realized she couldn't see. Her eyes were too swollen shut.

"It's alright, *Sihaya*," I murmured. "You're safe now." She whimpered, and the sound tore through me.

Mirijana returned with the healing plate, passing it over to me as tears streamed down her face. "What should I do?" She begged, her hands twisting.

"Towels and hot water. I need to see how bad it is." She nodded, sprinting out of the suite into the hallway.

Mirijana came back with the steaming towels, and I thanked her before getting to work. My eyes flooded black as I moved over Kael's body, my magic flowing through her veins as I worked. She groaned in pain, but I kept going, mending her fractured ribs and snapped fingers. Her skin went even paler than usual as she sucked in a sharp breath. She was going into shock.

"You're not allowed to die, do you hear me?" I said with a ferocity that surprised even me.

Shouting rang through the rest of the castle, but I ignored it, focusing on healing Kael. When I moved to her chest, I saw the torn skin where her piercings had been ripped out. A growl tore from my throat as I swiftly healed her wounds. My hands gently glided over the delicate skin with the healing plate, sending sparks of warmth throughout her body as I worked. The pale pink skin began to knit together, becoming smooth in texture.

"Her ears," Mirijana said, her voice croaking through the tears streaming down her face.

I checked to find those piercings ripped away too, but that wasn't all. The shells of her ears were no longer round but tapered to a point like mine.

I held the healing plate over them, being sure to heal every part of her head in case she had a concussion. The damage was so bad that it refused to heal all the way, as if her body didn't have what it needed to replace what it had lost.

When I finished with her head and chest, I moved down to her stomach and a wave of rage flashed through me, so intense I felt disconnected from my body. Semen spread over her skin amidst the dried blood, her thighs bruised. Someone had violated her in the worst way imaginable.

My jaw clenched as anger roared through me, but I held it inside, my only focus on taking care of Kael. Mirijana backed away as if she could feel the intensity rolling off me, but I didn't give in to my rage. Healing Kael was my priority.

She was my everything.

Finally, after what felt like hours, I finished healing her wounds. Her face was still slightly swollen, but she managed to open one eye and looked up at me in disbelief. Stripping to my breeches, I gathered her into my arms once more, stepping into the tub and bringing her with me. My chest hurt as I slowly washed the blood from her hair, carefully cleaning her limbs until she woke.

"Theron?" She croaked, her vocal cords bruised from being strangled.

"It's alright," I soothed, brushing a stray hair away from her face. "You're safe now." Mirijana stood by the bath as I wrapped an arm around Kael, and she started to cry.

Kael's tears tore me apart. I wanted to see her with her eyes flashing with anger or pleasure, not weeping as if her heart had been ripped from her chest.

I held her to me, never wanting to let go. "I'm so sorry, Kael. I should have been there to protect you."

She didn't respond, still crying as if she contained an ocean of tears. Slowly, she pulled away from me, her eyes dull. "It's not your fault, Theron. This is on me. I did this."

I looked at her in confusion. "What do you mean?"

Her eyes fluttered shut, her breathing slow and even as she fell asleep.

Mirijana handed me a pair of towels as I stood, water streaming from me. I dried Kael first before laying her in bed.

"Will she be alright?" Her hands hovered over Kael, arranging a blanket over her as if she wished she could do more.

"Her body will heal. She's just exhausted from her ordeal."

How long had Rhazien tortured her? Raped her? Icy rage filled me, and I stood methodically walking over to my weapon rack and grabbing my sword, not bothering with my armor.

"Stay here with her," I ordered, heading toward the door.

"Where are you going?"

"To kill my brother."

As I stormed down the hallway, my fury rose with each step. I was going to end Rhazien once and for all. The fear I'd harbored for so long was gone, leaving only a burning certainty that I had to kill him in its wake.

I didn't pause as I reached the door to his suite, kicking it open.

"Rhazien!"

I stopped in my tracks, staring in confusion. Rhazien's body lay in the middle of the room, surrounded by his dead concubines. Their bodies were contorted as if they had died in pain, and a vicious thrill ran through me. Rhazien's eyes were wide open in terror, his skin was puckered with dark purple blotches like bruises all over. The room reeked of death, a thick cloying scent that made me want to gag. My stomach churned, and I swallowed hard, as I analyzed the scene before me. In one corner, a hookah still simmered, filling me with dread as I realized they'd been poisoned.

My fists clenched at my side, my eyes watering from the smell.

"My lord? Your brother—" A courtier I didn't recognize stared at me in trepidation. Did they think I killed them? No, no one would ever believe that I'd use poison. Plus, I had just run into the room with my sword. Nobody would think I had done this. It had been… Kael. She'd told me it was her fault. She'd poisoned them somehow, and Rhazien had caught her and tortured her.

It was one thing for me to have killed Rhazien, but another to have her do it. If anyone found out, she would be executed immediately. Varzorn would never stand for a Remnant killing an elf.

I nodded to the courtier and turned on my heel, heading back to the suite. I had to get Kael out of there before anyone figured out what she'd done.

I hurried back, barely registering my surroundings. My mind raced with all the things I had to do to save Kael and get her away from here. This was going to change everything. My mother would find out and want to kill us both in retribution for Rhazien's death. There was no way around it; we needed to flee as quickly as possible.

"We have to leave," I said as I ran into the bedroom, already sprinting toward her clothing rack. "Get dressed. We're leaving. Now."

Kael blinked at me in surprise, still groggy. "What? Where are we going?" She mumbled, her jaw sore from being broken as she fell back asleep, the effort of staying conscious was too much for her.

"Fuck." I growled, running for my armor rack.

"Where are you going?" Mirijana asked, wringing her hands.

"I don't know yet, but I have to get her out of here. I won't let anyone hurt her again."

Mirijana stared at me, her eyes wide. "What did she do?"

I ignored her question. "Hide until Raenisa and Herrath return. They'll protect you. Tell them I took Kael to the rebels to keep her safe and will send a message when I can."

"Yes, my lord," Mirijana whispered, her eyes filled with tears.

"Go," I ordered, and she scampered off, running into the hall on quiet feet.

I dressed Kael quickly, throwing clothes for the both of us into a bag haphazardly before I scooped her up into my arms and ran through the castle, avoiding the chaos that was happening around us. I was casting away everything, but I didn't care. Kael was the only thing that mattered, and I had to get her out of here.

I ran down the steps, dodging servants and courtiers who were too busy scrambling about to notice us. I swore under my breath, my heart racing as I made our way down the stairs and out into the courtyard.

The vanira stable was a few hundred meters away, but I could already see it in the darkness of night, lit up by the moonlight. Kael was barely conscious, and I quickened my pace, determined to get her to safety.

A lump lodged itself in my throat when we reached the stable and I rushed over to Vaernix, calling her with a whistle. I carefully placed Kael onto her giant back, not bothering with a saddle, and climbed up after her, positioning her in my arms so she could ride with me as I tied on our pack of clothes.

"Where are the rebels? Where will you be safe?" I asked, her head lolling on my shoulder.

"Sailtown," she mumbled, still in a daze. I set off north, galloping through the night on Vaernix's back, Kael tucked safely against me.

The sky was midnight blue, Ydonja's stars twinkling above as the wind whipped around us as we traveled faster than ever before. With Vaernix's strength, we could make it there within a few hours—if we were lucky enough to avoid any patrols.

We rode swiftly across deserts, our journey lit only by moonlight; a faint glimmer of hope on an otherwise dark night. But soon enough, just as the first rays of sunlight began to appear over the horizon, Sailtown came into view—a small village situated at the base of the mountains.

It was an impressive sight, a trading town built into the sides of a canyon. It looked like a ship in full sail with red cloths covering the vendor stalls built into the stone walls and stairs carved into the canyon on either side. The canyon walls created a kind of amphitheater, allowing people to have conversations from any level within Sailtown without raising their voices.

We rode in further and I could see that there were two main levels; the lower level contained shops, inns, and eateries, while the upper level was where people lived, laundry lines snaking back and forth between the canyon walls. Winding cobblestone paths lined with colorful banners flew in the wind, men and women starting their morning chores before the heat became too intense.

Sailtown had been home to many before us who had sought refuge here, and it seemed like it would be our haven as well—at least for now. We had made it here just in time before anyone else discovered what she'd done or could come after us. The morning winds should hide Vaernix's tracks, making it impossible for any pursuit.

As we rode into the town, Kael started to stir in my arms. She moaned softly and when I looked down at her, she opened her eyes, blinking a few times before looking around us in confusion.

"Where are we?" she asked, her voice barely a whisper.

I smiled at her, my heart swelling with relief that she was awake. She was strong. She'd could heal, and I'd be there supporting her with every step.

"We're in Sailtown," I told her, confused at the agitation on her face.

"No. You can't be here," she said, her voice weak as she looked around. As if I'd be afraid of a few rebels. She was still delirious from her ordeal.

"Shhh, save your strength. They'll protect you. If you stay in Adraedor, my mother won't stop until she's killed us both."

"Theron—"

She cut herself off as I stopped Vaernix—the rebel I'd captured and tortured stood before us in the middle of the dusty street. His eyes were hard as he glared me, but his expression changed when he realized I was carrying Kael.

"Kael!" He shouted, sprinting toward us.

As he ran, others followed, rebels streaming from the canyon walls. They spread out around us, their faces stern and determined as they encircled Vaernix.

Fuck.

This was more than just a few rebels. Tension filled the air, like a wave of energy that surrounded us. I realized with dread that there was no way for me to escape now. Not without losing her.

Vaernix reared beneath me, sensing danger, but I didn't have time to worry about myself now—I had to protect Kael. I quickly dismounted, not wanting Vaernix to throw us both off into the chaos below and injure Kael further. I pulled off our pack, commanding her in Elvish to return to the stable. She scampered up the side of the canyon, causing one of the occupants to scream in fear before she disappeared. Kael stood, her legs weak as she clung to my arm. Haemir's son rushed forward and pulled her into his arms before I could protest; holding her against his chest protectively. *No.*

A pang of jealousy ran through me and I took a step forward, ready to rip her from her arms when she spoke.

"Hey, little brother."

Chapter 33

Kael

I took a deep breath and stared at Theron. Rebels surrounded him, holding swords to his throat. I could almost feel the cold metal against my skin as they pressed closer, waiting for my command.

Theron's eyes were locked onto mine, beseeching me to reveal the truth. "Kael, please. Tell them we're together."

I couldn't. If I did, the rebels would kill both of us.

His eyes begged me for an answer, one that I could never give him aloud. I refused, not looking his way as I turned to my brother, limping from my ordeal. The pain hardened my resolve as memories of what Rhazien had done rushed through me. The Carxidors were a stain on the world that needed to be rinsed clean.

Roza sneered at him, her words dripping with venom. "She doesn't look like your lover. She's wearing a collar like a dog."

Theron's voice was strained, desperate. "Kael, please. You know I care for you. Tell them the truth about us."

But I couldn't. Not yet.

Instead, I hardened my expression and spoke to Gavril, ignoring Theron's attempts to speak to me. "Don't kill him. He's the emperor's heir now, and he's more valuable as a bargaining chip. Tie him up."

Theron struggled, fighting against the men who swarmed him and tore his armor off piece by piece until he was shirtless and bleeding, forced to his knees in the sand. I couldn't stop staring at him as they bound his arms with leather ties. The betrayal that filled his gaze hollowed my stomach.

"Kael. Tell them."

"What is he talking about?" Gavril demanded, and I shot him a hard glance.

"I had to do... things to complete my mission. Don't ask me about it again."

"Kael..." My brother began, and I shook my head, unwilling and unable to explain.

"Don't," I warned.

"We're discussing this later." He scowled at me, running a hand over his face as he processed what I'd left unsaid. "Does that mean the Beast is dead?"

I nodded, and the surrounding rebels erupted into celebration, their voices echoing off the canyon walls. But I couldn't tear my attention away from Theron. He was glaring at me with such hatred that I felt it like a knife in my chest.

I stepped closer to him, glimpsing confusion and hurt warring in his gaze. He had just been learning to stand up against his horrible family, but my actions had ruined all of that.

"*Sihaya*," he breathed, and a stone dropped into my stomach. I couldn't hear this.

"Gag him," I ordered, and he thrashed against the rebels holding him, almost breaking free until they managed to tie him in a harness, forcing a leather strip between his teeth. One of them gripped Theron's long hair, sawing it off at the shoulders and lifting it above his head as they cheered.

Muffled curses spilled out of him and his eyes blazed with wrath, hatred emanating from him with every heaving breath. Every tender emotion he may have had for me once was gone, replaced with a profound loathing. I tore my gaze away, steeling myself against the shame threatening to overwhelm me. I wasn't even sure who I was betraying anymore.

Roza approached me with a familiar bone sword and Theron's eyes locked onto it, his struggles increasing as she smirked at me. "Bet you've been missing this."

She tossed me the sword, and I caught it, spinning it as if it was an extension of my hand. I looked at the carving I'd added to it five years ago, running my finger over the promise that I'd carved into the bone. "Where's his other one? I want the set."

"Catch, Striker."

Realization dawned on Theron's face like a lightning strike and rage twisted his features as he thrashed, uncaring of the leather cutting into his skin.

He knew the truth now.

The gag muffled his shouts of fury, but I understood the curses he lobbed at me. I smiled and pretended that it didn't hurt, hiding my pain until I could lick my wounds in private.

"We need to move fast. They won't be far behind." I commanded, holding Theron's gaze as his eyes burned into mine, promises of retribution crackling between us. "We have to go into the desert before they can track us. Then Teodosija's plan can begin."

"What about him?" Roza said, jerking her chin towards Theron.

I sauntered closer to him, ignoring the effect his body had on me as I gripped his loose hair and tipped his head back, forcing him to stare up into my eyes.

"He's mine."

Acknowledgments

Goddamn it feels good to get this book out of me! Last May, I was checking out Deviant Art and came across an image of a woman gripping a man by the hair as she forced him to stare up into her eyes. It stuck in my head, rolling around until I had almost a full story in my head in less than twenty-four hours. But I had a problem, I was already in the middle of the Inkwater series and wanted to continue it. So the Sands of Maeoris series became my reward, the project I worked on whenever I met my word goals for the day.

Until I had a bit of a breakdown.

Long story short, I have a weird gene that means I can't take some medications, but we didn't know that and we couldn't figure out why my anxiety had gotten so much worse until I was having multiple panic attacks a day. Finally, I did genetic testing and figured it out and I'm on a medication that is working for me now, but it put me behind on my release schedule for this year.

BUT that is not a bad thing.

Because not only did I dye my hair and adopt two more cats, that extra break down time let me world-build the fuck out of

Maeoris. I have plans for Snows of Maeoris after this (which is going to blow your fucking minds), with ideas for more series to come (Seas, Skies, Storms, Stars… It's a lot of S stuff, y'all. Go with it.) It's going to be incredible, especially when I dip my toe into reverse harem next year *waggling brows*

So now to the actual acknowledgements! First, my bestie Ginger Kane. You're the only reason that I could do this. The sand I shoveled you helped mold into a gorgeous castle and I am so thankful for all of your feedback and help. You were alpha reader, beta reader, editor and therapist all in one. I love and adore you forever. Next, I'd like to thank Frank Herbert for writing my favorite book, DUNE. You'll notice several Dune references in this book, and that isn't stopping soon. This is the book of my heart and that means lots of DUNE. It was so fun playing in a combined sandbox and I can't wait to really start unraveling more of the storylines. Next, when I had that picture stuck in my head, I also had a song in there that refused to leave, mixing inexorably with the story. Shout out to RAC's MIA, the Robotaki mix with Danny Dwyer. The chorus, "Don't want anyone if it ain't you," inspired a lot of Theron's energy.

My next shout out goes to Henry Zebrowski and the rest of the boys on the Last Podcast on the Left. After their podcast went wide and Apple automatically downloaded a few hundred episodes for me, I dove back into the pod, hard. To the point that my husband just sighed when I'd say things like, "You know what Marcus says, 'I'm not that smart, I just work really fucking hard.'" It was around the time that my mental health was unraveling—and sure I may have at one point wondered if my binging of LPOTL was the cause of it—but honestly, the podcast was one of the few things keeping me sane. And obviously I listened to the LPN deep dive on DUNE multiple times. (And shout out to Natalie Jean and Jackie for the ACOTAR pod! Fae baes go downnnnn) Thank you for being my companions during my dark year and helping pull me out of it, even if you didn't know you were. (Ben, did you think I forgot about you? Nope, I'm the Wisconsin-bred Hilda of your dreams and your future second wife. Just wait.)

A big thank you for my writing communities, both online and in person. You all have shaped me into the writer I am today and I couldn't be prouder. I think this is my best book to date and I hope you agree!

Lastly, thank you to my amazing husband and family. Things have been hard recently, but you have supported me and loved me unconditionally. I wouldn't have been able to do any of this without you. I love you, always. (Don't worry about that stuff I said to Ben, it's just a joke. Mwah)

(Ben– Hit me up after your first divorce)

About the Author

Atley Wykes is a lifelong reader and writer of fantasy romance. She adores writing love stories—the spicer the better—especially when her characters start off hating each other. When she isn't writing, you can find her daydreaming about her characters as they argue with one another and designing elaborate worlds for them to romp around in.

Sign up for her newsletter to receive free bonus content and announcements for new releases: atleywykes.com

You can also find her hanging out here:
  Facebook
  Instagram
  TikTok
  Reddit

Join the Newsletter

If you'd like to stay up to date with new releases, click the link below to join my free, bi-monthly newsletter.

Subscribe

and receive a FREE copy of To Etch a Promise in Bone. This prequel novella is set five years before the events of To Bind a Dark Heart and tells the story of Theron's arrival to Adraedor and Kael's beginnings as Striker.

Blurb for To Etch a Promise in Bone

In the unforgiving desert city of Adraedor, Kael is a survivor who knows better than to trust anyone. But when Theron, the disgraced Lord Marshal with a secret agenda, arrives in town, Kael's world is turned upside down.

As the rebel forces grow stronger and the empire's grip tightens, Kael and Theron find themselves caught in a dangerous game of cat and mouse. With Kael's thirst for revenge driving her every move, and Theron's own hidden motives threatening to derail her plans, the stakes couldn't be higher.

As they navigate the treacherous landscape of the city, Kael and Theron must confront their own demons and make difficult choices that could mean the difference between life and death. But as they draw closer to their ultimate goals, they realize that nothing is as it seems, and betrayal lurks around every corner.

In this heart-pounding thriller, Kael and Theron will risk everything to claim their own destinies, but the price of freedom may be higher than they ever imagined.

Maeoris Wiki

V isit atleywykes.com for full wiki, including: Maps, Family Sigils, Imperial Family Tree, and more!

The Pantheon
1. Mother of the Cosmos – YDONJA (EE-don-yah)
Alive

People: Humans and the other Gods

Home Country: The Cosmos

2. God of the Earth- ATAR (Ah-tar)
Alive, but missing

People: Elves (Two types of Elves, Light and Dark or Svartál and Sálfar)

Home country: Athain

3. God of the Skies - KEARIS (Kir-iss)
Deceased

People: Kyrie

Home Country: Cavantha

4. Sea Goddess - CETENA (Ceh-teen-ah)
Deceased
People: Sirin
Home Country: Ceaplaes

5. Nature Goddess- THANJA (Than-yah)
Deceased
People: Fae
Home Country: Haechall

6. Shifter God- RHAEDOS (Ray-dos)
Deceased
People: Zerkir
Home Country: Iafane

7. Fire Goddess- VETIA (Vee-sha)
Deceased
People: Inferi
Home Country: Eprijan

8. Ice God- SITHOS (Sigh-thos)
Deceased
People: Ice wraiths
Home Country: Plides

<u>Characters</u>

Kael "Bonesworn" Helekian – Rebel of indeterminate heritage who embarks on a mission to kill the governor of Adraedor after posing as a concubine for Theron Axidor

Theron "The Marshal" Axidor - Nephew of the Emperor and former Lord Marshal of the Niothe.

Raenisa "Fireclaw" Taelyr - Second in command to Theron Axidor in the Harvestmen

Herrath "The Paragon" Tavador - Only son of the Tavador line and in the Harvestmen as a known spy for the Empress and Nyana Carxidor

Zerek "GoldSparrow" Amyntas - Disowned son of the Amyntas family and member of the Harvestmen

Calyx "The Feral" Hareo - Former Harvestman killed during a slave revolt

Rhazien "Beast" Axidor - Elder brother and tormentor of Theron Axidor and Governor of Adraedor

Varzorn "Stonehand" Carxidor - Emperor of the Thain Empire

Nyana "The Weaver" Axidor - Sister to Varzorn and mother of Theron and Rhazien Carxidor

Raura Carxidor née Vennorin - Married to Varzorn Carxidor, the Empress

Caelia "Young Bear" Sarro - Eldest Sarro sibling, twice related to the throne and in line for heir

Xadrian "Darkstar" Sarro-Heliot - Second oldest Sarro sibling that claims his Sálfar heritage

Aracel "The Sweet" Sarro - Youngest Sarro sibling, considered too soft to rule

Theodas "Black Theo" Vennorin - Eldest Vennorin sibling, in line for heir

Trevyr "Silver Eye" Vennorin - Second Vennorin sibling

Tykas "Ox" Vennorin - Youngest Vennorin sibling who is mistreated by his siblings

Tannethe "She-snake" Vennorin - Third born Vennorin, who wants to marry Theron Axidor

Varzora "Zora" Rorel - Theron's cousin from the countryside

Osiel "Oz" Rorel - Theron's cousin from the countryside

Xavier "Iron Hawk" Amyntas - Brother to Zerek, contender for heir

Larion Axidor - Theron's father (Deceased)

Lyta Rorel née Axidor - Varzora and Osiel's mother and sister to Theron's father, Larion

Haemir - Rebel leader, father of Gavril and adopted father of Kael, Inferi Remnant

Gavril "Demonhide" - Rebel, brother to Kael, Inferi Remnant

Teodosija "Peregrine" - Leader of the rebellion, Kyrie Remnant

Cithara - Rebel, Fae Remnant

Niko "Shiver" - Rebel, Wraith Remnant

Roza - Rebel, sister to Orya, Sirin Remnant

Orya - Rebel, sister to Roza, Gavril's late girlfriend, Kael's late best friend (Deceased)

Carita - Works for Rhazien Carxidor and prepares concubines for the arena, Svartál

Zija - Rhazien's lead concubine, Inferi Remnant

Mirijana - Theron's housekeeper, Kyrie Remnant

Kadir - Rebel informant and royal tailor, Sirin Remnant

Aella- Unwilling concubine, Sirin Remnant

Rafe- Mine Overseer that sexually harassed Kael until she killed him, Human (Deceased)

Elven Nobles and Alliances
Royal Houses
Carxidor
Sigil / Colors: Vanira / Red, Black & Gold
Words: *"From Darkness We Conquer"*

Axidor
Sigil / Colors: Wyrm / Red & Iron gray
Words: *"The Eye that Sees Ahead"*

Daelor (Sálfar)
Sigil / Colors: Two moons & Star / Navy & Silver
Words: *"The Darkened Sun"*

High Houses:
Vennorin
Sigil / Colors: Viper / Navy & Gold
Words: *"Strike True"*

Rorel
Sigil / Colors: Wildcat / Purple & Bronze
Words: *"A Fool's Wrath"*

Sarro
Sigil / Colors: Bear / Green & Gold
Words: *"Awaken the Dark"*

Cairis
Sigil / Colors: Wolf / Teal & Iron
Words: *"Family Above All"*

Ceador
Sigil / Colors: Badger / Gold & Black
Words: *"Ever Deeper"*

Tavador
Sigil / Colors: Cavefish / Green & SIlver
Words: *"We Remain"*

Amyntas
Sigil / Colors: Hawk / Blue & Electrum
Words: *"With Eye & Claw"*

Heliot (Sálfar)
Sigil / Colors: White Bat / Blue & Platnium
Words: *"Light & Law"*

Minor Noble Houses:
Lazan

Sigil / Colors: Scorpion / Red & Yellow
Words: *"Worse than Death Itself"*

Gaeris
Sigil / Colors: Stag / Green & Black
Words: *"That Which Submits Rules"*

Velon
Sigil / Colors: Moth / Violet & Gold
Words: *"We Make Our Own Justice"*

Taelyr
Sigil / Colors: Fire Ant / Red & Yellow
Words: *"No Faith Betrayed"*

Hareo
Sigil / Colors: Boar / Orange & Black
Words: *"Stalwart Night"*

Kallith
Sigil / Colors: Stone Fox / Gray & White
Words: *"Stronger Than Stone"*

Orden
Sigil / Colors: Wasp / Brown & Cream
Words: *"Build Against the Wind"*

Rikkert
Sigil / Colors: Owl / Blue & Yellow
Words: *"Knowlege Soars"*

Findis
Sigil / Colors: Rat / Black & Bronze
Words: *"Know Your Purpose"*

Alliances
   1. Carxidor + Tavador + Vennorin + Lazan + Findis + Gaeris

Cousins in contention for the throne:
Rhazien Carxidor "The Beast"
Theodas Vennorin "Black Theo"
Trevor Vennorin "Silver Eye"
Tykas Vennorin "Ox"
Tannethe Vennorin "The She-snake"

2. Axidor + Taelyr + Velon + Cairis + Rorel
Cousins in contention for the throne:
Theron Axidor "Lord Marshal" & "Iron Wraith"

3. Sarro + Ceador + Amyntas + Kallith + Orden (+ Heliot)
Cousins in contention for the throne:
Caelia Sarro "The Young Bear"
Xadrian Sarro-Heliot "Darkstar"
Aracel Sarro "The Sweet Sarro"
Xavier Amyntas "Red Hawk"
Zerek Amyntas (Disowned) "Goldensparrow"

4. Unaligned:

Rikkert
Hareo

Printed in Great Britain
by Amazon